THE PENALTY BOX
a novel

To Jim!
With fond memories
of working together.

All Best,

Larry

LARRY O'CONNOR
THE PENALTY BOX

a novel

Kellom Books
An imprint of Canadian Scholars' Press Inc.

Toronto

The Penalty Box
Larry O'Connor

First published in 2007 by
Kellom Books, an imprint of Canadian Scholars' Press Inc.
180 Bloor Street West, Suite 801
Toronto, Ontario
M5S 2V6

www.cpsi.org

Gene MacLellan, "Snowbird," from *Now* and *Forever* (1970). Reprinted by permission of EMI Music Publishing.

Every reasonable effort has been made to identify copyright holders. Canadian Scholars' Press would be pleased to have any errors or omissions brought to its attention.

Canadian Scholars' Press gratefully acknowledges financial support for our publishing activities from the Ontario Arts Council, the Canada Council for the Arts, the Government of Canada through the Book Publishing Industry Development Program (BPIDP), and the Government of Ontario through the Ontario Book Publishing Tax Credit Program.

Library and Archives Canada Cataloguing in Publication

O'Connor, Larry, 1955-
    The penalty box : a novel / Larry O'Connor.
ISBN 978-1-55130-336-9
    I. Title.
PS8629.C656P45 2007   C813'.6   C2007-905068-9

Cover and interior design: Aldo Fierro
Cover art: "Ice Rink." © Joseph Gareri. iStockphoto 2726518

07   08   09   10   11   5   4   3   2   1

Printed and bound in Canada by Marquis Book Printing Inc.

Canada Council
for the Arts

Conseil des Arts
du Canada

Canadä

I saw now that we are not free to refrain from forging the chains of our misery and that however well we may know our own will, other people will not obey it.

—Marcel Proust

I was a boy who happened to love a game.

—Wayne Gretzky

To my dad,
the icemaker

PART ONE

chapter one

The best time to arrive in Saskatoon is on a summer night. When I see the moon hanging above that low-rise place of sandstone university halls and farm market stands, or the liquid flash of wild ducks and the dusky languor of herons on the South Saskatchewan River, something stirs in me. The summer moon is first golden on the horizon, then rises in various hues until it sheds such a perfect white that you can read a game sheet until midnight on an apartment balcony high above the river.

I could have used the night sky that August day I arrived in Saskatoon with Belle. It would have given me something good to reflect upon. Everything was pretty much all right. A little slow, perhaps, predictable, no more aches and pains than any other guy at my stage of life. But now I can't think of Saskatoon in quite the same way again. It's where I put my guard down. Where my troubles began.

It wasn't that the city itself got on my nerves. Not like Calgary or Vancouver or Edmonton, which try too hard to be something they're not. Saskatoon is like a deer that hasn't tasted the leaves of seed lettuce or a Canada goose that prefers the forest to the corporate retention ponds of Mississauga. Like a person who comes into the room and doesn't think twice about whether his pant leg is just so, or that her heels click at the right pitch on the parquet floor. Saskatoon's values are old, as old as the hills. A please-and-thank-you town where everybody doesn't just know your name; they know your place.

From the airplane window I could see the rolling hills of the river valley, the flatlands of the Prairies, grain elevators so many smudges on the horizon. The pilot told the crew to prepare for

landing and the stewardess flopped down the Murphy seat in front
of me. She pressed the flats of her hands along the sides of her dress,
smoothing the lavender polyester against her narrow hips. I knew
she had a good figure; she went up and down the aisle like a cat. I
look for that—a slim body, supple hips. She sat down not far from
me and her stockings swooshed as she crossed her legs. Long fingers
tapering gracefully to the tips stretched along the armrest. No ring,
not even a shadow. Once, a stewardess on a flight to Florida had
dropped a slip of paper into my hand. The paper had her name on
it and her phone number, and I tucked it into the breast pocket of
my NHL blazer. I didn't call her, which wasn't the point. In those
days, I had the power. On the flight to Saskatoon, I caught the stewardess's eye and she smiled at me—then looked away.

She had to be from Toronto, I told myself. Not a Saskatoon
girl. That come-hither look wasn't about me. She wanted something. To be close to Belle. Saskatoon wouldn't have gone there.
Not Saskatoon, the spiritual home of Gordie Howe, the most un-
derpaid sports star in history. In Saskatoon what you see is what
you get. A flirt is a flirt, a hockey star is a hockey star. It's a hard
lesson to learn that most folks aren't as they appear, not even close.
Howe trusted people, particularly Mr. Jack Adams, his boss with
the old Detroit Red Wings, who gave Howe a new jacket instead of
a raise when his teammates were urging him to band together and
insist on better pay. "Fight for our rights, for your rights, Gordie,"
they told him. "Lead the union and we'll all get a raise." "But Mr.
Adams just bought me this new jacket," Howe said. "I can't turn my
back on Mr. Adams." Jack Adams signed the paycheques, kept the
icemaking machine running, the wieners rolling on the hot dog rotisserie at the Olympia. Howe took his turn hoisting Belle over his
head when the Wings won their Cups, but no way would he mess
with me just to get close to her. A Saskatoon boy wouldn't dare.

Beside me, taking up two seats next to the window, was my precious cargo, the Stanley Cup. Belle, I call her. Like always, against
my side, in her simple blue trunk. (I like to think of her as being a
little shy.) Precious because she's been around. One hundred years
plus. Precious for the obvious reasons, sure. The symbol of hockey
supremacy, the Stanley Cup is the most recognized trophy in the

world. None other comes close. I took a navy blanket and covered her, tucked in the extra cloth between the case and the seat.

Of course, unlike Howe, I've never truly been with Belle. I'd played in the NHL, but never won a Cup. Instead, I'm reduced to memories. Late at night, the Bruins and the Canadiens in Stanley Cup overtime from the end of Mom and Dad's bed. Dad moves in sleep, I feel his knee against my back. The net an ocean wave, rising out and over the catching mitt of Boston goalie Gerry Cheevers. Jean Beliveau fires, and the puck is in, the game is over, and the Flying Frenchmen, magic in their speed, unsparing in their execution, have the ice to themselves, skating with the Stanley Cup glittering like a star above their heads.

I shifted in my seat and the airline safety belt dug into me. Pain shot through my back, riddled up my arm. I kept a bottle of Motrin in the skirt pocket of my blazer, and spilled four pills into my hand, downed them with a swig of water. Never knew when it would come on, the sharp pain from that old hockey injury. Hit from behind in the run-up to the '83 playoffs. Two hours of sitting weren't good for it. I flipped open the metal case of the buckle and relaxed the tension in the strap. Breathed deeply until the worst of the pain lifted. A dull ache I could handle, was everyday. As the landing gear groaned, I could feel the stewardess's eyes on me. But I didn't flinch. I had my rituals. In takeoffs and landings, I turned to Belle. Let the stewardesses look, try to catch my eye, but at takeoffs and landings what I've got is The Game in my head, the Stanley Cup at my side.

My girlfriend, Norma, once sent me a smile on a stick. She said she was tired of my scowl, that I was peevish (her word). Bad feelings sort of sneaked up on me like a hit from behind. People I met on the job didn't usually give me a second look—or if they did, it was only so they could get close to Belle.

Like an hour or so ago. I was drifting off when this guy, a couple of rows behind me, started barking, "Look, don't you see him? The guy with the broad shoulders and short hair. A former hockey player. I kinda recognize him."

You'd think the man would've got the message. Belle and I were under blankets and I was resting on a down pillow the stewardess had given me. I opened my eyes and saw the man standing in the aisle next to me. "Pardon me, is that by any chance the Stanley Cup next to you?" he said. The loose tie of his raincoat brushed against my hand. Tailored London Fog. Judging from the redness in his eyes and wheeze in his voice, I'd say he was a broker dying for a cigar.

"Nope, I'm sorry. Uh-uh."

I pressed the stewardess button and turned to see her begin to make her way toward me from the rear of the plane. An old man on his way to the restroom was blocking her. The broker leaned toward me. Three short hairs clung to his Adam's apple.

"I've been a hockey fan all my life. Is it really the Cup? I nearly died in '94 when the Rangers won. Could I touch it? Would that be okay? Just a peek?"

"You know," I said wearily as I bent to rise, forcing the broker to retreat a row. I was enjoying the look of fear in his eye as I motioned to the stewardess not to worry."For a Ranger fan," I said, "I'll make an exception. I'll tell you. I'm with the NHL Orchestra. And this," I said, gesturing toward my seat, "is my tuba."

The stewardess laughed, shook her head. Her blue eyes blinked a little too much, probably the contacts, I thought. Ironic touch to her full lips. When I was on the road with Belle, I often thought of Norma. And other women. I'd never come to not feel attracted to other women. "I hope you had a nice flight," the stewardess said as she helped me put Belle on a cart to be rolled down the jetway. "Come back and see us again." "I'll see what I can do," I said.

Back in the day that smile had had its conquests. And I wasn't done just yet. But I'd stopped looking in the glass of the airport shops to see my reflection. I used to not be able to go past a window or a mirror and not check myself out. Plate-glass windows on main street, the reflection in the sheet metal of a car door, my image in a roadside puddle. Never primping, just a sidelong glance, careful so that no one would notice. I had a comb in my back pocket that I'd use, make the necessary corrections. And girls would notice. Hell, they noticed a lot. Of course, those were my playing days. And my playing days were long over.

The prairie sun lit the arrival lounge of John G. Diefenbaker Airport like a Hollywood set. A farmer sat upright in a recessed grey plastic chair, reading the Money & Investing section of the *Wall Street Journal*. "With a Final Kick, Europe Beats America in Merger Race." A few seats away an old woman was trying to knit as she sat with a sullen-looking girl with turquoise hair streaked with gold. The old woman wasn't making much progress in her knitting. She kept looking up and around herself like a rookie cop on a stakeout. Otherwise, the place was deserted. My bosses in Toronto had told me Saskatoon was the perfect assignment. Dead. "Where God left his snowshoes," former Maple Leafs owner Harold Ballard once said. No one would get in the way of me getting Belle to her date on time.

I started when I saw a man from behind in a blue jean jacket, talking at a phone bank. Slightly bow-legged stance of the pro hockey player, thickening middle. Doug Cowpland, I thought with a shudder. We played together in junior and chummed a bit in the NHL but had drifted apart. After hockey, he had come home to Saskatchewan. The man turned, and I breathed a sigh of relief when I saw it wasn't Doug. Just another guy with dead eyes and nothing better to do but to hang out at the airport and watch travellers coming through.

My first impulse was to run when I saw my contact, Frank Cattel, a thin goof wearing a sky blue tie with about a million trout on it. Clean breakaway, right back into Norma's arms. If only I had the guts. But I was hemmed in by walls of glass and I couldn't bear to see what I'd become. Especially not in flight.

I rolled Belle up to him and we introduced ourselves. The first-term member of city council clapped me on the shoulder and smiled. "That's CA-TELL," he said. "Think Calgary Telecom, not cow pies." Frank had full frontal dental work. Sherwood surgery. They don't mess around in prairie hockey.

"Glad to see you—both of you," he said, staring wide-eyed at the FRAGILE wineglass stickers attached to Belle's trunk. When the Frank Cattels of the world met Belle for the first time, they forgot their small-town manners. Like menu pushers for a new restaurant. It was as if I were invisible. Every time, no matter what, that really got to me.

"And we're happy to see you."

"We got quite a crowd waiting," he said, reaching down to touch Belle's case. "Could I help you lift it?"

"Nah," I said, swallowing hard to tamp down my irritation. What does it matter if someone the likes of Frank doesn't give me the time of day. Just clam up, I said to myself. If you can't say something nice about someone, don't say anything at all. Mom's words. My girl Norma, on the other hand, says get out your anger. Speak your mind. Tell me what you want, what you have to have. I'd tried to do that, but so far had failed. I couldn't admit to Norma that outside of The Game I'd never been very good at wanting any-thing—or anyone.

For the past few years I'd been content to float, to let things happen to me. Norma and I had been fighting a lot about me drift-ing off, saying, "Uh-huh … Could be … You're kidding" in our more and more infrequent phone conversations. I didn't have to take the trip to Saskatoon. They could've got someone else. But Norma and I had hit a particularly bad patch, so I volunteered.

"It's nothing," I said, patting Belle's case as I swung her off the cart. The weight of her twisted my back and it hurt like hell. "She's my papoose."

I had Frank jump into the box of his pickup, the back of which he'd rigged with a sign: "Stanley Cup On Board!" I watched as he strapped in Belle behind the cab. Okay, so it's a little weird to give the Cup a girl's name. One escort calls her Stanley after Lord Stanley, who bought the original sterling bowl for fifty-five bucks in 1893 and donated it to hockey. I tell people I call her Belle for short because she's the star attraction in the Bell Great Hall at the Hockey Hall of Fame. She has silver bands—Bell rings—one atop the other, crowned by the replica of Stanley's 1893 sterling bowl, an upside-down bell. The real answer is more complicated, of course. All my love-hate re-lationships have been with women, and I can get spitting mad when Belle gets all the attention. Better that it's a woman's name and not a man's. Better a girl, not a serious threat. I mean, Belle's eight rings are engraved with the names of every single man who has ever been with her. And just like a woman, what rings she doesn't wear are locked away. In Belle's case, a former bank vault in the Hall.

A female name also softens people, encourages their best behaviour. Not enough if you ask me. Belle has more nicks and cuts on her than a Yonge Street hooker. Years ago she was abandoned on a street corner in Montreal, where players had forgotten her after they'd stopped to fix a flat tire. In the early days she was dropkicked to the bottom of the Rideau Canal. When she was fished out, an Ottawa Silver Seven took her home and didn't give her up for a year. Later, a photographer swiped her and demanded a ransom. He kept her around the house and planted geraniums in her.

Frank's pickup pulled out of the airport parking garage and into the hot sun. I put down the passenger window, rested my arm on the door. Roadside grasses rustled in the breeze. For the first time all day, I took a deep breath without pain. Prairie air—sweet, succulent. Like biting into the first Mac of fall, or bending to touch crocus blooms. That was something Norma and I shared in our first years in Toronto after hockey. Spring in Toronto could be bitter cold in those days, the wind off the lake, whipped to frigid by skyscraper corridors, narrow dreary streets. No snow on the ground, but a biting cold that seeped to the bone. We lived in the Beaches, along the Lake Ontario shore, and on the coldest spring days we would bundle up and walk under steel-grey skies until we spotted the first splashes of colour: purple, yellow, scarlet, violet, and blue, delicate petals on tender green shoots. Norma would bring a sketch pad and draw. They were so amazingly beautiful in the hard dark earth, those first crocus blooms, and before she did her little drawings we'd touch their velvet petals and kiss each other like we did when we'd first met.

Anne Murray's "Snowbird" was on the radio, and Frank leaned forward, turned up the volume. "Hey, don't you love this song?" Frank said, touching me above the knee. My flesh crawled at the spot he touched. He moved his hand back to the wheel, returning his attention to the road, and I clamped my left hand down on my leg. The air sucked out of me, and I looked out the rear window. The Cup's case was strapped in securely against the cab, and I took a deep breath.

The snowbird sings the song he always sings ...

I am the Keeper of the Stanley Cup. I played for years in the National Hockey League and now I work at the Hockey Hall of Fame. Some comedown, I know. For the Hall, getting Kyle Callendar as Cup escort was a stroke of good luck. Usually, guys taking my job were onetime hospitality specialists, the occasional ex-Zamboni driver. Flunkies, wannabes. About as deep as Broadway ice.

The thing that I want most in life's the thing that I can't win …

Me, the Hall took on as a reclamation project. I was five years out of hockey, had run through, I don't know, more than a million in savings on vacays in Jamaica, booze, restaurants, rent money through the roof. Then one day Norma said she had a surprise for me. I was blindfolded and taken to the Hall. She guided me through the entrance and around a bit until she finally squeezed my hand and then untied and removed the blindfold. Before me was the Stanley Cup. I literally staggered, stunned by the reflected light. For an hour or more I stood rooted before her. In all my years in pro hockey, I'd never held her. In more than a century, twenty thousand men have lived for that day, but only a fraction of them have ever had their names hand-stamped for eternity on her side. I knew then that more than anything I had to be with the Cup. For the Hall it was an easy call having an ex-NHLer as Cup escort. I had been drinking too much, was just a matter of time before I was going to flame out like Tim Horton, say, or Jon Kordic. In those days, outside of Norma, most of my friends were gone. Norma, I'm sure, was grasping at straws when she guided me before the Stanley Cup that day. This, I told her, I would be bound and determined not to fuck up. In my grey flannels, blue jacket, and white calfskin gloves, I would never let the Cup out of my sight. It would never be stolen on my watch. Better that I could stay in The Game. No matter what.

Yeah, if I could I know that I would FL-Y-Y-Y-Y away with you.

Frank snapped off the radio.

"The Shrivers are the big family in town, one of a kind, you'll see," Frank said as his truck rumbled over a level railway crossing. We'd come from the airport through the new motel developments and past Midtown Plaza, the city's mall pride, at parade speed for the election that I imagined must be coming up. At the feed store, men on the loading dock waved and Frank half-saluted with an index finger. A woman with a big butt strapping her kid into a child-safety seat stopped to watch as the pickup rolled past.

Saskatoon was home to Bobby Shriver, a forward for the Red Wings, the current Stanley Cup champs. Bobby was the end of the line, the last of the boys with visiting privileges. It's a summer tradition that each member of the winning team goes on a tear with Belle for a minimum of twenty-four hours. Every single member of the Red Wings—including the five European players who had Belle and me to their hometowns in Russia, Ukraine, and Latvia a month or so ago—had had their visit that summer except for Bobby.

"You can see Mr. Shriver in Bobby, that's for sure. Everybody says so," Frank continued, waving at two boys who'd stopped to gape before a corner dairy bar. He settled into the cloth bench of his pickup as if it were a covered litter before the Taj Mahal. A convoy of bicycles, red wagons, skateboarders, and scooter-like things were trailing us. The bicycles were gaining. We were going so slow a Second World War veteran with a bad leg could've kept us in sight on a straightaway for more than a minute.

"Mr. Shriver, the father, will be at the luncheon," Frank said. "You'll see what I mean. And you don't have to worry, I've briefed everybody about protocol as far as the Cup is concerned." He waggled his finger in his ear in a herky-jerky way. Bad wax buildup. Through the crook in his arm, I could see some kids had gathered on the roof of a five-and-dime. One had jabbed a hockey stick in the air, while the other was spread-eagled on the roof in a mock sniper position, his fingers on the shaft of the stick, taking deadly aim.

"We've made better time than I thought we would," Frank said as we pulled into the Agricultural Hall of Fame. "Let's soak up some local colour." At the entrance, a woman from the Ladies Auxiliary

was selling misaskwatomin jam. Saskatoon berry. "Sweet, not sug-
ared," she said. "My, that's really good," I replied, as I set Belle
down and tasted a sample. She slipped a jar into the hip pocket
of my blazer. Vaseline eyes widened as she pressed her finger to
her lips.

"That's where Saskatoon's name comes from, from that little
itty-bitty fruit," Frank explained. He stopped to talk to a clutch
of blue-rinse ladies from the Auxiliary. "CA-TELL," he explained
in a voice that mildly scolded. "As in, I CA-TELL you things." The
women tittered as I hurried away. Saskatoon might not get on my
nerves, but Frank Cattel sure as hell could. I was beginning to
think Frank must've escorted Harry Sinden around town when
the Bruin boss said he would fold the club before the shame of
being forced to relocate to Saskatoon.

"Hey, you can't get in without a ticket," a woman said from
the members table. She smiled as I put Belle down at my feet and
looked at her, a brunette with green eyes, shoulder-length curly
hair. She leaned forward, fingers clasped on the desk. A hint of
cleavage in her scarlet-red tank top. "You'll need a ticket for your
friend there, too," she said, laughing, looking at Belle. "Senior
rates, of course." Dimples and big teeth, early Farrah Fawcett
in that famous seventies pose. Like she was being held in a box:
nipples showing, big hair, and that wide smile that said, "It's okay,
I want it just like this."

"I don't have much time, so I don't think it would be worth my
while," I said. I dug into my pocket for my wallet and pulled out a
twenty. "Are the tickets good for all day?"

"Yes, they are," she said as she wrote something on the back of
a ticket. "That should be all you need." She placed the ticket and
the change from the twenty in my hand. Myra, her name tag said,
bright white against a backdrop of rust-red Saskatoon berries.

Wincing with the strain on my back, I picked up the Cup and
moved into the main hall. Myra'd written her name and phone
number on the ticket and I stashed it into my blazer pocket. Perhaps
I could salvage a decent time out of this leg of the trip after all.

I stopped in front of a sign that read, "This Way to the Bread
Basket of the World." No place in Canada produces more wheat

than Saskatchewan. And rape, cultivated for its seed, from which oil is made: a thick brownish-yellow oil used for lubrication and in the manufacture of soap. Saskatchewan is also tops in forage crops, not to mention oats, barley, and flaxseed, which bears blue flowers and makes an oil known for its healing powers. Weird, I thought. Rape for lubrication. Flax for the blues. Talk about organic farming.

Frank caught up to me as I stood before one of the founders' portraits in the main hall. A farmer who'd never been in a suit and stiff collar but that one time in his life. And from his look I could see the picture-taking had been going on for way too long—like Frank's conversation.

"Some damned fool Yankee newspaper," Frank said, gasping for breath, "once said that a vacation in Saskatoon was like driving all day to dig potatoes. Not anymore, that's for sure. You'll see. Saskatoon is some sophisticated … It's too bad you won't be staying into the weekend. The Saturday farmers' market is well worth sticking around for."

Sure, I thought. Only if the brunette ticket taker had the weekend off. And even then, you wouldn't be seeing us. We'd rent a car and head off to a riverfront cabin somewhere. I'd tell Toronto that I'd "Gone Fishing"; Norma, that I'd been forced to stay on business.

"Better come along," Frank said finally, sweeping the air with his long arm. A curling skip, egging on his slow-footed second. "We're getting late. I'd say there's close to two hundred people waiting for us at the Lions Club. C'mon, whaddaya say we get going?"

Before I turned to leave, I noticed a particularly grim-looking founder in the portrait gallery. Emmett Noble Shriver, a man in a bow tie and a hard face with deep-set eyes. "That's Bobby's great-grandfather," Frank said. "C'mon," he repeated, looking at Belle, not me. "We got to go." The ancient Shriver looked like someone I knew and a shock went through me. Mom used to say when you got that feeling you'd entered a wrinkle of time; you were dead and someone was walking on your grave.

chapter two

Lions Club hockey banquets were my life. When I was growing up, Mom would slick down my cowlick, using her mouth to wet it while we sat in the front seat of the Impala on the way to the annual affair in Keppel, Ontario. Ice hockey is all in Keppel. Like the sea in a Caribbean village. And the village boy who could dive the longest, find the prize oysters, the pearls that gleamed more than other kids' pearls—that's what mattered.

I wore a bow tie yanked tight under my collar, a white shirt and blazer, and rode as silent as could be. Mom and Dad groomed me something special for the Lions Club banquet, where I'd be presented with the scoring trophy for most points, the cup for the most valuable player. Keppel applauded, held me up as a spectacle. I was not only good at hockey, I was the town's miracle on ice, the banquet a tribal rite. Like they'd give on the island for the boy who held his breath longer and dove the deepest. For presenting to them the most beautiful pearls they'd ever seen.

Mom was in her two-tone dress, orange and black, the team colours, the dress she saved the whole year in clear plastic. Lipstick, full-blown red. Even Dad wore a suit and tie. Shaved himself close, Old Spice ripe in the air. I don't remember much about what I looked like. When you grow up with people fussing over you, the others become more real than you are. At special occasions, a part of me has never stopped looking over my shoulder to see who people were really looking at.

The night of the Lions Club banquet, Dad would draw a lint brush along my blue blazer and grey trousers, tug my tie into a

sharp knot. It was Mom's job to make sure my hair looked suf-
ficiently wet and neat. She traced a line along the top of my head
like a heart surgeon does an incision. Steady and clean, no pain.
The patient is numb, after all.

In the Impala, they told me where to sit. When it was okay to
speak. Shaped my hands in a proper fold on my lap. None of the
actions I took were my own. It's silence I remember because as a
boy I didn't own a thing.

Except on the ice—and in my dreams. Those days I dreamed
only of skating. With a hockey stick in my hand, on frozen lakes
that never ended, blue sky, the swoosh of cutting blades. Wind
whipping my sweater, my hair. In the grim silence of the Lions
Club banquet, I longed only for a return to my solitude, to my
place of skating in my mind.

So I knew something of what Bobby Shriver was going through.
Bobby's grin as he entered the banquet room that day in Saskatoon
was like a baby's, wide as the world and sweet, trusting. But his was
no baby's body. It seemed the wheel on his Red Wings windbreaker
could have fit the tire well in the trunk of my Honda. He was so
squeaky clean and smart-looking he must have come straight from
The Bay after first showering and shaving in the stockroom. Even
his trouser buttons shone. Bobby stood at the back of the hall, where
grey-haired men slapped his back, reached for and shook his hand.
Bobby barely flinched. Once his dress Timberlands were rooted to
one spot, he couldn't be moved. Not without a body block.

Bobby walked up the aisle as if it were a patch of half-grown
corn stalks. Once, he stole a glance over his shoulder as if he were
looking for something. Or someone. He couldn't quite believe this
was happening and he wanted to be reassured the people he had
just passed hadn't somehow vanished. That the whole thing wasn't
a dream.

The applause that drenched Bobby took me back. To Lanny
Stenholm and his wife, Carolyn, the town pharmacists; Bill Carter,
the insurance guy, and his wife, Betty; Frenchy Benoit, of Benoit
Auto Body. Clapping and hooting and hollering for me, their own
man-boy hockey hero, Keppel's number one son. Hairdresser
Wilda Nelson stood on her chair, whistled and cheered. In Keppel,

Frank Cattel was John Wright, who wholesaled team uniforms, Tom Jonesed the microphone. "The boy who has made this all happen, we all remember him as the kid who wouldn't quit, who gave us all so many exciting moments, who we've been following with such pride and delight over the years that all of Keppel stands as one to celebrate. Let's all give a rousing, hometown welcome to the pride of Keppel, our own Kyle Callendar."

Mom and Dad, wet with tears of joy, clung to each other like sweethearts. Except for the Lions Club award nights, I never saw them as much as touch. The sound of those hometown cheers and the look of pride on my parents' faces at first churned my stomach, made my lips quiver, my palms moist. But then I began to feel a power in my legs, my chest filled with air, my mind with words, all the lines of the speech I'd rehearsed. As I pressed my hands to the tabletop in rising to the podium, I really seemed in command.

No matter how many celebration nights I attend every year, I have these feelings. Except in my case, there was never any Stanley Cup. Keppel's shame is that Kyle Callendar failed to play on a Stanley Cup winner. Instead I place the Cup in the hands of those who do.

In the Hall you can go right up and touch her. We tell folks they can, but most don't. They stop inches from her: trace with a finger M. LEMIEUX, 1990–91 Penguins; P. FORSBERG, 1995–96 Avalanche; W. GRETZKY, 1987–88 Oilers. Find the typos in NEW YORK ILANDERS, TORONTO MAPLE LEAES, BQSTON BRUINS, the four misspellings of J. PLANTE. One day I took Belle to the Chicago Lighthouse, a place for blind kids. We told the kids it was a cup and they expected it to be something for drinking milk or juice. One boy floated his fingers up her side so slowly that I imagined he was absorbing each name, slipping each one into a piggybank like a prized penny. Another pressed his face to Belle's side, then his ear to her and held it there a long time.

It doesn't matter how far I've gone with Belle, what town we pull up in, whether by jet, float plane, barge, train, bus, pickup truck, or little red wagon, that moment sets my hair on end. The kid and the Stanley Cup. A quizzical, slightly embarrassed look. Could this possibly be okay? Can I touch the Stanley Cup?

From my seat on the dais in Saskatoon, I touched her with my white linen gloves. Felt the engravings, the little cuts, dents, metal of a Chevy Vega. Before Belle is given over to a champion, no one is to touch her with bare hands. Only the champions are allowed to hoist her in the air. The room was heavy with heat, stifling, but even through the gloves Belle felt cool. Before leaving Toronto that day, I'd polished her. I started at the base with the Gorham. A thin layer, not too much so that it goops in the etchings. I rubbed her hard, from bottom to top, until I reached the upside-down bell itself. I stood on a chair to get a good position and worked until the bell, too, was glowing, blinding in the early morning sun. Then I put on my gloves and placed her in the velvet bed of her carrying case.

"Thank you," Bobby Shriver said as the cheering subsided. Tiny backlit hairs spoiled the round perfection of Bobby's head. His face was smooth and flushed, sweat beading on his forehead. He caught my eye and although I had never met him before—would not have recognized him from his hockey card the Hall had me bring—I could sense a strange fear in him. Bobby Shriver did not know where to look before his own hometown fans and admirers. I thought for some reason that wasn't immediately clear he didn't feel safe.

Bobby's fingers shook and the paper in his hand rustled at the microphone. A hush fell. Bobby couldn't read his prepared speech unless he'd memorized it, the paper was shaking so much. Finally, his eyes lifted from the paper and landed on Belle. He stared at the Cup, gleaming under the floodlights, ran his eyes down the list of names: G. HOWE. H. MORENZ. D. KEON. R. ORR. R. SHRIVER.

"Thank you," Bobby mumbled, staring at Belle like a two-hundred-forty-pound stroke victim.

"No, thank you! Thank you! We thank you, BOBBEEEEEEE!" the crowd replied. Minor hockey scoring leaders threw their Roots caps in the air, pounded the floorboards with their Doc Martens. Tears streamed down the cheeks of the Ladies' Auxiliary. I smiled to think the moose head over the fireplace might soon burst into an ear-to-ear grin, when I noticed Bobby's father, Sheldon, clapping like everyone else but not looking at his son. He never took his eyes off Belle. And me.

Sheldon Shriver rose from his chair on the dais and ran a hand over his dark blue Brooks Brothers suit. His garnet and silver ascot set off big white hair. As he was taking Bobby's place at the microphone, applause halted like a talk show audience before a flash card. "As everyone here knows," Sheldon said, holding his palms forward in submission. Blue eyes shone from deep Shriver sockets. "Bobby is not only my boy. He is Saskatoon's boy."

Cheering and noisemaking shook the walls and when the table on the dais began trembling, I jumped to my feet to steady Belle. I pulled her close and glanced toward Sheldon. He was calm, taking a sip of water, smiling at me.

After lunch and an afternoon autograph session at a summer hockey school, I stopped at a payphone and called Myra's number. The voice on the machine was huskier than I remembered, a touch vulnerable. I told the machine the location and time of the Cup party, that this should be considered an official invitation.

Beautiful women, I'd have to say, don't seem to mind playing second fiddle to Belle. It used to be only pro hockey players could line up such action. But that was when the Stanley Cup was little better than a provincial sideshow, with girls in farm country who could drink soldiers under the table and over-the-hill gals in Toronto hitting on balding men in blue blazers and grey flannel slacks, tassel shoes. Now Belle is Hollywood, escorted from Laredo to the Arctic Circle. We escorts are still porky in our blazers and baggy pants, and the white gloves can be a little much. But the girls are certainly looking better these days.

Bobby took my arm as I put the receiver down. It was an odd gesture from such a shy boy, but not unnatural. Like he'd been taking the arm of strangers all his life.

"I'll show you the way to our car, Mr. Callendar."

"Kyle, son," I said. "Just call me Kyle."

Bobby took his hand off me and said, "Kyle," like he was taste-testing it. Too bland. Needs salt. "Here, it's this way."

Bobby walked ahead as I tucked the ticket with Myra's phone number into my breast pocket and carefully hoisted Belle onto my shoulder. "It's really something, isn't it?" I said. "Like you just can't believe it."

"How's that, sir—I mean, Kyle?"

"C'mon, boy, loosen up," I said, gently pushing his shoulder. "The Cup, man. Your name on the Cup."

"Yep," he said, the hint of a smile at a corner of his mouth. "Yep. You're right there," he said. His head bobbed like the poodle toy Mom and Dad kept at the rear window of the Impala. We walked on and I fingered the ticket in my pocket. A better man would've slipped the phone number into the boy's hands, told him, "There you go, son. Congratulations." I'd never met a boy in greater need of the love of a woman.

The white stretch limo was parked along a side street before a donut shop. It was only a bit after 7 p.m., and the brilliant light of a Saskatoon summer night hadn't let up. The neon letters of the donut sign glowed amber, matching the blinking caution light over the intersection. As if Anita Bryant, the Florida sunshine girl herself, had bewitched the city.

At the curb Sheldon was sipping sparkling water in a tall glass with a wedge of lime on the rim. We shook hands and I was surprised by the strength of his grip. Not overpowering but without a trace of limpness.

"Put the Cup here on the seat, Kyle," Sheldon said as he opened the car door. "I'll sit beside it. You boys get comfortable across from me."

Between us, Bobby and I probably tipped over four hundred and fifty pounds, but we slipped into the back of the limo like a knife through butter. As I sunk into the deep-piled cushioned leather of the seats even the dull ache in my back eased a little. Sheldon sat cross-legged on the edge of the seat, the heel of his Italian leather shoes grazing the Cup's case.

"What'll it be, boys?" Sheldon asked, opening a mini-bar to his right.

"A beer would go down nicely," I replied.

"Sure would, Dad," Bobby said.

The driver started the limo and pulled out as Sheldon took a couple of Old Viennas from the icebox and poured first my beer and then Bobby's into steins. I drained half the contents in a wink. "Man, I can't believe it," I said. "O Vee. I haven't had one of these in ages."

Sheldon smiled, his long white teeth bright in the waning light. A single gold tooth glistened. "With beer, like just about anything else, what you want, you can get. You just have to know what you want.

"Tell me, Kyle," Sheldon said, fixing his powder-blue eyes on me. "What do you think of our little Saskatoon so far?"

At the curb before a domed Ukrainian church, a tramp in a dirty maroon toque and a bomber jacket gave the limo a double take as we turned a corner and sped down a straightaway. I shifted in my seat and returned Sheldon's gaze, took a sip of O Vee.

"Tasty beer. You can get very tasty beer here."

"With our compliments," Sheldon said, half-saluting.

"I like Saskatoon. It's a lovely town." I didn't know what he was after, but I was tired, wasn't in the mood for anything but a programmed response as I downed the rest of my beer. "Tell me about where we're going."

"My private camp about an hour from here. You'll really enjoy yourself. Another O Vee?"

"Nah, not right now."

Having finished his beer, Bobby stowed the bottle in the icebox and turned his head into the back corner of the limo to rest on an airline-style pillow. He was as far away from the Cup as he could be.

"We don't get fellows like you down this way very often," Sheldon said. He paused, but I didn't bite. "What Saskatoon has to offer often takes people by surprise. For example, I'll bet you didn't know that Saskatoon claims more PhDs per capita than any other place in Canada. Or that Saskatchewan is known as the museum capital of North America. You really must pay a visit to the Mendel. Very significant Inuit pieces. A few pieces we donated, right Bobby?"

Bobby seemed to be out like a light. Slow and deliberate as his stretch limo, Sheldon invited comments but they weren't required.

He told me after he'd graduated law school and worked for a developer in Regina, he served a term as a provincial Conservative Party member, was being groomed for the leadership before he dropped out of politics and returned to private life. Now he owned things. Office towers, hunting camps, shopping malls. As we motored up the Yellowhead Highway, I had the sinking feeling that Sheldon Shriver was just warming up. The evening sun beating through the tinted glass, the beer in my belly, and the prospect of listening to Sheldon for I didn't know how long was making me drowsy. Perhaps I was wrong about the applause at the Lions Club banquet. Perhaps the guests had cheered and carried on because Sheldon had cut his speech so short.

"Of course, the sad part is, Saskatoon remains a big mystery to most people," Sheldon said, his eyes trained on me. "But last year no single place in Canada had faster tourism growth than this city."

"And Gordie Howe," I said. Shadows fell on wheat fields along the banks of the North Saskatchewan River. "Lest we forget, Gordie Howe."

"Floral, Saskatchewan." Sheldon seemed to like my leg pulling. Maybe not enough people take him on, I thought. Maybe Sheldon was flashing me looks at the luncheon because he was looking for a rival. Somebody he couldn't push around.

"It's a common enough misconception, of course, that Gordie hailed from Saskatoon," he said, leaning toward me. I couldn't believe how perfect his face looked. Not only had his nose hairs been trimmed and his eyebrows shaped, but his whole face looked as if it had had a wax job. Emmett Noble must be rolling over in his grave.

"But Gordie did play his junior here," Sheldon continued. "Gordie Howe ... there's a hockey player you can talk about. Present to kids as a role model. Real statesman for The Game," he declared, shaking his finger. Resigned to the rant, I slid down the seat, stretching my legs and tucking my arms behind my head. A puff of hair clung to the synthetic pillow cover.

As Sheldon Shriver droned on, I nodded, said "uh-huh," made the expected comments. If Sheldon Shriver were looking for a fight, this Stanley Cup escort was willing to concede the first round.

chapter three

There was an edge of darkness to the day when the stretch limo turned down the lane into the Shrivers' camp, a reconstituted Hudson's Bay Company factory along the North Saskatchewan. The blockhouse, which I imagined three hundred years ago served as lookout for Indian traders and English explorers, was decked out as a glittering terrace. Men in tuxes and women in long gowns waved Red Wings caps and cheered, saluting us with their cocktail glasses. Red Wings banners flew from the ramparts above a sign that proclaimed "Fort Stanley." Above the walls, an oversized Canadian flag waved lazily in the evening breeze.

"What do you think?" Sheldon asked, his teeth still remarkably shiny in the purple light of dusk.

"Nice," I said as I looked again, sure that one of the women in a sheer black dress on the terrace—waving perhaps harder than most—was Myra, the ticket taker from the Agricultural Hall of Fame. "Very nice."

Champagne corks popped. Bubbly and applause rained down from the blockhouse terrace as Bobby, his legs stiff from the ride, struggled to get out of the limo. I took Belle out of her case and handed her to Bobby, who was gumming an unlit cigar that was popped into his mouth. Photographers flooded him with flash, throwing light on a forest of spruce behind him. My head swam with the smell of pine, and I thought of Norma. Funny how that is, no matter what happens between people, there are smell memories that become forever linked to a lover, an old friend. On a trip we took to Alaska last summer, Norma had snapped roll after roll of film, saying she'd heard a rustle in the trees, seen figures moving through the bush. But when we had the photos developed we had nothing but trees. Snapshot after snapshot of northern pine trees, growing in every which way. "Blue spruce, not moose," she said.

Bobby touched my arm that was resting on the car door.

"Mr. Callendar—"

"Kyle, son."

Bobby had set down the Cup and one hand was holding the cigar while the other was jammed in his trousers, jangling something. Keys, maybe coins. Bobby had the nervous habit of narrowing his eyes while he talked, like he wasn't just feeling for something inside his pockets. Like there was something on his mind that he would never in his life talk about. If I were going to see that there was a lot of Sheldon in Bobby, I was going to need more time. Or a team of investigators.

"Kyle, could I …" Bobby started. With that, the photogs backed off him as if they'd received an order. They were like no press guys I had ever seen. Blue jeans washed sometime during the past year, weren't grabbing for cigarettes every five seconds, or poking their lenses at Belle like seagulls on raw liver.

"Kyle, could I keep the Cup for a while?" Bobby asked, his eyes closed as if he were reading lines on the underside of his lids.

"Yes, of course," I said.

What a waste, I thought. Thousands of guys are more deserving than this one to be with the Cup. Twelve guys on the ice and Bobby was the last one you'd notice. "Not so mobile going backward on his skates," scouts wrote. "Has trouble defending on attack left … hesitant to take charge, lets the play come to him."

But about once a game Bobby cold-cocked somebody. In junior, he hit the points leader so hard the boy missed the next ten games with a muscle tear, caused him to lose the scoring championship, his shot of being picked in the first round. Finally, the Bruins took him in the seventh, when Bobby went too—to the Ducks.

At first Bobby didn't get in his big hit a game, and he was traded to the Red Wings as the player to be named later in a four-man deal. The guy everybody forgot about. The season he made it to the

NHL the Wings' top draft pick suffered a mild concussion when he collided with Bobby on a line change. In practice, a month later, a goalie prospect tweaked a groin muscle, stretching for Bobby's snapper from the slot. Coach began to think Bobby was a jinx and he was benched.

Then the Wings started beating everyone in sight on their way to the Stanley Cup. That saved Bobby, who Coach began to see as less a curse than a necessary evil. In the run-up to the playoffs, Bobby played some, managed his occasional game-stopping hit. But he didn't get on the ice in the playoffs. Insiders said his days as a Red Wing were numbered.

I gave Bobby the drill. Ten minutes with photographers then bring the Cup into the compound and take her to a display area at the back of the fort. Bobby nodded, said he understood, and I left him as photo flashes burst around him and Belle. Once inside the compound, Sheldon steered me toward Frank Cattel, who had shed his trout tie for a black silk one, and grabbed the hand of a beefy man in a tuxedo that fit him like skin. The old man thumped the back of his friend as they walked off together.

"Told you the Shrivers were something else, eh?" Frank said, tugging on the collar of his tux.

"Uh-huh," I replied. "How long have you known them?"

"The Shrivers?" he said as he cupped my elbow in his hand, guiding me toward the drinks table. "How long have I known the Shrivers? May as well ask how long you been breathing, or in my case," he said, parsing the thin strands of hair on his head with his free hand, "how long you been going bald."

"A long time, I take it."

"Now that's a little personal," he said, screwing up his face in mock offence.

"Sorry, I'm just interested, that's all. Comes with the job. So what's the story? How did you come to know them?"

He was about to say something, but checked himself. Then he looked beyond me as if I were invisible.

"What comes with the job? Being a snoop?" he whispered in my ear. He waved at a TSN sports girl. She and her toothy grin began to make their way toward us.

"Jesus, Frank," I said, surprised by his chilly response. "I'm just asking."

Frank suddenly stiffened and glared at me. "I can assure you that you needn't worry about the safety of the Cup. Mr. Shriver wouldn't want you to worry. It wouldn't make him feel very good."

"Listen, I'm—"

"The escort to the Stanley Cup. That means a lot to me. It means a lot to Mr. Shriver. We will take very good care of your Cup."

"I don't believe this, I—"

A big-busted woman with a slight man stepped in front of the TSN interviewer, but Frank moved between them and me and turned his back on the three of them. "You strike me as a guy who likes his ale," Frank said, his Dale Carnegie switch snapped back on. "But try the Iceberg. Mr. Shriver has some connections. Usually, with vodka I can take it or leave it. This stuff, though, is heaven itself."

I'd been good, hadn't had anything stronger than beer in years. But Frank's changed manner unnerved me. A vodka with ice appeared in his hands, and I took a sip. He was right about one thing. That Iceberg was smooth.

Frank nodded toward some men with hunched-over shoulders, a gathering of question marks. "The press," he said as he winked at me and shot over toward them.

What was it with Frank? I wondered as I drained my Iceberg. Why was he so testy? Usually these hangers-on were as pliable as ten-year-old skates. Something had set Frank off, I thought. Something about the Shrivers.

I went back for another Iceberg and began to look around. I'd been to a few forts. In public school, we'd once visited Sainte-Marie among the Hurons, the former Jesuit mission built to bring Christianity to the wilderness. Old native women fussed with dried grass—making baskets while a volunteer yakked away. Then, during my junior hockey days, I visited Fort Henry, a limestone fortress in Kingston, Ontario, which was built to defend against the Americans in the War of 1812. Never a shot was fired in anger. Old Fort Henry was just like its name: dull and antiquated, ideal for its idleness.

Fort Stanley, though, was of an entirely different type. Oak tongue-and-groove floors as shiny as ice covered the compound's interior. Along the dark-wood ramparts, the revellers mingled, peering over the top and into the woods as if they were taking first watch. Young couples dallied, women sipping from martini glasses, men holding long snouts of ale. Heads tilted skyward, with one man pointing where the morning star would appear in the opalescent sky.

"It retracts," Myra said, touching the hollow of my upper arm. She had come up behind me as I was looking at the sky. Faint smell of gardenias. "In the fall, before the weather turns, the roof covers the whole compound. You can imagine the snowfall out here can be amazing … Before it gets too much colder tonight, I'm sure Sheldon will push the button," she said as she pressed her finger into the small of my back.

Applause erupted as Bobby and Sheldon, carrying Belle between them, climbed a set of stairs at the back wall of the compound. A shelf halfway up the side of the wall had been installed to hold the Cup. The lights dimmed and a floodlight covered the Shrivers and glinted off the Stanley Cup like a star on earth. Bobby had shed his team jacket and Timberlands for a red tuxedo and black dress shoes. He looked like a shorn Santa Claus slimmed by Pilates. Sheldon held his hand up in some kind of benediction, while Bobby squinted in the light.

"Are you pushing my buttons?" I asked Myra.

"You tell me," she said, smiling, her green eyes peering over a half-filled martini glass. Her curly hair was pinned up, revealing a long graceful neck. A triangle of thigh showed through a slit in her evening dress. Even her ankles weren't covered but surrounded by raw leather strands of Hellenic sandals.

Suddenly, a spotlight blinded me. An old woman near me almost keeled over. I felt Myra's hip graze the skirt of my blazer as she slipped away.

"Please, let's everyone give a down-home round of applause to Kyle Callendar—the one-time NHLer and escort to the Stanley Cup," Sheldon said into a microphone. The crowd cheered for a beat, and then the light swung to others: the president of the Chamber of Commerce, Frank Cattel, the publisher of a seed catalogue.

A man with Pringles ears in a farmer's haircut caught my eye and took a step toward me. "Quite a show, eh?" he said. "Of course, it's probably nothing to you given what you see every day."

"Yep," I said, still half-blinded. Beyond the farmer, a stone's throw away, Myra was talking to two women in suits. Hockey coaches or equipment suppliers. I couldn't catch her eye, so I headed to the drinks table. If I were going to hook up with someone like Myra, I'd need some more liquid courage. Something to push down the guilt I was beginning to feel about Norma. At the drinks table were tubs of ice filled with champagne. And Jameson's Irish whisky, and cases of a Finger Lakes chardonnay that people were saying went down like cool silk.

"You were some player yourself, Kyle," said the guy with the farmer's cut who'd followed me. He pointed to the back wall where Bobby was holding the Cup above his head. "It should be you up there."

He was an older guy, pushing sixty. I'd got pretty good in my job of placing people and the work they did by my first impressions. The tux was a size too small, particularly across the throat, which had suffered the worst for aging. Even in the half-light, I could see flesh gathered under the pressure of the collar. I thought financial adviser, peddling stocks and bonds to farmers on the verge of unloading a thousand acres. No, a financial adviser wouldn't have rented a tux. Insurance, I settled on. He sold insurance to schoolteachers.

"Ginger ale, lots of ice," he ordered at the bar. A recovering alcoholic. And for some time, too. He was very comfortable taking the lead with strangers.

"Wilbur Stanfield," he said. For a big man his bones were surprisingly delicate and as we shook hands I crushed them in mine.

"Sorry, fella."

"Listen, no, no, not at all," he said, flexing his fingers. "Think nothing of it. As I certainly know—I've seen you often enough on the ice—you've got the hands. I got to tell you, best hands I've ever seen in close."

"Not anymore, I don't think," I said as I took my Iceberg and moved away from a crowd at the bar. "You're going back a lot of years."

"Maybe, but to me it was like yesterday."

A thin man with a fuzzy-caterpillar moustache squeezed in beside Wilbur. Propelling the man forward was the woman with the enormous bust I'd seen when I was talking to Frank. She was holding a martini glass at an angle, with pale yellow contents dribbling over the lip.

"Pardon me, but I couldn't help overhearing you," the thin man chirped. "My name is Bruce Rangford and this is my wife, Wilma."

I nodded at Laurel and his Hardy-in-drag, who smiled grimly and jutted her hand toward me. After the experience with Wilbur, I let up on the pressure and Wilma yanked my hand down like she was pumping for well water.

"Kyle Callendar, what an honour," she blurted. I drained my drink and handed the glass to her husband, pointed toward the drinks table, signalling with two hands coming to a peak. Bruce snatched up the glass and, with Wilbur to assist, was off to the bar.

"How about that, as I live and breathe. Kyle Callendar. You're the one, the reason I'm here tonight," Wilma said as she swabbed her forehead with a handkerchief. "You gave me the memories, I can tell you. The night of nights was against the Leafs in the old Gardens … Easter weekend … Can't stand those Leafs. Never could. Bruce doesn't feel that way. Ask him, he'll tell you. Me, that's a different story. Hate them like topsy. Anyway, you came into the game on the checking line, assigned to shadow Darryl Sittler. Remember?"

"Yeah," I said, "listen, I've got to—"

"Just stop him from scoring and you've done your job. But no, what do you do? You score three goals. Three goals. Your only hat trick, as far as I know. With also-ran Pittsburgh. No good, no-account Pittsburgh."

Wilma was startled by someone's loud laugh, and I moved to step around her but she seized my arm. She was milk-maiden strong. The smell of gin, dog meal, and five-dollar perfume was making me sick.

"We didn't let the Penguin thing get in the way, though—you being a Keppel, Ontario, boy and all—'cause for that one night every gosh darn person in gosh darn Maple Leaf Gardens rose up as one and threw a hat onto the ice when you scored that third one." I smiled lamely at Wilma. I remember. Like a walrus at play, she reeled back in a throwing motion. Wilma threw her Easter bonnet with yellow ribbons trailing from way up in the greys. It went sailing through the blues, the reds, and the golds of the Gardens among fedoras with mallard feathers, pillbox hats, and made-in-Taiwan baseball caps. A sea of swirling headwear. The scoreboard screen did a close-up of only one hat on the arena ice.

"Remember that hat? My grandma's Easter bonnet? You gotta have remembered that hat," Wilma said, leaning into my face. Sweat dotted sprouts of hair on her upper lip.

"That was from me," she said. She grabbed me in a bear hug and kissed me on the lips. "Your biggest fan."

Finally, I managed to stagger away from her. I remember all right. Stick to Number 27. Sittler. Curly locks of Adonis. The slap of Coach's hand. Out there Callendar. Stick to him. Like Velcro. Jar his hands. Get in front of him. Behind his back. Slap the stick on the ice, Callendar. Force the pass. To your wing, not his. And back to you. Sittler's tired, not up to banging you, he's got no Number 27 to cling to, to shadow. You're in. Deke the goalie. Mike Palmateer gives up goals through the legs. Goal! Goal! Goal! Coach is punching the air, the fans cheering like mad for the Ontario boy, throwing hats, hundreds of them. Like snow in a paperweight. They see your arms raised, smiling for all you're worth, kissing the puck you retrieve from the Gardens' net, but what they can't know is what that roar does inside your head. Me, as a boy, my hair wet and flat to my head, my father kneeling before me. You look at your skates as you're chasing down Adonis, and it's Father you see, tightening your laces. Fitting your wings. You see the top of Father's head, the bald bit, the soft pink spot, and then as his head slowly rises, his smile, eye teeth like fangs. You've got it, boy. Don't disappoint me. Get out there and do what I told you, do it for me, for all of us, do you hear? I'm talking to you, boy. Did you hear me? Uh-huh. Of course, Dad. Sure. I'll be watching you, son. Remember what I told you. Thanks Dad, you say as you feel the pressure building like a blow to the head.

But you push it all down, down. None of that is ever supposed to matter. None of it will ever escape. If you can't say something nice about someone, don't say anything at all. It gets in the way. Nothing is outside The Game.

chapter four

My father did wallpaper. He came back from the war and he wall-papered the house. Tiny roses in the kitchen. Blue pinstripes in the dining room. Pale burgundy in the hall. Cream and charcoal in the master bedroom. He even wallpapered rooms that he'd set aside for the boy he was going to have. With thousands of tin soldiers on dark orange. Then he did a room with glossy ballerinas, but Mom never did deliver Dad a girl. Later, he'd turn it into a sewing room. Yolk yellow, with tiny blue dots.

Somebody once wrote that for soldiers there's no such thing as after the war. That was so with my father. He was always on a campaign. Each glued strip of wallpaper that he put up in our house was carefully planned, meticulously placed. No overhang. Strip after strip after strip of wallpaper was done in this way.

Father's first fight was at Dieppe in 1942. He was a kid, not yet twenty, one of the five thousand Canadian soldiers who landed at the Nazi stronghold that August day. He survived while nine hundred of his fellow soldiers were slaughtered in the time an office worker puts in a day's work. Perhaps after Dieppe, Father felt that only order and discipline could save him and his fam-ily. That the only authority he could trust was of his own mak-ing. Father marched out of Europe and into Keppel believing in himself—and only himself. He married Mother, bought a house and an abandoned barn, wallpapered the house, then went out on the road alone, trucking. When he didn't have any kids at first, I think he was content with his life, because a dozen years later he wasn't home, was on the road when I was born. Then, for my second Christmas, on the coldest nights of the year, Father watered the floor of the barn and made ice. He installed plywood boards for shooting pucks at, built pine benches for players to rest on and for people to watch.

Then Father bought a Super 8 camera. I remember only a few flickering images, me in the blue and white of the Toronto Maple Leafs, a navy cap on my head. I'm on our rink in skates, struggling to stay up, a hockey stick in my hands. As an adult watching, I wait for those tired little legs to give out, for the teeter and fall. Instead, I dash to the end boards, back and forth, again and again, never once going down, until I finally shudder to a stop for my close-up before my father, the camera's steady hand.

But Father wasn't one for skating. He made the ice, but as far as I know he didn't even own a pair of skates, didn't go out on the rink except in his buckled-up galoshes carrying a shovel, a hammer to fix the boards, or the garden hose for flooding. Maybe it was the war that took the play out of him. Or maybe that was just the way he was. In any case, when I was growing up, Father was either on the road, in his basement workshop, or in the barn making ice. For long hours in the winter, he'd flood the ice, make repairs to the barn. Me, my task was clear. I played all hours on the ice, later made the travelling hockey teams, squads of Keppel's best.

I was small for my age, but I beat the odds to make those teams. In wartime, odds aren't just against a Canadian, they're stacked against him. Most of the thirteen hundred soldiers taken prisoner at Dieppe would spend the next three years in a stalag. Dad was one of the lucky ones to make it safely back to England. After the war, Dad had to win, at all costs. And he'd be damned if a son of his wound up a loser. "Any player worth his salt thinks he's better than you," he told me more than once. "Maybe they are. But don't you ever let them believe it."

"Why yell when everyone else is yelling?" he'd say in the car after the game. "What's the point of that? No one is going to hear you." In the cold hush of a thousand games in Keppel, it was my Father's voice that broke the silence. Thick red cords bulged along his neck. "You're a goof, ref ... Put the whistle in your pocket ... What, are you blind?" He yelled at other players, coaches, parents

who told him to shush. But Father was unshushable. I shoot right
but played left wing because Father preferred the west side of the
rink, a place ten rows above centre ice where no one else dared ven-
ture and the acoustics were best. If Father had sat on the east side, I
would have played right wing. I skated up and down the ice, never
veering more than a few feet from the wall. The only way I could
play The Game was to stay as far away as I could from my father.

An eerie silence fell when Father yelled. Like the one that follows a crazy person's outburst on a subway. Or in a bar before the
first punch is thrown. Parents of ten-year-old boys watched to see
if he would carry out the threat in his voice. Climb out and onto
the ice and beat to a pulp a volunteer referee—a postman or fellow
truck driver helping out at the rink on his day off. Many's the time
it seemed like he would, but he never did.

Times were different for truckers in those days. Before price-
cutting brought on by deregulation in the States meant that anyone
with a worn cap and an affinity for caffeine could buy a rig and
start a business. Dad drove for Fleming Cartage, a moving company
that was expanding into other types of freight. Founder and owner
Bob Fleming was my coach the year I played for the junior Keppel
Grey Devils. Dad and Bob got closer when I played for the team and
broke Bob's own record for goals in a single season: forty-seven. I
scored fifty-one, my most ever in a season, and the *Keppel Advance*
splashed a front-page picture of the three of us—Coach Fleming,
my dad, and me. About this time, Dad began getting more regular
short-haul accounts—palettes of Home Hardware catalogues and
Reader's Digest from the WeB Press, white goods from the General
Electric plant to Toronto, London, and Kingston. Rarely an over-
night. From time to time, he won a lucrative run to Florida to pick
up fresh-cut flowers. He carted toilet paper south and picked up
flowers for northbound, a two-way that weighed a fraction of what
any other job would, cut fuel expenses nearly in half. Father never
made better time than when he went on a flower run. It was a treat
for Mother and me, too. For a week or more after a flower run,
Father would be in a good mood. High on roses, Mom liked to say.

For hours, it seemed, he'd sit on the pine bench in the barn
and toss pucks toward me. Black disks floating along a pristine

blue-grey surface that I'd slapshot into the boards. Harder, faster, he would say. Don't look down. Get used to the rhythm of the shot, let the stick be an extension of you. No, not like that. Pay attention. Yes. That's it. Attaboy.

I used that stick, forehand and backhand, flipping pucks into the open flaps of a cardboard box that Father moved around the ice. Ten in a row, backhand; ten in a row, forehand; alternate to twenty. At fourteen years old, I could flip a puck into a moving cigar box eight times out of ten, either hand.

In those days, boys would come over. Neighbourhood kids, but also boys from away. Come to Callendar's barn, they said. Father lit the place with three naked bulbs on a string and flood-lights in the corners, and we played ice hockey until the wee hours on holidays, hour-long games after dinner on school nights. In summer, I stooped to pick pennies from the street and kept them in a jar. Then I'd paint the coppers fire-engine red and sky blue and before the nights turned cold place them, my lucky pennies, on the dirt floor of the barn so that during the long winter nights I could see them sparkle under the lights, like pieces of a dream that I could catch and hold while I skated on the foot-deep ice my father built.

Dizzy from my encounter with Wilma, I excused myself and made my way through the crowds to the bathroom. I'd been do-ing a good job of keeping the past in check, but the combination of booze and the stirring of memories from the likes of Wilma were sure to bring me down. For decades, it seemed, I'd managed to keep my memory swarm at bay. But now I could feel it com-ing on, like the rumbling in your gut before the retching started. What I needed was a distraction; if I had half a brain, an ounce of strength to resist temptation, I should have blown the place right then and there. I know that now. I should have left the Cup with the Shrivers—which was the plan anyway—and got a driver to take me back to my motel where I could ring up Norma and talk with her into the night. That would have been smart, would've kept my life intact. Instead, I would go down the tubes. Get what I deserved.

Sheldon, it seemed, was more than my match. Talk about distractions. Take the bathroom, for instance. When I walked in I couldn't believe it. Stadium size, with stalls labelled wolverine, beaver, muskrat, grizzly, black rat snake, and fisher cat. The stalls were empty, so I peeked in and each toilet seat was lined in the hide of the labelled animal. The walls were something, too, carved in University of Saskatchewan greystone. I entered that room and all my thoughts of escape vanished.

A man wearing thick glasses was fingering a chunk of the wall before a urinal. He was lanky with the settled posture of a former athlete, overdeveloped back and leg muscles. When ex-hockey players stop training, begin to relax, their backsides balloon. But the man holding himself up before the urinal in Sheldon Shriver's fort bathroom was anything but fat.

He turned to look at me as I moved to a urinal and unzipped. His right eye was powder blue glass and wandered, but the other was clear. Something about him was very familiar.

"Some kind of party, eh?" he said.

"Yeah," I said, beginning to feel myself again. Piss splashed on pink mint. Next, I'd check out the feel of the fur-lined toilet seats. Butt-test the black rat snake and the wolverine. That would be something that Norma would get a real charge out of.

"I could understand you not recognizing me," the man said, looking down to the floor as he zipped up. "It's been a while. Jim Cowpland. You played with my brother, Doug, at Kingston."

"Yeah, yeah, that's right," I said, startled. "I thought I recognized you. I can see a lot of Doug in you … I—is he here?"

"Nah, but my dad is. Just outside. I know that he'd love to see you."

I stared at him for a beat and said, "Sure, tell your dad, sure. Later."

I went into the black rat snake stall, closed and latched the door behind me, and listened as Jim left the room. I pulled down my trousers and sat on the seat. The surface was surprisingly slick and hard, no give. I slumped against the wall of the stall like a sack of feathers.

Ron Cowpland. I hadn't thought of him in years. Gone Ron. December 1978—I'll never forget it. I was in Pittsburgh blue, the jaunty Penguin dial on the front. One Friday that December, Doug, Ron's first born, had been called up to the Toronto Maple Leafs. The next day was *Hockey Night in Canada*, the Maple Leafs against the Chicago Blackhawks. Everyone in the country had a version of the truth, but Doug and I were close then and he told me what really happened.

The summer before when Doug was working in Ron's garage, Gordie Howe had come to call. Ron looked up from under a car he was working on to see the great man himself. Gordie was shaking his boy's hand, saying he couldn't stay long, was just passing through, but that he was an admirer, that he really thought the boy had what it took. Framed by the open door of Ron's Repair, massive clouds chasing each other across the sky, Saskatchewan's Own stood with Ron Cowpland's first-born son. Ron could've got up, wiped his hands of grease, and shaken the hand of hockey's greatest player of all time, but the weight of the moment pressed down the small of his back, kept him there on his creeper unable to move, not wanting to miss a word. "Pardon me, but I've got to go," Gordie Howe said in dulcet tones as he grabbed Doug's shoulders with both hands. "I'll be watching you."

Minutes before puck-drop on that *Hockey Night in Canada*, Ron shut the lights in his country home and cranked up the volume on the colour set bought on loan that week. His heart thumped against his rib cage as he pulled up a hassock from the easy chair and sat before the screen. "JimBoy. Rose. C'mon." Rose dropped her apron on the counter and Jim, who was working on a motorbike outside, rubbed his hands on a rag, threw it down. They both came running and perched on the sofa to watch.

A simple announcement followed, read by the cool CBC voice. The one that interrupts this program for a special news bulletin. That says this is a test of the emergency broadcast system. Only a test. A voice that isn't selling anything. It's unironic and unprovoking, inevitable and invincible. "The game previously scheduled between the Toronto Maple Leafs and the Chicago Blackhawks is not available at this time," it said. "In the meantime, we will broadcast the game between the St. Louis Blues and the Vancouver Canucks, already in progress."

What followed was a blur. Sound bites, ellipsis, snapshots passed through the hands of jurors ... A fist through the kitchen wall ... Shotgun blast into the TV screen ... Murderous threats to the answering service of the Dogrib television station ... A car with a man and his daughter veers off the road to avoid collision with a pickup, barrelling down the centre line ... The television reporter no more than a girl, a specialist in soybean oil futures, winter wheat varieties, a shotgun to her head ... Eight reporters against the newsroom wall ... "TAKE THAT GAME OFF THE AIR. PUT ON MY SON'S GAME. I WANT TO SEE MY SON ..." "Please, sir, there's nothing we can do. Please don't ..." Ron out the front door, still holding the gun, and three Mounties appear. "Hold it right there." Ron wheels and fires, and an officer's down, hit in the foot. The Mounties return fire. Three shots. One in Ron's left shoulder, another in the mouth, a third through the armpit, piercing a lung. He falls, rolls bleeding in the snow.

Across Canada, sympathies were with Ron Cowpland. Flowers by the carload arrived at the hospital; well-wishers jammed the switchboard. After it was certain he would recover, Ridley Appliance Store in Keppel ran "Gone Ron!" sales, half-price discounts to replace your destroyed TV. Expansion was killing The Game, according to Grant Ridley, so it was only natural to slaughter your old TV. Just do a "Ron," bring in your smashed-up set and a copy of the TV listing of the game that set you off—Pittsburgh Penguins vs. Buffalo Sabres, say, or Minnesota North Stars vs. Los Angeles Kings—and you had a deal.

"It's good to see you again, boy," Ron Cowpland said just outside the bathroom door. He was holding Jim's arm, leaning on him. Next to them on the wall were framed action shots of Bobby Shriver in a sequence of games at Joe Louis Arena in Detroit. Except for the tiny lights on the photos in eight-by-ten frames, it was dark. "You haven't changed a bit."

I couldn't say the same for Ron. The life drained out of a beech tree in winter. Gnarled arms that looked as if they would snap at the slightest pressure.

"You don't look so bad yourself, Ron," I said.

Ron shook his head and smiled. "Yes, I do. But if you're of a mind to humour an old man, I'd like you to do something for me. Would you be so kind as to join Jim and me on a little drive?"

I looked up at the lights on the Cup, scanned the room for Myra, who for the life of me I didn't want to miss hooking up with. And what about Norma? I thought with a shudder. Why did I always find myself so quick to betray Norma?

"It'll be all right," the old man said, patting my wrist. His palm was rough and bony. "You've met your obligations here. You've other obligations. If you'd allow me the opportunity, I'd like to introduce you to them." He put his arm around my shoulder and the three of us headed for the door like *Ponderosa*.

I don't do well with road silences. When Norma and I take motor trips, we talk non-stop—about family and friends, hockey, her art, gardening plans. When I'm alone I must have books on tape, say a Jim Harrison or an Elmore Leonard, or oldies music, Creedence Clearwater, Croce, Chapin, *Frankenstein* by Edgar Winter.

My feelings about the road started with my father. Father drove for miles on end and didn't say anything. He was a man who could travel across two prairie provinces and not change his facial expression, his lips sealed except for the occasional yawn. Deep inside him there was a hurt or an anger brewing. I never knew which. He was slow to boil and the telltale signs of his temper coming on were subtle, barely detectable. In a rage Father's eyes stopped blinking and narrowed ever so slightly. It was only a moment, and if you noticed it you could try to prepare. For a fury that you'd never forget.

Ron didn't look anything like my father. Father was like Jean Beliveau, tall and distinguished, while Ron reminded me more of Walter Gretzky, Wayne Gretzky's dad. A shy man who on long trips doesn't know what to do with his hands, so he sits on them. A man who could live alone in the forest for seasons on end and not feel that he was missing out on something, who would say with a straight face and humble bearing that for all those years he had no regrets.

For longer than I was comfortable we drove along a country road with no one saying anything. As different as Ron seemed from my dad, I sensed that he, too, had a bad temper. With a father like mine, I was an expert in pointless rages.

Jim's hard thigh and hip were pressed into mine. On my other side, Ron hunched over the wheel like that Picasso of an old man cradling a guitar. In the dashboard light, I could see Ron's fingernails were blackened. He'd put on a battered feed-mill cap that narrowed even further his ferret face.

With his good eye wide and a wry smile, Jim unlatched the glovebox, pulled a flat board from under his seat, and laid it on the open cover. Then he took a Drum tobacco pouch from his shirt pocket and plunked it down on the board, laying two cigarette papers alongside. He poked in the cigarette lighter, rolled and licked two cigarettes, and put one cigarette in his father's mouth. The lighter popped out and his old man lit the tobacco. It smelled pungent, delicious. I hadn't smoked in a dozen years and I couldn't believe how much I craved a cigarette. Jim rolled and licked a third one, which I greedily accepted, and the old man lit mine and Jim's cigarette with the dimming coil of the car's lighter.

We smoked and drove for another mile in silence. The lights of the old pickup barely dented the darkness. As I looked at the frail man relaxed behind the wheel and his son, stretched out as serene as you please beside him, I, too, began to ease into my seat. For the first time all night, I felt my jaw go slack, my bowels loosen.

I rolled down the window. The dark plain and blast of cool air made me think of France, where Father spent the war. Of course, I asked my father about the war. But he was silent. "No son," he said once. "I won't talk about that. Not now." What could I do but imagine the horror instead? What the dying say, that the sky literally falls on their head, that the worst is in the waiting and the fear, the fear of waiting, the waiting of fear. How could I begin to know? To begin to put it in words if they weren't my father's? The enemies I'd faced were commonplace: the playground bully, an on-ice rival, women scorned. My father, on the other hand, wasn't so lucky. He was a survivor, a man with real blood on his hands. Who was I to ever stand up to a man like that? One whom I couldn't let go of.

I took a last drag on my cigarette and flicked the butt out the window. Try as I might, I'd never been able to say no to the power of a certain kind of man.

"Over there," Jim said, jerking his head to the right. Ron Cowpland eased the pickup off the road and turned down what looked like a dirt lane. Jim pulled out a six-pack of Sage Grouse Ale from under the seat and a flask of Four Aces from the glovebox. The truck rolled to a stop. "We're going to have us a little Stanley Cup celebration of our own," Ron said, his words leaking like mincemeat from a grinder.

We were sitting on a picnic table at a pullout. Ron sucked on his cigarette and took a slug of whisky, offered me the bottle, and I took a long swallow. He touched Jim on the knee, made a hand-pump gesture at his mouth pointing to the truck, and Jim ran off, a bloodhound in a posse.

"It's not been easy for that boy," Ron said.

"How so?" I'd lit up another rollie but the second drag tasted foul, and I stubbed it on the tabletop and flicked it toward the bush.

"He could play, too," he said, ignoring me. "But where Doug was quick and shifty, Jim was aggressive and mulish."

"I know from Doug he lost his eye playing. I'm sorry. That must have been really hard for all of you."

Ron sucked his cigarette and blew a puff that enveloped him, made him look like a hologram of the creature from the black lagoon. He swigged some Sage Grouse and dropped his butt, ground it under the heel of his work boot. "A high stick carved his left eye out of his socket as clean as you please. Blood was just pouring out of him like a geyser."

"I really can't imagine," I said, with another swallow of Four Aces.

"Yeah," Ron said. He wheezed, couldn't at first catch his breath. "His mother covered her face and screamed, while I saw my boy's eye on a blue line button until the trainer gathered it up. They say it was only seconds, that they were on it quick, but something like that happens and time is as black as space. You can't see to the end of it."

Ron stared toward the bush. "Jim went as far as any one-eyed player could be expected to go. But he would never be like his older brother."

Jim returned to the picnic table and gave Ron an inhaler, which the old man puffed. Ron closed his eyes for a time and when he looked at me again he seemed very tired, as if he'd aged a decade. He touched his son on the face and traced a finger up the cheekbone toward his glass eye. A harsh shadow fell on Jim's face so I couldn't see the hand clearly, but something in the old man's body language as he leaned over his son got to me. A lump rose in my throat as it hadn't since I was a boy, and my eyes filled with tears.

"Do you have boys, Kyle?" Ron whispered.

"No," I said, knuckling the corners of my eyes. The cool night air evaporated the tears on contact. I popped the cap off a Sage Grouse and downed half of it.

"Perhaps I've overdone it. Sad memories. An old man's folly."

"Nah," I said. The booze, the travel, and the strangeness of the night suddenly hit me like a ton of bricks. "What did you bring me here for, Ron?"

"Conversation. Insights to humour an old man. Answers maybe."

"Okay," I said. "What do you want to know?"

Ron folded his hands in his lap just as I used to do in the back seat of my dad's Impala. He was as still as a raccoon in a tree hollow. "I want to know about the Cup. What it's like being with the Cup."

"I don't know, Ron," I said, staring at my hands. For a moment I saw them as they were thirty years ago. Boy's hands. "I don't know what I can tell you. It's a job that I do. Just a job."

"No," he said, slowly shaking his head, "I've been watching you and that's just not so."

"Huh? What do you mean you've been watching me?"

Ron touched the back of his son's hand, and they smiled at each other. "My momma called it the sixth sense. Ran in the family, she said. I can't vouch for that part of it because most of my kin's dead now, but I do have a power to see things. Mostly it's about time, like I felt that day when Jim here lost his eye. Most people don't do anything but live in those tiny sweeps of the second hand across the clock. Just go about their daily business. But the fact is, what is known or seen along that dimension of time is only a fraction of what is there. Of what is possible."

I stared at Ron and he shook his head. He sipped his beer and motioned toward Jim, who walked into the dark.

"I don't know whether it was being shot up or old age," Ron said as he touched my knee. A tingling sensation ran up my spine and I shifted away from him. "But this sight has gotten right powerful as I've gotten older. I don't do much with it, but believe me when I tell you, this is not just a job for you … Now Kyle, please. Tell me about the Cup."

"My first memory was during a broadcast of an on-ice victory party. My father's black and white television," I said as I emptied the flask of whiskey, tossed it into a trash barrel with a clang. Ron had lit up another rollie and was nodding, his eyes closed.

"In Keppel, we lived in a clapboard two-storey with no basement. Not much, you know. Mother wore cloudy beads on a string around her neck and plastic cream-coloured earrings that snapped on. Father's gold-plated watch, a wedding gift from Mother, was tarnished and mostly it was on his wrist on a road faraway. Where he was when I was born, the first week in October, a birthday I share with Mario Lemieux and the opening of the NHL season. There was no money for fancy toys or board games, but we bought a TV set—a colour one—when I was ten years old, so when the games came on I began to believe that my birth was hockey itself, the beginning of the Stanley Cup run. To my eye that Cup glittered on TV like a glass house. Men on silver skates scampered round and round on ice with the most beautiful thing I would ever see.

"Ron, even Mother was a fan. Not really of The Game, exactly. Something deeper. She'd sit forward in her seat listening to Bill Hewitt, the television play-by-play man, and on radio, his father, Foster. Faster, Foster, I joked, but Mother took in every word. Twenty years or so before, she'd sat by the radio the same way listening for news about her fiancé in occupied France. Later, she sat listening the same way to Foster and Bill. Maple Leafs on the rush. Three abreast. The Canadiens are on their heels. A melee breaks out. Conacher's hit. Conacher's down. Apps is in alone. He shoots! He scores!

"Today, Keppel Feed Mill is boarded up, the five-and-dime is on its way out, and there's nothing much left of Main Street, except for The Beer Store and, on the outskirts, the Esso. There's the Church for Salvation, the Rink for Everything Else. Without hockey, Keppel would be like a dog with a full bladder that doesn't piss on the rug. The poor thing just curls into itself and sleeps.

"I've never done a thing in my life without the Cup in mind," I said, suddenly clear.

"I hear you," Ron said. "You're doing well. Don't stop. Go on."

"I love the stories of the Cup, you know. The shenanigans. We're not to talk about them, but–"

"I'm not telling anyone. This is just for me."

"There's a slew of them, of course," I said after a pause, a swig of Sage Grouse. "The Dallas Star who tossed Belle from a balcony into a swimming pool. Or Clark Gillies's dog lapping water from her. The baby who was baptized in her. Phil Bourque prying off the plastic base, finding the signatures of two handymen. 'Enjoy it, Phil Bubba Bourque, '91 Penguins,' he wrote. The only player with his name outside and inside the Cup.

"When the Rangers won, they took the Cup to Belmont, where a horse ate from her. Naked girls sat on her, made her so bent out of shape she couldn't hold the contents of a shot glass. 'Touch the Cup all you want, but keep your hands off the dancers,' a club owner said. After reforging another version of the trophy, the Hall said Belle can go into regular bars, but not those other kinds.

"My favourite tale, though, is of Ken Kilander, a Canadiens fan. The story that brought about the first of the escorts.

"He was in the stands of a Cup game in the Chicago Stadium. 1962. Bobby Hull, the Golden Jet, skated onto the ice, and Kilander froze. While the crowd was going nuts for Hull, Kilander had a vision. No way, he thought, could his beloved Canadiens stop this force of nature, this man who seemed capable of carrying his team-mates like so many hay bales. Montreal was ahead in the series, two games to one, but Cuchulain had appeared and as in Irish legend, in the rage of battle, Hull swelled to giant size. Finally, Ken Kilander fled the horror, his heart racing, his goal clear: to get to the Cup and smash the glass behind which she was kept at the time, in the lobby of the arena, and lift her from the wall.

Ken Kilander made a getaway, ran down the street with the Stanley Cup in his hands.

"'Your honour, I was simply taking the Cup back to Montreal where it belongs,' Ken Kilander would tell the judge. After that, the NHL began to think like the anthem. That we'd better get some guys like me to stand on guard."

I told Ron about playing junior, the endless bus trips out of Keppel and then Kingston. A stint in the International League, Hershey, Norfolk. Finally, the break with Pittsburgh, where I played before Mario, when we never really got close to the Cup. Then traded to also-rans Los Angeles, Winnipeg, and finally, the Sharks.

"Now you know," I said. "I lived to win the Cup, to be one of those big men gliding on ice. And it didn't happen."

"So why take the job? Why be reminded of that failure every day?" Ron said, leaning in toward me. Tires of a lone truck groaned on a country road. I groped to answer and nothing came.

"It was at Joey Kocur's Cup party," Ron continued. He rubbed his nose with the index finger and thumb of his right hand, once, twice, three times, as if the strokes massaged his memory. "You were there, about a thousand people for a corn roast out Kelvington way. I sensed something different in you then. Something missing. Like the wonder you talk about now was hidden. Tamped deep inside."

Jesus, where was he going with this, I thought. "I want to go now," I said. "I gotta be getting back."

"What do you think of the Cup now?" Ron asked, softly but firmly like a surgeon who wants to operate but needs consent. "You're with it every day. Tell me. Has it been a help?"

What else did I have but the Cup? For years Keppel had not been home for me. Mom and Dad have moved from the house I grew up in to a place on a lake. Father built the walls, the doors, the ceilings, the picture window. Installed a state-of-the-art heating system, underground pipes that work on the same principle as the plant for making artificial ice, but instead of making cold, they blow heat in winter, cold in summer. His phone bill is next to nothing; e-mails he sends to me are maximum three lines, part of his obsession to save. The weather, news of his curling bonspiels, the failing health of a former trucker pal I'd never heard of. On a computer in the mud room, he'll play Free Cell, the solitaire game, for hours. Hitting reset every time he doesn't win, so that he always has a perfect score. The first time I went north after he'd built the house, I asked if Dad would go out to see the sunset with me, to spend the last evening of my visit with him. He looked me in the eye and said, "No."

A taste of metal, like water from rusty pipes, rose in the back of my throat, and I gagged and spat to the ground. "I don't know," I said, feeling weak, suddenly out of breath. I felt faint, my knees buckled. "I wanted the Cup, that was all. It was the Cup or nothing. Always. Now—take me back to the fort, would you?"

Ron paused, a poker player who had planted an ace in the hole that eventually would fall. "I know, son," Ron said. Ron Cowpland could see right through me, down to the smallest part. He could see that I was in the fight of my life. He could see that all along.

chapter five

"Twenty-four Blue."

"An Ex, cans."

"Party Pack. No? Make it a Pleasure."

"Half a Crystal."

It was my last summer living at home and I was working at The Beer Store in Keppel. Most days I didn't work on the mike at the front; that was Fern Goodbar's job. He'd graduated from the community college broadcasting school, figured in the alumni report that ninety-five per cent of graduates had found work in their field. I didn't doubt that was so. Before or since, I've never heard anyone speak with greater authority into a mike than Fern Goodbar. He gave the customer the sense that his order of "Twelve Canadian" had the solemn reckoning of a noble act. Like driving a spike on the national railway, or tapping a century tree for maple syrup. On the way to the Keppel Beer Store, people warmed to the thought that Fern Goodbar would be at the mike, calling in their order.

Fern had slipped out to the dairy bar to get some smokes and I was behind the mike when Dad came in. It was a Tuesday afternoon and pretty slow, the only sale to Merle Kendall, the postie on late lunch who'd bought a six of Blue for the purpose.

Dad had the pinched look of indigestion. "Do you think you could get away for a bit?" he asked. "I'd like to talk to you about something."

"Dunno, Dad. Maybe when Fern gets back. I got the mike, eh?" I tapped the mike and the store crackled with sound. The Roxy on

49

Saturday night. Father had never before made such an appeal to me. I'd stopped asking about the war when I was small; press it, I thought, and he would blow for sure. Instead he would lecture me, tell me what he thought about this or that. But we'd never in our lives actually had a father-and-son talk. I resented it, had settled on the idea that the least said the better, so for the past couple of years I'd been avoiding him. We'd been nothing short of strangers living in the same house.

Dad smiled at me and his gaze lingered on my Fudgsicle-brown work shirt with KYLE sewn above the pocket. Dad was in his Fleming Cartage shirt on which Mom had hand sewn CHARLIE an inch or two higher than mine.

Coach Fleming had arranged the job at The Beer Store for me. It was the best gig in town for profile. People would come in for beer, sure, but also to hear Fern on the mike and shake the hand of Kyle Callendar, future hockey star.

"So then, let's hear you on that thing," Dad said, pointing to the mike.

Dad, always the one to test your performance. Five hundred people in the room and I'd do just fine, but Father's withering gaze always got to me. The Gobi in my mouth, a stone in my stomach. When Fern went for smokes, he usually took his time, I thought with a shudder. He would flirt with Gail, the cashier at the dairy bar. Or leaf through the dirt bike magazines if Joanne were on duty. Fern knew that Tuesday afternoons were dead, that there was no point in rushing back.

"Fern is likely to be back soon," I said in a rush of breath. "He's the one you got to hear."

"I heard him plenty," Dad said with a grin. From where Dad was standing, he could see the route that Fern's Camaro would have to take. Instead, a late-model Chevy pulled in. But there was no sign of Fern. "Give it a try," Dad said, folding his arms on his chest and stepping to the middle of the floor to better judge the sound system. "C'mon, you've got a minute. Let's hear you."

"Dad, I don't think …" The Chevy pulled up directly in front of the store. "Here … here, let's wait for the customer."

A woman pushed through the door, her head down. Hair of
straw raked by summer sun. Her hands like a non-skater on slick
ice, afraid to fall down. She was tall but skin and bones, draped
from collar to ankles with a rust-coloured trench coat cinched at
the waist. The spectre wafted along the linoleum, moving not to the
front of the store—as everyone did, to place their order—but along
the far wall where we kept the display of bottles and cans, the menu
of beers we had in stock that never changed so it didn't make any
sense to look them over because you knew what you were going to
get when you walked in, went to the mike and ordered, and waited
for Larry in the back to run the case, or half, or six, or sleeve of cans
up the rollers and out. Of course, the timing changed a bit if you
had to redeem. But never mind. Nobody ever consulted the menu.

"What the Sam Hill," Dad whispered. "That's Joan Hawthorne,
the artist."

I had heard of her, the woman artist from Toronto famous for
giant canvases of butter tarts that didn't look like butter tarts at all,
more like muddy tires needing retread. A piece I read about her in
the *Advance* said she got material for her Canadiana series during
road trips. Keppel, they reported, would soon get a visit.

Eventually, Joan Hawthorne careered to the mike. Her eyes
were grey and flat like the half-blind tabby that lived off the A&P
dumpster.

"What'll it be, ma'am?" I said, covering the mike with my left
hand.

"I want some beer," she said as she tried to twirl a lock of hair
in her fingers. It was so brittle it didn't take.

"Well, you came to the right place," I replied as I looked toward
my father, who stifled a laugh.

"Oh, a father-and-son store?" she said, raising her hand toward
my father as if she were going to touch him. "How cute." She took
an unsteady step toward Dad. "Perhaps Father could recommend
a beer for me," she said, staring hard at him. "Tell me, what's your
brand, sailor?" Dad's smile vanished as he blushed the colour of
Joan Hawthorne's coat.

Finally, Fern burst through the door. "Hey, there," he said, and
we turned to look at him. A couple of years ago, comedians Johnny

Wayne and Frank Shuster visited the Keppel Winter Carnival, and rumour had it they were impressed with what folks were saying about Fern on the mike and they were going to drop in for a visit. Fern got wind of the talk and even missed the Ski-Doo races, never left the store for a minute, even for a smoke break. But Wayne and Shuster never showed up. He was beginning to think he would miss his chance at being discovered.

Fern's beard had better than adequate covering that day, with only an angry splash of acne above his right cheekbone. In the parking lot, he'd surely have run his back-pocket comb through his hair and fiddled with his brown-frame eyeglasses. With a flick of his wrist, he gestured for me to move and when I did he galloped to his post behind the mike and grinned toward the famous lady.

"If you would come up to the counter here, ma'am, I'd be happy to help you," he said. The words hung in the air like icicles.

Joan gave Fern a once-over and shook her head. "It's quite all right … Fern. I was just asking a question of … Charlie, here. And if it's all the same to you, I'd prefer if … Kyle put in my order for me," she said, sucking her teeth. Each time she called us by name, she paused, eyeing the sewn script on our shirts. I felt as if I had a button unfastened. I touched the top of my trouser fly, felt the metal tongue of the zipper.

"Well, sure," Fern said into the mike as he slowly stepped away, his long arms at his side. Fern was particularly proud of his "sh" sounds, which were most like Lloyd Robertson. He got an "A" on his finals because he spoke for a week with four marbles in his mouth to master the "sh" sound.

Joan Hawthorne returned her full attention to my father. "I'm waiting, Charlie," she said. She'd interlaced her fingers and dropped her hands to her pelvis.

"I don't know," Dad said. "There are plenty of beers. It's just hard to say." He smiled at her in a way that suggested he was enjoying himself. But until that point in my life, I had never imagined that Father could enjoy anything in which he wasn't in control. And particularly not if that person getting the better of him were a woman.

"Hard can be good," Joan said, smiling like a girl on a carousel.

"Ex," Dad said, matter-of-factly. "Ex is the smoothest, a long way better than Fifty. And it's brewed not far from here, in Barrie. Go for the freshest is what I say."

Joan Hawthorne nodded and then walked to the other side of my father and looked him up and down. Dad had a farmer friend and from time to time we went to the stockyards. Joan nodded in the way the farmers did studying cattle or pigs, when they came upon something that was good enough to go. Not the best in show by any means, but ample.

"That'll do," she concluded, moving away from my father and coming toward the counter where I stood at the mike. Fern was sulking in redemption.

"Ex," the artist said.

With my hand covering the mike, I took a deep breath and at the moment that I pulled my hand away, I said, as clearly and as distinctly as I could, "Ex, a Six."

Joan Hawthorne smiled thinly. "Thank you," she said, before she collected her beer. "That'll do just fine."

chapter six

I woke up in my room at the Airport McLaren thinking about wallpaper. The thousands of tin soldiers in my father's house. How motels will do fake wood panelling and wall board and seconds paint like they did in the room at the Airport McLaren. Never wallpaper. Above my bed stand was a pot of fake woodland plants, looking as real as can be. Mother had ones just like them all over the house. Called them her perfect arrangements. They looked remarkably lifelike and unless you went right up to them you'd never have known they were fakes. She'd dust them from time to time, but for all the years I lived at home, Mother never replaced her perfect arrangements.

Myra moved in sleep and mumbled, a small animal sound. Dark coils of hair splayed across a pillow and onto my belly as I lay on my back on the bed. Used to be I thought this was a perfect arrangement: sex with a beautiful woman in a distant place. That night, though, didn't seem so perfect. I found I wasn't feeling very well at all.

After the Cowplands dropped me back at the Shrivers' fort, I called the phone number that was on the ticket to the Agricultural Hall of Fame and Myra answered. She agreed to meet me at the Airport McLaren. At the fort, there were only a few stragglers— Sheldon, of course, and Frank Cattel and a half-dozen insurance salesmen types, guys with little wrists and chests of lard, and their wives, old before their time. Sheldon winked, threw me a set of car keys. "Take the brown sedan out front," he said. I snapped open the lid of Belle's case to take a look at her. Gleaming just like I left

her. "Don't worry," Sheldon said, "we took good care of her." I
said, "Sure, I really appreciate it, thanks for the party—for everything," popped a half-dozen Motrin, hauled Belle onto my back
and was off.

In bed with Myra I was thinking about how if independent
operators like McLaren's hung wallpaper instead of cheap panelling in their dozen or so rooms they'd make people feel more at
home and do more business, when I felt the tightness in my chest.
Alarmed, I sat up and rested my back against the hard plastic headboard. Myra's hair slid from my belly and lay in the moonlight
against the white cotton sheets. I felt a little shock in my chest but
nothing in the groin. Tiny pulls at my heart like I once felt after
shovelling snow. Yet why now, I thought, on a Saskatoon summer
night, when I was propped up in bed, not soothed by the scent of
a woman I'd just made love to, but jittery and uncertain, thinking
of wallpaper of all things?

Maybe it was the cigarettes after so long not smoking them.
Or all the booze I'd mixed. Or the hockey memories, the thoughts
of home that Ron Cowpland had stirred up. Seeing him after all
those years had been a shock. Why the hell did I have to go with
him? I should've just stayed at the party. What compelled me to go
off with a man capable of taking a loaded shotgun to the head of
a reporter girl in a TV newsroom? My chest was pulled tight like
an over-strung instrument. If I shifted my weight on my left elbow
and held my right arm straight to my side, the pressure eased a
little.

Willy Chesterton, who for years ran the camera stand at the Cup
in the Hall, complained of chest pains once and he was diagnosed
as suffering from stress. One afternoon, in the middle of snapping
two Czech girls, he felt woozy, needed to hold the Cup's pedestal to
steady himself so that he wouldn't keel over. Doctors couldn't find
anything wrong, just told him it was stress and that he could use a
change. So Willy transferred to office staff. It was a shame because
Willy was a natural with the camera. He pinched the cheeks of
tykes, flirted with Scandinavian tourists, swapped stats with the
true fans. Now Willy's a computer operator in marketing. He's
miserable, with stress chewing his hands, not his heart.

I wondered what it was that Dad wanted to tell me that day at
The Beer Store. Maybe, I thought, the war story that he'd promised. He had promised me, hadn't he, the day I asked about the
war, when he said "Not now," that he would one day tell me about
it, about his war? I was going away and this was his chance, wasn't
it? If only I'd been more respectful, shown him that I cared.
Instead I bucked him, sent him sprawling. If there was any one
thing I'd learned from home, it was how to shut people out. Like
Father did years later in his new place, when he wouldn't join me
to see the sunset.

After Joan Hawthorne left the store, Father turned to me and
said he had to go. What he had to tell me could wait, he said. The
way the famous artist looked him up and down like a piece of meat
must have humiliated him. But there were no telltale signs of anger: the pursing of his lips, tightening of his fists at his sides that
would precede an outburst, a volley of insults, so out of control
that people just backed off, as if it were steam from a cranky boiler
that any minute would blow.

Me, I kept my feelings inside. That was why I was suffering this
pain. Norma was right, of course, saying for my own good I had to
get out my anger and shame. But I hadn't been able to find my way
of doing it. Father drove a rig every day until he was seventy-five,
and still went on the occasional run. Since the war, he'd never seen
a doctor for anything serious. I shimmied up in bed and looked at
the clock radio. 4:45. Time for the first session of minor hockey, I
thought. Time to get dressed and head to the rink, yell like mad at
the referees of six- and seven-year-olds. Threaten them with bodily
harm, maybe even thump one on the back of the head in the corridor during intermission. That's what the doctor calls for—a little
hockey violence for good health. Like father, like son.

I couldn't laugh for the pain. If I took shallow breaths, the hurt
subsided to a tweak. After sex, I usually slept like a baby but my
head was swimming. Then I remembered the dream I'd had before waking. I was in a dark lane, not so different than the one the
Cowplands had taken me to. In the distance was a brilliant light. I
crept forward, and as I got closer I saw that it was the Cup, reflect-
ing light, but I couldn't see the source. I ran my finger under the

names etched into the Cup and only one name was repeated line after line. I took note of the name and then I woke up, but the devil of it was I could remember everything to the smallest detail—but the name repeated up and down the Stanley Cup I couldn't for the life of me recall.

I turned to Myra and ran my hand under the covers and along her hip, down her buttocks and thigh. "You're the one, baby," I said into her ear. She stirred, touched the hair at the back of my neck, traced a line up to my ear. I swallowed and the ache in my chest eased.

"Tell me something that's true," she said, with a sigh.

"You're fine, very fine," I said, cupping her head in my hands. "If I were a poet, I'd write you a sonnet. A carpenter, I'd build you a music box. But I play hockey—"

"So you'll make a bad pass."

"Touché," I said, taking her hand and placing the index finger onto my breastplate.

"C'mon, Kyle. Tell me something that is true," she repeated. Her green eyes looked liquid in the light of the summer moon.

"I want to make love to you. Slowly this time."

Afterward, the tiniest beads of sweat in the hollow of her breasts glistened in the moonlight. A cheap motel room can shine like a czar's bedchamber on Saskatoon summer nights. Such beauty can take your mind off most things, and after an ideal night of love, send you into such slumber that you've never known. More than anything else, that was what I was after. Sleep, escape. Myra, whose round, soft shoulders and billowy curls lay against my chest, shuddered with pleasure. She held my hands, whispering, "Such beautiful hands, beautiful hands …" before she fell asleep. Me, it was no go. The nasty pulling feeling in my chest came back, was getting worse. Had the Gobi in my mouth and my breath was shallow, halting. I thought of half-crazed Ron and Jim, his glass eye a flare in the bush. Brown water stains spotted a ceiling tile directly above my head. The Stanley Cup was in its case, up against the wall by the door. My tie and blazer were strewn on a bureau, where I'd thrown them in the frenzy of lovemaking. The NHL crest on the lapel loomed in the moonlight.

Father wasn't alone in his obsession with winning. Coach Fleming was the same way. During one practice my first year with the Keppel Grey Devils, Coach had me flat on my face, pushing a puck along the ice with my nose. Everybody on the team was doing it. Coach, arms akimbo, barked at us while we crawled around like insects. The game before we had skated hard, passed and shot well, but we hadn't body checked enough. We were big strong kids. We needed to hit the opposition. Hit somebody. If you don't hit, you don't win. And if you don't win, what's the point?

As I grew older, it became clear to me that most people, even those you least expected, believed as my father did—that winning was everything. At Kingston Central High, where I went to school during my years as a junior with the Kingston Canadians, new kids in town were invited on the auditorium stage to be introduced to the student body. "Class, this is Kyle Callendar," the principal said. A perky brunette, a bleached blonde, and a sloe-eyed Italian girl caught my eye. I glanced at the principal, who gave me a sly smile. "Central is proud to have you, son."

That year I took a seat at the rear of classrooms, in Typing, Business Practice, Industrial Arts, Man in Society. Lollipop courses where the fix was in: work like a winner on the junior Canadians and just show up in school, and I'd get a passing grade, while daughters of architects and plant managers, a willowy blonde who looked like Bibi Anderson and was planning a career in television news, were drawn to me like moths at a light. When it came to women, I thought, my father was half-right. Winning was the point, but you didn't have to work hard.

With my father, though, I never knew if he was proud to have me. He was a soldier following his own set of rules. Bring order to the home, a strong work ethic to his boy. Fight the ultimate Canadian battle, the necessary failure. Surrender is not an option.

I've never been very good at keeping Father's judgments out of my head. "Shoot, boy—shoot the puck. No, no, not like that. For God's sake, Kyle, no." I don't know if Dad was pleased or not when I took the job at the Hall of Fame, but he didn't openly object. I never knew how he felt, good or bad. Even when I was playing in the NHL, he never told me how proud he was. What it meant to him. Now I was a grown man, responsible for my own actions. "Get on with ya, boy. Suck it up. There's no other way."

Winning was about how you looked, too. Particularly, my hair. Always cut to the same length, the part a thin line on the right side of my scalp. Dad had upholstered the barber chair in burnt orange vinyl, no hint of a wrinkle on the seat. Not soft but smooth as polished bone. I sat as still as could be when Dad cut my hair. The lid of his haircutting kit lay open on the table: "If You Can Comb Hair You Can Cut Hair." A boy smiling sweetly, his dad standing behind him with a shit-eating grin as if they'd just shared a joke. Not us. Not while Dad cut my hair.

"Hold your head still. Still, I told you."

He taught me how to concentrate on a single object. "Something on the windowsill, boy. Just keep your eye on that, don't twitch or squirm in your seat. Do you want me to lop your ear off?"

I chose a ceramic dog. A beagle with a glossy coat. Something Mom got as an extra, a throw-in at Stegner's department store. Hal Stegner was always throwing in knick-knacks for Mom, a miniature totem pole, a frog, rainbow, angel, pilgrim. "The doodads," Mom called them.

I watched the beagle as Dad grabbed the back of my neck and pushed my head down. The clipper roared at my ear as he yanked at the cord, which caught at something near the floor. The cold blades scraped at the back of my neck as I watched the iron filings of my hair fluttering down and away. The neck done, then I went back to looking at the beagle for all I was worth, until the haircut was over, the lid shut and I was told, "Attaboy. Good for you."

So I was carried along by events. Father cut my hair, made the ice and I played on it. At eighteen, I left home for hockey and school. Grades were fixed and beautiful girls flocked to me. Pittsburgh drafted me and I signed for more money than I could have ever imagined. Never had I made a decision on my own. A couple of months ago, Norma and I were about to take a big step together, get married, maybe have a kid, when the Hall offered me more escort work. They said with the growing popularity of the Cup in North America, it would be a winning formula, the ex-NHL player as designated Stanley Cup escort. Hockey had become big business, a giant theme store in Manhattan—marketing deals on jerseys, peak caps, videos, action figures. Every week now Belle had a gig out of town. It meant, of course, I would be in Toronto less and less. Norma argued against it, but she more than anyone else had to know that I couldn't say no to hockey. We'd have kids someday, I told her. Just wait.

But the last time I returned to Toronto, Norma was away, visiting her mother in Muskoka. And there was nothing in the fridge. Not even a box of baking soda. About a month before that she got particularly pissed off with me. The fridge was chocked full. With pucks.

Good things had seemed to come pretty easily to me. Even when they went to hell after I was cut from The Game, I never once thought that someone, somewhere, wouldn't be there to protect me, to help bring me back from the brink. But in that motel room in Saskatoon lying with the brunette ticket taker after a night of sex, I couldn't sleep. More pressure was building in my chest, and for the first time in my life I was beginning to have serious doubts.

chapter seven

Somewhere a phone chirped. I sat up in bed, but Myra didn't budge. Deep in the luggage, stuffed in with my boxers and socks, the cellphone chirped. I got out of bed and quietly unzipped the bag, pulled out the phone. Who the hell could it be in the middle of the night? Only Norma and the Hall curator had the number to the cellphone—and both called only in case of emergencies. One of the early bosses at the Hall was an astronaut nut, and code talk he had introduced over the cell had stuck. "Any heat on entry?" meant are you encountering any trouble. If I responded "Burning up," the police were alerted. "Splashdown" was the Stanley Cup victory party.

I crept into the bathroom, gently closed the door, and sat on the toilet. To the right of the door was the cast-iron arch of a bottle opener, with hundreds of layers of paint, the last one caramel. "Yep," I whispered into the phone. "Kyle here."

"Has the albatross landed?"

"Eagle, Norma," I said in as even a voice as I could muster. "It's eagle for success of a mission." Naked, I sat up out of a slouch and crossed my legs, something I never do on the toilet. Ran a hand through my hair.

"Well, aren't you uptight, Mr. Callendar, sir." The pout in her voice was neither playful nor serious, could go either way. "And why are you whispering? Is there someone with you?"

"No, of course not," I snapped. "I'm exhausted, that's all … But dear, you know the rules about this phone. Only emergencies, remember? … Never mind, though. What's up?"

"Nothing," she said. "Nothing at all." She hung up. I rang back the apartment but she wouldn't pick up. I left a message on the answering machine, a long one, urging her to answer, not to hold my tone so much against me. It was a gruelling assignment, I told her, and I couldn't wait to see her. Phones weren't my thing, she knew that. But Norma didn't pick up. Knowing her, she probably stormed out to the 7-Eleven to buy smokes and cool off. She'd smoke a couple and drown the rest of the pack 'cause she's been trying to quit. I'd have some more explaining to do, but leaving a long message on the machine was the right beginning. Before the flight I'd try her again at the airport. A second long call that would certainly win her over. If she were in the apartment, she might even answer.

I pushed myself up off the toilet seat and stood in front of the mirror above the sink. Between my thumb and forefinger I pinched a glob of flesh at my cheekbone. It seemed there wasn't much you could do with a fleshy face. It came with drinking, the fatty foods, a boy's love of french-fried potatoes from the Keppel chip wagon. Only a spray of grey had infected the wave of brown soft hair at my temples. My eyes were still ocean blue, with no deep lines at the corners. From the earliest age, I had deep-set mouth lines. Finally, at fifty, they looked distinguished.

Norma would be there, I told myself. She had always been there. Norma Hanford knew me, not from Keppel, but from Kingston. In high school typing class, she once told me the letters for "typewriter" had a row of their own so that thick-fingered gun salesmen for Remington could better pitch their new product. I could never get it, but Norma mastered the home row: ASDF for the left hand, JKL; for the right hand. "All words are available to you when you know the home row," she had said.

Norma was there when I was waived through all the NHL teams, too. When nobody wanted me. A footnote to hockey nerds, card collectors, small-town historians. Kyle Callendar scored that hat trick while shadowing Sittler, and one year, with the Los Angeles Kings, scored twenty-three goals. A defensive specialist, dealt to Winnipeg, the San Jose Sharks, and at thirty-two finished. Washed up.

While with the Sharks, I lived in a five-thousand-dollar-a-week apartment overlooking San Francisco Bay. People on our point of land on Napier Lane kept tidy little gardens, and on my balcony during off days I used to like to water big flowering plants where the most dazzling hummingbirds fed at sunset. Hummingbirds move so fast, yet so controlled, and when I studied them I began to feel that I could somehow pick up my pace on the ice, turn quicker, anticipate, and dart like they did. Be one step ahead of the other guy.

But after San Jose, nobody wanted me. For a month after I was waived—I don't know, maybe longer—I didn't return calls. The answering machine got clogged with messages—as did the apartment, with Molson Golden and rye liquor bottles, empty Chinese food containers, balled-up socks. From an open window, I shouted at men and women, teens in hoodies, geezers on big-wheel bikes. I went out once in a month—to put out my hockey trophies in the trash. I had hardware in all sizes, from fist-sized action figures to skyscrapers of chrome and mahogany. I flung them everywhichway in heavy paper bags, grocery boxes, see-through plastic. A heap of mangled metal.

Even hummingbirds have their season. Careers are over if you can't do split-second transitions from defence to offence to defence. The rearguard breaks up the play at the blue line and hits the streaking winger across the opposite blue. Attack the net in less than three seconds. Coach has a stopwatch. Make the split or you're out. Out on your stupid fat ass.

Norma took a month's leave from her job at *Gardening Now* magazine in Toronto and flew to San Francisco to be with me. I watched and re-watched Bruce Willis in *Die Hard 2* while Norma stroked my hand, told me it was going to be all right. I could make it, she said, if I could learn to open up. If I confided in her. Told her what I was feeling. I promised her I would. Then Norma cleaned the apartment, and when it was spotless she went out one afternoon and came back with a moving van and packing cartons. She wrapped my hat-trick puck from the game at the Gardens that earned me one true fan in Wilma Rangford, helped me lift my Jennifer Convertible, stereo, and TV set into a U-Haul, and we went north to Toronto.

I studied my body in the mirror. Fat ass, all right. And Jesus, the tire roll around the middle had really got out of hand. I bent down to try to touch my toes. In my day, I could get the flat of my hand to the ground—and the back of my hand, sweep in a wide arc about my body. But I couldn't get close to the floor. My muscles were as stiff as a board. This is the end, I thought. Who did I think I was kidding? I flopped back onto the toilet seat and hammered my thigh with my fist.

The handle of the bathroom door turned and it opened a crack. Before I could see Myra's face, I cried "No" and sprang to the door, slamming it shut with both hands.

"Hey, Kyle, are you okay?" Myra said.

"Don't just come barging in on me like that. Leave me alone!"

"Huh, what's that? What's got in to you?"

I threw open the door and roared, "Would you really like to know? Would you?" My thighs burned and I chased her into a chair. The big push you need on a breakaway, the first one that sets you free, in all alone. Just you and the mythic one, the spirit in the mask.

"Take one more step and I'll scream," a voice said. It was disembodied and faraway, anonymous. Where the words are plain enough but the tone is cheapest sheet metal. Tin cans attached to string.

I looked down as if from a high place. Hovering over a woman who finally took shape, a stranger wrapped inside my NHL jacket, curled up in a ball on an easy chair. Masses of dark hair. She was shaking and crying, her head turned away from me.

I dropped to my knees before her and touched with a fingertip the skin above her ankle. Her leg jerked under the skirt of the jacket so that only her toes showed. "I'm sorry," I gasped. "You startled me. If you had've knocked—"

"Don't touch me. You're crazy. I thought ... the look in your eye ... I didn't know what would ha—"

"It's over," I said. "Let me lift you back into bed ... If you want me to leave, I'll leave."

Myra stopped crying but was trembling like a leaf. She burrowed further inside my blazer, and deeper into the chair.

"I'll put my stuff in a bag and be out of here in a minute," I said, moving to the edge of her chair. Faint gardenias. When I talked her hair rustled. "You just stay where you are. Keep the jacket."

She turned toward me, and as she did I kissed her, my fingertips on her chin. Then deeper, teeth on teeth, and she threw her arms around me. One hand grabbed a fistful of hair as she kissed me back. I lifted her from the chair, and still kissing her, took her to bed. Once in bed, we began play-fighting. She pushed at me, struggled under my weight.

"It's not going to be so easy," she cooed as I got more and more aroused. "You can't go psycho on me and expect me to just fall back into your arms."

"Psycho? Who are you kidding? I was changing the mood. You like this mood, don't you?"

"Don't be so sure." I was straddling her, with my hands on her wrists, holding her down. She tried to move but was pinned.

"Like I said, beautiful hands," she said as she finally relaxed under me. " 'Beautiful hands,' that's what they say in hockey, isn't it, Kyle?"

"Soft hands," I said, as I took my weight off her wrists. I flexed the fingers of my right hand as I looked at them. " 'Soft hands' is what they say."

"It somehow doesn't seem enough. To call your hands soft hands. They're very special hands, Kyle. You're a little crazy. But you can talk. And your hands are very special."

"It's not the only part of me that's special."

Suddenly, Myra thrust a knee into my groin. Bitch slaps and blows rained on my face and head as I covered up as best I could. "You bastard," she cried. "You scared me half to death! Special? You think you're special? You're shit, mister, worse than nothing." She pounded my back like a banshee, a thousand blows. Finally, she grew tired and stopped, tore the comforter off the bed, and retreated to the easy chair.

I lay like a fetus, my eyes wide, trying to think, to see, to find something to hold on to. But I couldn't. My mind was blank. I stared at tiny hairs on my pale skin and couldn't come up with a goddamn thing.

chapter eight

The next morning my taxi passed Ron Cowpland's truck at the far end of the departure lane at the airport. My head was pounding from too much drink and not enough sleep, but I recognized the pickup. An hour before, I'd woken up to an empty room, the scent of gardenias. When and where Myra went, I hadn't a clue, but she'd left the blazer. Good riddance to her, trouble with a capital T. Let her spend her life at the Agricultural Hall of Fame. A school group leader, with a specialty in cash crops. Hitting the seniors' homes on membership drives. I laughed to myself and my back twinged. But the hurt in my chest had subsided and my breathing seemed fine. The cabbie pulled over. I gave him a handful of toonies, he scribbled a receipt, and I stepped up to the curb with the Cup and my luggage.

Ron wasn't in his truck. Pages of a colour magazine lay crumpled and dirty on the floor of the passenger side. Not a girlie mag, I thought. Or sports, either. Bears and big-rack sheep and ads for lumberjack shirts and a collapsible house with a heating unit. Survivalist stuff. The seats and floor were strewn with the half-shells of sunflower seeds. Little heaps. As if Ron and Jim had driven the night through, eating nothing but sunflower seeds, one after the other. But precisely, getting so they could cut and spit out the shell and swallow the nut in one go. Like you would do to calm your nerves, concentrate on a single action until it was reflex.

I opened the driver's door, reached in, and pulled out the cigarette lighter. It was stone cold. I was about to put the lighter back into its slot, but then slipped it into my pocket and started into the terminal.

The airport coffee bar in Saskatoon isn't much to speak of. A hutch with a few muffins, over-brewed coffee, an array of tables like forest mushrooms. A pocketful of change from a twenty and you're still hungry. Sheldon and Bobby Shriver had come to see me off and were at the coffee bar. From the Air Canada ticket counter I could see Sheldon fluttering his hand in that faggy way of his that stood out like a foreign film director on a rural shoot. He was in a straw boater and seersucker suit. Bobby, wide as a car with his hands jammed in his Red Wings bomber jacket, stared at the floor. Frank Cattel was avoiding my eyes, too, looking toward a nearby group of middle-aged women who were poring over brochures to a Yankee gambling destination. Potential voters, he was thinking. With them were three others: a bearded fat man in dark glasses and two athletic-looking guys.

"The Stanley Cup, gentlemen," Sheldon said, pointing to Belle as I approached, pushing her aboard an airport cart. The men rose from their seats. "And, of course, may I present to you, the Keeper of the Stanley Cup, Mr. Kyle Callendar."

"Very plees to meet you," said the first athlete. His palm was cool and hard, surprisingly strong as we shook hands. His accent wasn't Eastern European exactly. Musical, less gruff. Finnish, maybe. He was a tall drink of water, muscle on his frame but no hips. An amateur on the big ice, where he could escape trouble. His friend was all Russian. Round face and thick chest. Huge bones but with a spring to him that could tip a two-hundred-pounder over his backside in the bat of an eye.

"Yah," the Russian said as he pounded my back with his open palm. "I have seen this man play," he said, looking toward his comrades. "Kyle Callendar, he was a good one."

"Thank you," I said. The thump of the Russian's hand hurt like hell, but I didn't let on. Just what I needed, a hockey freak show. I tried to catch the eye of the fat man behind his glasses and full beard, but he looked away as he sat down. Then everyone took their seat. I put Belle's trunk beside me, peered inside, saw that she was fine, and snapped the case shut.

"You've given Saskatoon something to talk about for the season, perhaps even longer," Sheldon said. "Rest assured, I'll put in a good word for you at the Hall. A helluva good word." A waiter poured me a cup of coffee, splashed a refill for Sheldon.

"Thanks, but there's no need," I said. "It's just my job, what I'm hired to do." Suddenly, an icy feeling tingled down my spine. I spun around, sure that someone was watching me. But no one was there. Only a security guard at the gate I was to go through for my flight to Toronto.

"Is something wrong?" Sheldon asked, sounding genuinely concerned. "Are you all right?"

"Fine, fine," I said, running my fingers through my hair. "A little tired, maybe. Didn't get much sleep last night." I popped a couple of Motrin with half of the lukewarm coffee. My head was banging like a gong.

"Yes, well, like you said, it is what you do," Sheldon said, smiling. Frank Cattel beamed a Dale Carnegie, tapped me on the shoulder. Even Bobby grinned. Only the fat man was impassive. He was still looking away from me, as if he were putting in time until a hot date arrived.

"Whatever … here are your keys, Sheldon," I said, handing them over. I told him where the sedan was parked at the airport motel. He tossed the keys to Frank, who stashed them in a trouser pocket and stood up to leave. I rose and Frank pumped my arm, said something trite, palmed me his business card, and left.

"I know you don't have much time, Kyle, but I wanted you to meet some friends of mine before you go," Sheldon said. "You might recognize Bjorn Skajjit," he said, gesturing toward the tall drink of water. "A few years ago he was Norway's big hope, the country's best shot at being its first native son in the NHL. I saw him play junior in Peterborough. Like Thor cutting a path to some northern heaven." Bjorn was impassive, as if the praise were nothing new to him. All in a day's work for Norway's Great Hope.

"And this is Vladimir Rostov," Sheldon continued. "Parts of Siberia refer to Rostov as their Gordie Howe. How's that for putting Saskatoon on the map, eh? Like Gordie did, Vlad here gets better with age, has led a Petersburg club in plus-minus for a decade."

Vladimir crushed my hand in his grip. Then he grabbed my aching head with both hands, pulled my face forward, and kissed me first on the left cheek and then on the right. I gagged and nearly fainted from the smell of an overly ripe ground vegetable.

"Listen, I'm flattered to meet these guys," I said, looking toward Sheldon but trying to catch Bobby's eye. Poor Bobby. He never once looked up. I know my job and pride myself at recognizing by sight the players of every decent club in the NHL. From nasty bastard Chris Simon to eggs-in-his-pocket Sergei Zubov. But Bobby, even after spending two days around him, I couldn't keep straight. As a reminder of what he looked like, you needed a copy of his Topps hockey card. Even in that he looked desperate and a little sad. "Maybe this could wait for another time," I said. "I'm tired and I got a flight to catch."

"And may I introduce Brian McConachie," Sheldon said, ignoring me. "He's my business associate on this matter that I assure you won't involve any more time than it takes to finish our coffees."

Damn it, I thought. I forgot to call Norma. I glanced at my watch. Norma would be beside herself by now, so angry that I may as well not go home at all. Who could I stay with tonight? I wondered. "Sorry, gentlemen," I said, "I'd really like to hear what you have to say. But it's getting late and I gotta go."

"Seriously, Kyle," Sheldon said as I rose and grabbed for the Cup. "No more than a minute of your time, that's all we're asking."

"Sorry," I said, dropping my business card on the table and swinging the Cup back on the cart. "Please do shoot me an e-mail, tell me all about it. You'll have to excuse me, though, I've got an emergency call to make before my flight. Very nice to meet you both," I said, shaking hands with the Shrivers. "Gentlemen," I concluded, tossing off a half-salute to the others before I raced to the gate.

Rather than chance missing my flight, I decided to use the Airfone or my cellphone on board to call Norma. That way I could leave a long message. I'd tell her the truth. Consider the poor escort to the Stanley Cup. Pity me having to deal with the tiresome likes of Frank Cattel, the Shrivers, the Cowplands, the Rangfords. When Norma hears what I've had to put up with, she couldn't help but forgive me. If she wasn't there, I'd put the full catastrophe on the machine.

As rushed as I was, the smell of Drum tobacco stopped me in my tracks. Ron Cowpland stood in the doorway of the men's room. There was no smoking inside the terminal building, but Ron was making an exception. Perhaps Jim was inside the restroom, and he was waiting for him. He smirked and waved me on.

A minute later, at the security checkpoint, I turned to look for Ron and Jim. Except for a colour poster of the Star Alliance global airline marketing deal, the corridor was empty. With my back turned, a luggage inspector picked up Belle, which was too big to run under the X-ray machine, and placed her on a table.

"Hey," I said, showing my NHL ID card. "I have to be with that when it gets hand-checked."

I stepped around the electronic security portal and bumped into a big man in a uniform. "I'm sorry, sir," he said. "You have to go through the security checkpoint first." I lost sight of Belle as another inspector came up on the other side of me. A mother with big hair in a trench coat was being frisked by an East Indian woman. Two towheads were sitting on the floor with plastic trucks, staring at me.

I walked through the portal and it beeped. The solid-built worker took his electronic wand and began to run it down the outside of my leg.

"G'wan," I said, lifting my arms as the device ran up my body. "Don't miss the lymph nodes in the armpit. Give 'em a good dose."

"Funny man," said a third inspector. "There's not a trace of radiation in these things."

I glanced toward the empty security conveyor belt, and then turned to face him, a beefy man with a scaly nose and an enormous head. Yeah, right, I thought.

The big man's wand squealed like a mouse.

"What's in your coat pocket, sir?"

I pulled out the cigarette lighter and the bottle of Motrin. In the other pocket was the jar of misaskwatomin jam. I gave him the items and he put them on a tray.

The woman and her two kids had left, were probably at the gate by now. The East Indian inspector moved in behind me. "Here,"

I said, my voice cracking, "just let me go, would you? You can call my employers at the Hockey Hall of Fame ... Maybe you're a hockey fan. I played in the NHL myself. Kyle Callendar?"

I walked to where the Cup's case had been placed on a table. "Here, take a look and you'll see what I mean."

The woman flipped open the case and the inspectors crowded around the Stanley Cup as if it were Inca gold. I lowered myself to look through the channel of the conveyor belt. The corridor was empty, a void. With only a trace of Drum tobacco. And the pain. My chest pain was killing me.

PART TWO

chapter nine

Times have changed. That seems obvious, but growing up in Keppel you got the impression that some things never changed. Every June there was the Main Street Sidewalk Jamboree; in July, the Royalist Day parade—and in the cold, hockey tournaments. But it's a global village now and everything changes. Except human behaviour, that is. We may have the latest devices and high-tech measuring tools for observing human behaviour, but what does it amount to? We're nothing but park workers with sharp poles collecting and discarding scraps of wisdom like so many bits of paper. Like Coach Fleming, who never tired of repeating his favourite saying, a quote by Nelson Algren: "Never play cards with any man named Doc. Never eat at any place called Mom's. And never, never, no matter what else you do in your life ... sleep with anyone whose troubles are worse than your own." A never-ending stream of paper.

I don't like the in-flight magazines the airlines stuff into the pockets of the seat in front of you. So I always ask for the bulkhead for Belle and me. That's the first thing I remember telling the doctors. I need legroom, and when there aren't any screaming kids in the bulkhead—say the flight is predominantly business people—then I can just drift off.

And don't think the Hockey Hall of Fame is a top-drawer operation either, sending us first class or even business. It's not. Whenever the Hall can get away with it, it flies coach. After five years of flying with Belle all over North America, I don't get motion sickness anymore. Well, that is, unless we're approaching or leaving Denver. Something about the wind currents out of the mountains causes wicked turbulence on takeoffs and landings. I don't actually toss my cookies flying into Mile High, but no matter how much Dramamine I take I feel terrible. And sitting at the bulkhead with Belle everybody sees you. A grown man in an NHL blazer turning various shades of green, with his head in his hands, fathers and sons pointing at him, whispering, sniggering.

I could've been lying flat on my back for a week or more, a month, I didn't know. The doctors said it was the morning after. You fainted, suffered what looked like a panic attack, and were brought to a safe place. Try to calm down, they said.

Uh-huh, I nodded. I was in a private room on a hospital bed. And not a particularly comfortable one. Under me was a rubberized cover snapped to the mattress like a condom. On top a bedspread, gold-bead polyester. A plastic food tray hung near my elbow.

At first there were just voices. Deep, too-serious. Men who said one thing and meant another, but whose reserve was so deep they'd lost touch with what it was they meant. That explained their edge of anger.

Finally I saw an old man. His ears stuck out like wings, strangely at odds with the rock face of his forehead. Hair so far back that when I first saw him I thought I'd been taken away all right. By extraterrestrials.

"How are you feeling?" he asked.

"Tired … I could sleep for a week … What about the Cup?" I said, suddenly remembering. I tried to lift myself up on an elbow. "Where is it? Is she all right?"

"Don't worry," he said, patting my hand. "The Cup is safe and sound. It was shipped in secure cargo back to Toronto. It's in the Hall of Fame as we speak."

ET turned to go, and before he left the room I fell asleep and had a dream. Of course, everybody dreams, but for years of my adult life I honestly couldn't remember a single one. I'd wake up with a start in the middle of the night, and Norma being a light sleeper would wake up too. A moment before, my head was filled with images, but as soon as I opened my mouth to describe it, the dream vanished. I was blank, staring at the shadows on our punch-board ceiling tiles. Norma tried to draw the dream out of me; she rubbed my temples, laid her head on my chest, toyed with a hair curl behind my ear. But it was no go; I couldn't remember a thing. She'd turn over and go back to sleep. Me, I'd sit up for hours, wide awake, my mind an empty slate.

But this dream I remembered. Father was taking me to the bush to cut a tree for Christmas. In life this never happened. For weeks before Christmas, Dad was on the road. The dream father said this was the only way to bring home a tree. With each step Father took in the forest, the snow shook from the pine boughs. We settled on a full blue-green one, with needles like velvet, blunt tips. He lifted me to the highest branch to test it for strength, because he wouldn't bring a Christmas tree home that couldn't hold his baby in its arms.

"Tell me, Kyle, what's it like up there," Father shouted from the ground.

Perhaps it was the overpowering scent of the pine. Or the glare of the sun on the miles upon miles of snow-laden trees. Fairies with tiny wings bore me in their arms, higher and higher, farther above my father. Up into the heat of the sun until I was sweating and awake, wide awake, and bursting, calling down to him, "Magic," I cried, "It's a magic tree." And my father whooped and cried from below because that was what he'd been waiting to hear.

Dad didn't take me many places when I was young, but once he took me to the Hall. In those days, the Hall was on the grounds of the Canadian National Exhibition, where in summer there was the Ferris wheel, the Champagne ride, the Tilt-O-Whirl. It was a long drive from Keppel to Toronto. I was only twelve years old, but I remember everything about that day. From the backseat of the Impala, I marvelled at the look of Dad behind the wheel: dark glasses on a round face, not a line or a crease at his lips, his brow. Wavy hair, with grey highlights in the afternoon sun—feathery and touchable but never touched. Not even by Mom at his side because Father, a Buddha in meditation, serene in his concentration, was driving. On the road, you'd best let him be.

We weren't much beyond Tiverton, I remember. Father had pulled out to pass with a curve coming up. He timed it perfectly, of course, speeding ahead of his quarry, a red Trans Am, a good second or two before the car on the curve, a Dodge Dart, barrelled into us. Still, it made me nervous, so I pulled on the seatbelt, snapped the clasp into the buckle. At the loud sound, Dad glared at me in the rearview mirror. In those days, Father never wore a belt. The very idea an insult to his manhood.

"Am I going too fast for you?" he asked with a mocking smile.

"No Dad," I said. "But I don't know. I … I think I'd like to wear it."

Dad shook his head, then tramped the gas on a straightaway. We roared along in silence until Mom reached out and touched Dad's arm and he slowed to the speed limit. Me, I didn't take off the belt for the rest of the ride and Dad never so much as gave me a glance in the rearview.

Our first visit was to the Better Living Pavilion. Mom brought Dad to the exhibit for the electric carving knife. A man sawed the thinnest of slices of boiled roast beef and held them out like wafers to non-believers. "That's something I can see you doing, dear," Mom said as Dad munched a free sample. I walked away and stopped to watch the water flowing against gravity in the giant faucet of the Culligan Water display. Water escaping, not to the outside but back to the source.

Finally, we entered the Hall. With plaques and pictures of old pockmarked white men. "C'mon son," Dad said, forgetting the tiff in the car, "let me show you a few things." The Leafs were Dad's team. King Clancy, inducted 1958; Charlie Conacher, Dad's namesake, 1961. "See these guys, boy," he said, grabbing my elbow and guiding me a step closer to the picture of Clancy, his looking-glass smile. For a moment, I couldn't believe it, but Dad seemed happy. I felt it in the turned-up corner of his mouth, a sparkle in his eyes. His face was red as a beet, a little giggle caught in his throat.

"Clancy was okay, Kyle, no great shakes. Not Apps, Howe, or Lindsay, certainly not Morenz," he said. "But he did it all—a player, a ref, a coach. What a joker. Once, a player threw a glove in the air to protest a call that Clancy had made on him: 'If that comes down, you've got a game misconduct,' Clancy told him. Howse about that, eh? And look, there's Ching Johnson. He was some card, too. Only ref ever to have bodychecked a player after his pro-playing days were over. 'The old habit was too deep within me,' he said. 'I forgot where I was and what I was doing.' "

Dad took me before the glass cases, hockey sticks of the greats: Eddie Shore, Red Storey, Conn Smythe. Like spears of a warrior caste, heavy and worn in battle. Sweaters with their simple geometrics—the Boston B, first naked, then raised upon a shield; Montreal's slender H in the jaws of the C; the regal headdress of the Blackhawks. And the Maple Leaf, pure and sculpted, the line leader, the one.

"This is as good as it gets, boy," Dad said. What he said next he muffled, a whisper that sounded like "love you" but was so out of character that I think it must have been something else. I grabbed his hand, and Dad and I went in search of the Stanley Cup.

My head was as big as the room. I couldn't hold any thoughts for long. I must've had a high fever too, because hospital workers were forever lifting me out of bed and into a chair so that they could change the sheets. Workers' round backs, the colour of spring ice. Beyond, the Grain Elevator, where the fishermen go, to burrow and sit, like lizards in the desert.

I'm beside my mother at church. Someone has thrown a rock through the stained-glass window. The image—garment of a boy, face of a woman—is jagged now, and before me on the cushioned prayer bench is a broken piece of the stained glass. Blue and green and red, and I stoop to pick up the glass, stuff it in my pocket, and take it home. I look through the stained glass every chance I get, marvel at how it changes not only the colour but the shape of things.

Norma is sitting on the bedspread beside me. Her pageboy cut has grown out since I'd last seen her; wisps of black hair on the top of her head are illuminated by the light from the hospital window.

"I came as soon as I heard, Kyle."

I gently push her back and look at her. Sad smile of promise that she rarely shows. What strangers take for interest because Norma cannot, will not hide. I take a tissue and dab the mascara that leaks with her tears. She plaits her fingers in mine like we did when we were in high school and kisses me hard on the lips.

"Kyle, there's so much you don't tell me."

Slowly, I push back the collar of her white cardigan, put my hands on her shoulders. A thumb in the hollow of her neck. My fingers on her collarbone, the balls of my hands on her breasts.

"Home row," I say, struggling to smile.

Sluts, puck bunnies, dirties, daddy's girls, nymphs. Mostly nameless ones, they sat in the cold of Keppel Arena under the grey metal box suspended from the rafters, heating coils Ferrari red. Suzy Hunter. The fire in her eyes could've stoked the hot dog rotisserie in the foyer. And Peggy Simpson in the back of the Lincoln Continental. Beautiful hair brushed to a copper-penny shine. A daddy's girl and a year older than her friends. Her old man was a doctor, always on call, but in the Ford Pinto, his wife's car, because he'd let darling Peggy have the Lincoln. "Dahling," he called her in a Southern drawl.

Victoria Blackwood was sitting next to Suzy. Once in a blue moon, Victoria joined us in the Lincoln, but mostly she didn't, was a Salvation Army girl, so her parents wouldn't let her out unchaperoned. After the game, she was picked up by her father and taken for Bible reading and tambourine slamming on her ass, cheeks like melons. Her hair was short, set off her round face, a face you cupped in your hands like a rosebud. So sexy, that gap in her front teeth.

"When are you going to let me out of here?" I asked ET. "I'm feeling fine to leave."

ET said Sheldon Shriver had been concerned about me, as were the airport-security workers, even Myra, who the doctor said Frank Cattel went to the trouble of looking up. In a mirror I watched as the doctor moved alongside the bed and picked up a hard plastic juice cup and was staring at it like it was made of a foreign substance he couldn't quite recall. He put down the cup and looked in the mirror, too. His orbs were shiny grey.

"My name is Dr. Wayne Strachan. You can call me Wayne."
The cool of the sheets skimmed my belly, my thighs. Penis
scant, invisible.

The soldiers never marched. Hour after hour, I stared at them.
Tin soldiers in red coats, beige pinstripe slacks at dusk, fading to
silhouettes, slightly raised patterns on the wall. A street light made
shadows of oak leaves dance upon the soldiers' faces, suggesting
movement, orders received, a forward march. When Father was
on the road, I could sleep in the room with my battalion of fighting men, but when he was home, in the bedroom with my mother
down below, I lay awake and willed for the soldiers to attack. To
plunge their bayonets into the heart of the enemy.

From the hospital window, I could see a willow tree blowing in a
breeze. I wanted to take Norma with me to the base of that tree and
spend the day there. Maybe the month.
    If you look deep enough in Norma's eyes you get lost. There is
no escape. The pain can't get to you there.

Belle is the sun to her orbiting planets—the Calder, the Hart, the
Art Ross, the Vezina, named after goalie George Vezina, the father
of twenty-two children. In the Hall, we chaperone her, take me-
mento photographs of her for tourists. Hoist up a two-year-old,
pose with a girlfriend, give grandpa a special treat. Touch her, sure,
but sorry, you can't pick her up, hold her over your head. That is
only for champions. Willy snaps a picture, and moments later the
photo sheets appear. From eight-by-ten to wallet size. Forever im-
mortalized in picture frames from coast to coast, now in Europe,
too, Russia. And after the Nagano Olympics, Japan. You and Belle.
The Stanley Cup. The oldest sports trophy that is continuously
fought for. Where it all begins—and ends. The only one to love.

Keppel was the worst for grey skies. So many different levels of
grey, from white silver to near black. Plumes of exhaust, motors
old and new, and the voluminous cloud of Dad's truck. Clinging to
the stout pipe above the cab in the frigid morning air.

One February a thaw came. The grey split and carved into the sky the mirror image of the ice on the lake, the clouds matching the ice, the sky the lake waters. I jogged around the lake as if suspended between the two, while two lovers walked on the thin ice, moving toward open water.

Toward blackness. I could never open my eyes in it. In a shower, my eyes are screwed tight as a drum. Boys in Keppel went to the mill dam—where in spring melt the salmon leapt, stabs of darting silver—to learn to swim under the waterfall. But I lost my way in dark water, couldn't begin to feel safe. Instead, I ran on hard surfaces, for miles alone along country roads, my eyes open, forever open.

The couple walked until I couldn't see them anymore.

The rink at dawn—dank, smell of an abandoned chest.

In Keppel, Clem Cunningham was the rink rat. Dark skinned, thin, angular, like century-old household pipe. The rink had catwalks bolted into a network of ceiling rafters, and Clem slept in a cranny under the rooftop. Figure skaters and hockey players in dim light. Backstage, Yankee cigarette butts strewn on wet wood.

I picked at fluff from the bedspread, and brushed the surface with the flat of my hand, pressing out the wrinkles. Clem, at the wheel of the Zamboni, cut a cool line down the centre of the ice. Did a steady circumference, speed a slow walk. Never went over a place more than once. With the driest, smoothest points at the faceoff circles.

"Folks wouldn't think of interfering in the ice, any more than the sunrise or the deer hunt," Clem said.

Clem wheeled the Zamboni into the corner so that the wet rag of the trailer reached the ice that met the boards. Folks studied that first turn, watching to see if Clem were dropping too much water, if the ice was freezing on contact, coming up hard and fast. If the plant was working right, by the time Clem was beginning to make the turn at the other end, the first corner was frozen clear and smooth.

The net was a two-man job. Floodwater was sucked out of the holes with a turkey baster, the drill placed into the heart of the hole and thrust deeply and firmly. Three twists and pulled up hard and quick so the ice chips scattered, didn't fall back into the hole. The number two popped in the net pegs and Clem slammed the net down. Take out too much ice from the hole and the pegs wobbled, the net would go off its moorings at the slightest push.

Do you observe the salesman on a call to the five-and-dime? The housewife getting a dust bunny out from under Johnny's bed? Hardly. No one in Keppel lived a more public life than Clem, the Zamboni driver.

Parents tell kids to go outside, play in traffic. Wash windows for Mom, hold boards at the circular saw for Dad. With no MTV. No Sony PlayStation. No quality time with Father, the emotional cripple leading a failed life in a house full of strangers.

We didn't believe in Santa Claus, or aliens from outer space, or the goddamn Easter Bunny, but we believed in Clem because Clem was the miracle maker. Clem made ice.

"How's it hanging, bud?" a voice said. I wouldn't have known it was Doug Cowpland if not for the fingerless black gloves. Ever since junior hockey, Doug wore half-gloves, cutting the fingers off in loud, angry bites. It hid the chilblains, the frostbite scars on his hands that never quite healed.

"Doug? Doug? Is that you?"

"It ain't Commissioner Gordon," Doug said. When he smiled, I could see he'd let his teeth go. Skid marks of green, ground down to nubs. Eyes were sunk in his head, a limp ponytail with flecks of grey. But the body was all Cowpland—big angular shoulders and a ruddy neck. At the drop of the hat, he would be on the ice. And make me pay, for sure.

I shifted on the bed and tried to sit up, but was wracked with dizziness and fell back on the pillow.

"Whoa, man," Doug said, as he moved to my side and touched my brow. "You just take it easy. That's what the doctors say."

I closed my eyes and gasped. Not with pain but weakness. The breath of a sparrow.

"Oh man, who put out the lights?"

"It wasn't me this time," Doug said. He had slipped off one of his gloves and was touching my arm. His hand was as cold and damp as a root cellar.

"Don't you get me started," I whispered. "Don't you forget who got who in that open ice hit."

"Oh, ladies and gentlemen of the press, may I present to you the great, the incomparable—"

"Put you right over my back. Gasping for air, the wind knocked out of you—"

"Kyle Callendar."

I opened my eyes and Doug showed me a closed fist and two quick pumps. My gesture when I scored a goal in my playing days.

"Stick around man," I said as I drifted off to sleep. "I don't want to lose it."

"Count on it," he said, squeezing my hand.

chapter ten

Doctors forced nitro pills into me, hooked me up to monitors like an astronaut before a moon shot. Bits of wires and tubes sprung from every non-erogenous zone of my body as I walked and then ran on a treadmill. Tests were coming up empty on serious heart problems. There was no heart disease in my family. They gave me a super-aspirin, anti-anxiety pills as big as bumblebees, talked to me about unstable angina. With nothing showing up in the tests, they continued to think panic attack. When adrenal glands over-respond to stress and exhaustion and trigger extreme reactions—like my bizarre outburst in the motel that Myra reported, or the chest pain, loss of breath, and dead faint at the airport. Tiredness and alcohol are causes, but the main culprit is stress, the doctors said. Stress alone will bring it on.

I'd have to come back to the hospital for more tests, but the doctors released me when the chest pain and hallucinations subsided and I could walk to the john on my own. The Hall arranged for a few days at a strip motel. Some nondescript chain with clean sheets and a three-way lamp. Norma brought some changes of clothes for me and for the first time in months, it seemed we were playing house.

That first night Norma was reading proofs from the most recent issue of *Snow Grower* magazine with the lamp at the dim setting so I could rest on the bed. She was wearing black-rimmed glasses—Donna Karan, with their original lens. She brushed back some strands of hair, held her hand at her neck. Occasionally, she'd dash a squiggle of blue non-repro ink.

"What's this issue? Avalanche protection?" I asked, as I raised my arms above my head and stretched.

"Tundra travel," she said, not looking up from the tiny desk. "Blooms on the permafrost, likin' the lichen. It's getting bigger every year."

"Bigger than the annual seal hunt?"

"*Snow Grower* doesn't do the seal hunt, Kyle," she said. "*Snow Grower* is the publication for winter gardeners."

"Bigger than snow pumpkins?"

Norma smiled and put down her pen, carefully folded her glasses and put them in her case. "Coming back, are we?" she said. Her eyes met mine as she slowly lifted her negligee over her head and dropped it to the floor. In the butter-coloured light of the hotel lamp, her body looked slightly tanned. I stripped off my jeans and boxers and licked my index fingers and rubbed her nipples with the fingers and thumb. She grabbed the back of my neck and we kissed and then made love with a recklessness that surprised me. Like we were kids again.

Afterward, Norma's head lay nestled in the crook of my arm. The smoothness of her body calmed me as only Norma could. The smell of her hair was not of rosemary shampoo, or eucalyptus, or a sweetly sad designer perfume. Just her sex. The pure, simple power of Norma Hanford. What always pulled me back from the edge.

"I've been having these dreams, hon," I said.

"Really, you're remembering your dreams? Tell me."

"One that I had is about my father. Well, some are with my father, but others involve a man who at first I don't recognize. The man in the dream says we are Tannenbaums and every year at Christmastime we go to the bush to chop down our tree. 'Family tradition,' he jokes. 'Tannenbaum, O Tannenbaum,' we sing as we traipse off into the bush looking for that year's tree. There are many of us Tannenbaums, but I am the youngest, scurrying behind to keep up, so small I'm almost swallowed up by the deep, wide footprints in the snow. I stumble to keep pace with my lumberjack dream dad who's slicing the cold with an axe and singing 'O Tannenbaum' so loud and full that snow shakes from the pine boughs.

"We trudge and trudge. There are plenty of trees, but we don't stop, we don't even as much as look at them or inspect them as we go by, and I realize that we were never meant to actually pick one, that we will sing to beat the band but never do what we have set out to do. Eventually I wake up with the image of this strange man's back, and the tune 'O Tannenbaum' droning in my head.

"But finally it comes to me. The old man in the dreams. It's Emmett Noble Shriver, the ancestor of this man I told you about, Sheldon Shriver. And there's another thing. When I was young there was one funeral home in town, Tannenbaum Funeral Home. Christmas Tree Funeral Home."

Norma hung before me like the saint in the stained-glass window. But with no rock, no shard of glass. She was still, not a tremor or a crease in her face.

"That's quite a dream, Kyle. And after so long not remembering. How do you feel?" She said, teasing my hair with her fingers. "How does that make you feel?"

"I don't know. I really don't know," I said, leaning on the fake wood headboard. I looked up and noticed brown water spots on the ceiling tiles. Same look as the McLaren. I smirked a little with the thought of Myra, the crazy sex we'd had.

"Now what are you smiling at?" Norma asked.

"I don't know, nothing."

"Tell me, dear, I want to know."

"Jesus, Norma, I'm trying. Telling you my dreams, isn't that enough? Give me a little room, would you?"

"I'll give you a little room," Norma said as she pivoted off the bed. She was fighting back tears as she stooped to pick up her negligee from the floor. "More than you can imagine," she said.

"Norma, I—"

"I'll tell you what, Kyle," Norma said, stifling a sob. She paused and took a deep breath. "Why don't you type the dream up? I like the imagery. I could use it as a back pager."

I jumped off the bed and grabbed her shoulders. "Norma, I'm serious—"

She twisted out of my grip and turned to get away from me. "Could be just stress, hon," she said, wriggling into her gown. "Like the doctors say."

"No, Norma. Not you too. I need you, can't you see? I mean, this could bring on another episode, I—"

"Kyle," she said, slowly shaking her head. "Okay. Let's try again." She turned to face me, her eyes red with tears. "Please talk to me. It's not enough for me to have you just report your life. You don't think you do, but you keep so much inside. Don't you understand? For us to make it as a couple, I need to know you, to hear you. All of you."

"Eh? Well, I ... Listen, Norma, you know I'm not comfortable with this stuff." I went back to the bed, fished through the bedding, found my boxers, and put them on.

"Kyle, you don't think I don't know what's going on with you," she whispered, moving to my side. I could feel her breath on my lips. I lifted my gaze from my bare feet to Norma, the tip of her turned-up nose.

"I've always wanted what was best for you," she said, touching my cheek. "But I have needs, too. Remember in the hospital I said that there is so much you don't tell me? I meant that, Kyle. I have to begin to feel that you can open up to me." She placed her hands on either side of my face, her dark eyes narrowing to beads. "How many times have we talked about this, Kyle? You know it's been the single biggest obstacle to us being together." She paused but kept her hands on my face. "From us really being together."

I'd seen Norma in hundreds of different moods, but never this one. Her square jaw was set, her brow furrowed. Using my name like a violin bow.

"It's not about the other women, Kyle," she said.

"What? I mean, how—"

"Oh, Kyle, you chump," she said, with a thin smile. "There are some things you can't hide. And you don't even know it."

I slumped on the bed and folded my hands onto my lap. I watched Norma in the mirror above a chest of drawers put her glasses back on and move over to the bed, snap the three-way lamp to the medium setting. She sat down and picked up a sheath of *Snow Grower* proof.

"Don't get me wrong," Norma said, not looking up from the proof. "It's good that you're remembering your dreams. I'm happy for that. But I can't stand it anymore that you don't really talk to me. That you have this whole side of yourself that you don't reveal."

"I'm sorry, Norma. I'm sorry I disappoint you."

She threw down her pen and snatched off her glasses. "You just don't get it, do you?" she said, glaring at me. "If you're going to be sorry, be sorry for yourself. This isn't about me. It's about *you*. It's this behaviour, your withholding of feelings that's bringing on these attacks, not anything that can be traced to me."

"Then what do you want from me?" I said, looking up at her.

"It's so simple," she said, pushing aside the proof and meeting my gaze. "I want you to tell me how and what you feel when you feel it. What's inside. If you'd like to know, that is what the doctors told me, what that Dr. Strachan said. That you've got to find a way to open up. Not just take anti-anxiety pills. Not to be sorry and silent, but to talk."

Jesus, I thought, what's going on? If I lost Norma I didn't know what I would do.

"You want to know how I feel?" I said as I pushed myself up on the bed. "I feel the ground under my feet giving way. You, more than anyone else, you can't abandon me now. You've got to help me."

Father couldn't dance. The beat was lost on him. On the open road, he never knew when the asphalt would dip, a pavement cut appear. His rig would hit a bump and he held onto the wheel, rocked not to a beat but to the shock of the unexpected, a blow underfoot. His life was not a rhythm, a sensuality, the smooth rock and roll, bend and sway, swing and step of salsa, never varying, feeling the beat, like water in a river flow—not on the road, where the bump was the beat, and he couldn't keep all the roads of America in his head. Instead, he sat and held on to the wheel for life. Not for dear life, because what he held was outside himself. Father was not raised to listen to any inner voices. He knew what he didn't want a hundred times better than what he wanted. The proper way to take a hit.

The roads of late winter stayed with Father. The time of year when even after a rain, the edges of sight were more brown than green. Trees so many sticks like men without dinner, cream-coloured warehouse buildings, and concrete barriers, some twenty feet high, keeping the sound hemmed in, the whir of spinning tires, a sound that never ends so that you can't hear your heart, the breath in your lungs.

Father never beat me. Not once. In Keppel, you never heard any stories about that, about fathers beating their sons. Not in the good families, anyway. Not in the good schools, in the good hockey clubs, in the good homes.

Self-restraint has its limits, and occasionally Father would give me a blast. And like a nuclear test in the desert, you'd never forget it. Or anything about it. What the weather was like, what you were wearing. Like the nuclear test, there were no casualties. Or at least none that you could at first detect. Yelling is a blow, sure, but it's silence that kills. Silence cuts in millions of tiny ways, destroys by inches.

I remember, too, my father flooding the rink. Every night when the weather turned cold, Father went to the abandoned barn and stood, his lips frozen shut by the damp and frigid air, the back spray from the garden hose, and flooded the rink so that his only son could play The Game.

"He's doing this for you," Mother told me once.

But as long as I've known him, Father never skated, never got a moment's joy out of the work he put in. We were never truly together on the ice. In my dream, Father put me in the Christmas tree, lifted me high above the ground so that I imagined I were a bird, soaring through the crystal blue sky, leaving what I knew behind. The message for me was that my father was not there. On a road far away, not really taking part. "Tell me, Kyle, what's it like up there?" he shouted to me as I sat in the tree in my dream. Somewhere deep in my bones I knew. I was alone in the world.

chapter eleven

Doug didn't call first. That wasn't his style. Even before "Gone Ron," there was nothing ordinary about him. Nothing that you could predict, or not with any degree of accuracy. Take that free night we had in London, Ontario, while we played for the junior Canadians. After spending the night drinking beers, Doug insisted we hop a freight to get home. In those days, trains shunted through north London for all hours and we tumbled into an empty moving freight car, laughing to beat hell on the coldest night of the year. We stayed on the train a little longer than we should have and didn't find our way back to the hotel until 3 a.m. Coach was pissed and he let us know it, but he couldn't bench us. Not his two star players.

It was 6 a.m. and I heard a light knock on the motel room door. Norma was sleeping soundly next to me, so I eased out of bed and tiptoed to the window and peered out. Doug held two Tim Hortons bags, steam rising from them in the morning cool, on either side of a goofy smile. I pulled on my jeans and a T-shirt, slipped on my shoes, and quietly opened the door so as not to disturb Norma.

"A little brekkie, bud?" Doug said.

"I don't know, man," I said, carefully closing the door and stepping outside. "Norma is still resting, I can't go far."

"That's why I've brought the brekkie to you," he said, brandishing the Tim Horton bags. "Allow me to escort you to your seat." He gestured with his head to a black Cadillac, pointed in the direction of the rising sun.

"Okay, but just for a few minutes," I said warily. "I don't want to leave Norma alone for long."

"Of course. We wouldn't have it any other way."

You could've eaten off the floor of Doug's Caddy. The spacious legroom and the tilt of the bucket seats made it seem as if I weren't sitting at all but hovering above the deep-piled leather cushions of the bench seats. I sipped the coffee and burned the tip of my upper lip. Doug took the cup from me and slipped it into a java jacket. He snatched a hunk of cruller from the other bag and handed it to me.

"Feeling better now?" Doug said as we chomped our meals. The golden-brown cruller melted in my mouth. Through the Cinemascope of Doug's windshield, I watched as a squirrel jumped from the roof of an apartment building to overhanging branches of a maple. It scooted through the tree and over the city street, jumped into the branches of another maple that formed a canopy over the road, and disappeared onto the roof of a house.

Doug took a sip of coffee and eased into his seat. He was wearing stone-grey trousers, a zip-up Gore-Tex-like top, and Reeboks. Deep wrinkles on his forehead, thin mouth lines. Amphibian scaling on his hands, the telltale age marks, and the chilblains. But his muscle tone in the light of the morning sun looked great—like he stopped playing hockey yesterday.

"Yeah," I said, "I guess. Thanks." Suddenly, I felt very uncomfortable alone in the car with Doug. It had been too long. A shudder rippled through me like an icy draft. Thank God I'd taken that anti-anxiety pill the night before, I thought.

"I should drink up and get back inside, though. I didn't leave a note or anything."

Doug slowly nodded his head in an absent-minded way. "My pop said he saw you, Kyle."

"Yeah, he and Jim took me for a ride the night of Bobby's Cup party. It was okay." I glanced up looking for the squirrel on the roof.

"For a man a few bricks short, you mean," Doug said. He pressed a button on the console and a readout flashed the time, temperature, humidity, and what I imagined was the latitude and longitude. There was no cigarette lighter.

"Hope he didn't embarrass himself too much."

"Nah, not at all."

"How's your old man? Are you keeping in touch?"

"Sort of. As much as seems reasonable."

Doug shifted in his seat and we both fell silent. He dropped his hands on his legs and rubbed them twice from his groin to his knees.

"Legs never used to stiffen up like this after a run. Does that happen to you, Kyle?"

"Yeah, they do get stiff. When I get out. My schedule hasn't allowed for it much, though."

"Right, you got the travelling job. Others have a little more time on their hands." He glanced into the side-view mirror as if he were expecting someone. He wiped his lips with a paper napkin and handed me one, but I declined it.

"Tell me about your work," I said. A year or so after hockey, Doug had taken a job as manager of Old Woman's River Community Arena, near North Battleford.

"Nah, not now. Maybe later," he said. We settled in on finishing our meals. After breakfast, Doug stacked the coffee cups, crumpled the bag and napkins, and stuffed the debris into a little wastebasket on the floor.

"I meant what I told you at the hospital, Kyle: that I want to help you," he said, staring blankly out the windshield. He fidgeted on his seat, like he'd been benched the second period and had only one more shift in the game so he had to make it good. "You have to trust me in that," he said, turning to face me. "Do you think you can trust me? I mean we've known each other a long time, haven't we?"

I looked away. A woman in a housecoat with a dog the colour of wet kindling hurried along the street.

"Sure have, I guess."

"I know Pop has taken a liking to you, but there is something you should know about him. A little story that I think might help give you an idea where he is coming from. It certainly has helped me." We looked at each other and he smiled. The pain in my back twinged and I leaned against the door for relief. "Maybe," he said, his mouth widening to a grin, "break the ice, so to speak. We've known each other forever, but wouldn't it be nice to get to a place of better understanding? That's what I'd like in any case."

I cut a glance to the empty street and then back to Doug, gave him a slight nod to go on.

"I don't know whether you know it or Pop told you the other night, but the old man loved Eddie Shore," Doug said. "At first because he was a Saskatchewan boy. Fort Qu'Appelle, down Regina way. Of course, Eddie was before our time, but to hear Dad tell it, he was the greatest pound-for-pound hockey player that he ever saw. One hundred and sixty pounds of muscle. Hockey players may be bigger now, but they don't have The Game in their blood, Pop says. Not like Eddie Shore did."

Doug paused to pick a shred of fried dough from his jacket and put it into his mouth. Dark veins, a Manitoba watershed, etched his nose.

" 'Play The Game hard, son. Like Shore,' Pop would tell me. And I did, to the best of my ability. But Shore was the pilot light that fired Pop's heart. Not me, not ever. I was never going to re-place him.

"What I didn't know in my playing days was what Pop meant by hard," Doug said, leaning his head on the wheel. A glimmer of light in the sky peeked above the rooftops. "Later, I learned that nobody in the history of The Game ever suffered the way that Eddie Shore did. He was patched up with nine hundred and seventy-eight stitches; he broke his back, his hip, his collarbone a dozen times, his jaw five. When he was buried, frostbite scarred his hands from a game-day drive in the dead of winter, during which he travelled in a car without a windshield from Boston to Montreal. Imagine all those bones—bruised or broken. Only his wisdom teeth left in his head.

"The books will tell you about Shore's violent hit that ended Ace Bailey's playing career, but what they don't tell you, Kyle, is how a man who plays The Game like that cannot only be forgiven but be a hero. Pop called it the dirty little secret. A lesson from the men to the boys who thought they could get by without the hard lessons. That bones were broken outside the rink, too."

Then Doug shot his head straight up with a jolt as if he too had been thumped. He glared at me and then his face slowly relaxed.

"To Eddie, love was being hit, Kyle. And although my old man never actually told me, the same must have been true for him. Not that he ever hit me, you understand. But Pop lived vicariously through Eddie Shore, cheered his violent life because he felt the memory of the pain of every blow his own father had given him.

" 'You see this scar, boy,' Pop told me the day he got out of prison. Pop was some squirrelly then, and he'd pulled open the front of his shirt like Superman and with his two hands was making like he was opening the cavity of his chest along a scar that stretched from his sternum to his gut. 'A piece of Eddie Shore was buried in here when he died,' Pop said.

"I reached out and touched the rope of cold red flesh. 'What piece was that?' I asked.

" 'His guilty pleasure,' he said. Then Pop smiled, so that his face was open and clear. The mouth of a river."

As a boy I liked to push in the cigarette lighter on the console of my father's rig. Through the minutes of quiet, while I waited for my father to come back from a delivery, I'd daydream after I'd depressed the metal knob with my thumb and imagine the warmth and feel of Dad's thumb, because he often used the lighter, was a big smoker then, always had a cigarette dangling from his lip, the smell of his smoke on my hair, clothes, and skin. The lighter would pop out, and I'd stare into the centre of the knob, smell the tobacco. Export A, green package on the dash. Circles of angry red to the heart of rage, lightening like the morning sky, then darkness, grey, nothing. Once, I slammed the knob back into its slot on the dash, frustrated in the waiting, because it had seemed forever that Father had left me in the cab of the truck while he was on the delivery, a meaningless one outside Lion's Head, with six pallets of paint, wallboard, nails, a couple of hundred board feet of lumber. A minute later, the cigarette lighter popped out again and I let it sit.

Once I was waiting outside Gwen Martinson's. Her general store on a dirt road north of the village of Lion's Head, which I never saw but people told me wasn't much to look at, let alone stick your head in to. Gwen's was end of the line for Dad's rig. A quarter-mile in off the highway, the road narrowed to a logging track, fit for Jeeps in mud season, snowmobiles in winter. Dad backed the rig down the road as I sat slumped in the cab, watching for signs of life in the treetops, spruce and white pine, sprays of needles and black arms that swaddled the dim sun. It wasn't hockey season, so we weren't talking much. I laid back and eventually the rig ground to a halt. "Wait for me," Dad said, as he opened the door to get out. "Gwen and I have to do the business first, then you can help me with the unloading. I won't be long."

I couldn't listen to the radio because Dad took the keys with him. Would drain the battery, Dad said, and he could tell if I were to use it, by how the engine sounded at the turn of the ignition, so it was just as well he didn't leave them. It wasn't much of a temptation, because near Lion's Head you couldn't get Motown or even CBC, only the hog and feed market reports, sermons on life after death. Instead, I wound down the window and looked out. And pushed in the cigarette lighter once every ten minutes or so because it didn't drain the battery so much, or not so Father could tell.

A murder of crows was making a racket somewhere nearby. Crows didn't need much of an excuse to talk. Like Itchy Phil Stokes, the town fool, who in spring traipsed Keppel with his hundred-pound lawn roller, and talked a blue streak to himself or anyone who would listen. Once, we gave Itchy the job to roll our lawn and I walked alongside him. Itchy talked about the weather, the way the smell of the first spring rain will get in your woollens and stay there until the snow. After he finished rolling the lawn, he stood over the cracks on a pavement square in our lane and read the future like a palm reader. You are going to meet a dark stranger. You'll have two children, a girl and a boy. You can expect to work in sales. He'd never see anything bad in the lane. If he did, he said he'd crack it into pieces and repair the job, pour the concrete, make it like new. Not only would we protect against being sued by the person who would slip and break an ankle, we could smooth over the past, Itchy said.

The crow cawed in the dying light of the late afternoon, until, as I was drifting off to sleep, wondering if my father would ever come back from doing the business with Gwen, I heard a light tap of metal at my ear. I jerked up in the seat and looked out the window. From the height of the cab, I saw a woman smile as if from a divide, the open water between the dock and an ocean liner turning toward France. Her arms had slipped out of the sleeves of her sweater, ragged deer in a forest, and she was hugging herself, protecting against the cold because where she had been moments before was warmer than I could ever yet have imagined. Her eyes met mine and she reached up her hand toward me and mouthed the words, "Come, Kyle. Come inside with me."

Norma finished with *Snow Grower* and was working on her king-fisher. *Kingfisher in Context*. Norma took photographs of animals, then blew them up on slightly larger canvases, distorting them with very bright oils. Putting colour where there was none. Even in high school, Norma had an eye, was always sketching, endlessly talking about the shapes of the clouds, say, or how light changed the colour on a cluster of rocks in Kingston Harbour. Now friends in Toronto said her work reminded them of early David Hockney. The colours, in any case. She hadn't yet managed to mount her first show, but she always worked as if she were about to, said she'd quit her day job in a heartbeat when she could.

With *Crow in Context*, she'd layered colours to bring lustre to the crow's coat and did wonders with leaves of the oak tree, alternating light and dark green to best show the direction of the light. But *Kingfisher in Context* was going to be something else. She'd painted shades of blue, daggered texture of the throat, the lordly crest. And the water. It was one thing to do cat-o'-nine-tails and black water for *Red-winged Blackbird in Context*. But a rushing river. That you had to prepare for. A slow build. A series was not a random collection around a theme, but a forward march, Norma once told me. We cannot fly. We cannot be beamed aboard. But we can get to where we want to go if we're on the move.

"Norma, do you have a moment?" I asked, leaning against the doorway. Light from the open window formed a rectangle on the wall above Norma's head. She flicked her hair behind her ear and onto her shoulder. Her mouth parted as she began to say something, but then her coal-black eyes averted my gaze. Girl-shy, she shook her head, and then looked back into my eyes as tears formed in hers. "No," she said as she rose from her chair and approached me. "No, I don't. Not just yet."

Norma kissed me and slipped my T-shirt over my head and tossed it to the floor. I raised my hands to her face, but she grabbed my left wrist and squeezed hard. Once a woman touched me, I usually took over. If a woman kissed me, I kissed her harder. If I wasn't in command, I felt alone. Unloved. And I couldn't bear that. She mouthed the word "no," wet her index finger, and traced a half-moon along my chest hairs. My head was light as air and I groaned with delight. Norma stepped out of her painter's smock, an old Original Six NHL business shirt of mine. Her hair fell to her shoulders. A limpid smile. In all our years together I had never wanted to touch her more than at that moment. To bury my face in her sex. But my wrist was still red from her grip, the warning "no" too loud in my ear, so I did nothing but watch her as my beautiful Norma pulled at my hands and we eased to the floor.

"No," she whispered over and over like a mantra, until the sound of it crashed in my head like waves against rocks. "No," she said, as we lay back in each other's arms, legs intertwined, spent from our lovemaking.

We lay like that for a long time, drifting in and out of sleep. I opened my eyes and Norma's face hovered above me like an angel's.

"Kyle, remember your promise. We have to keep talking. I need that. Tell me. What was on your mind when you came into the room? What were you going to tell me?"

For the life of me, I didn't know what she was talking about. I closed my eyes and saw the Cup, felt the uncommon warmth of Gwen's gaze. "Sure. Yeah, I remember. Don't worry," I said.

"But I am worried—about us."

"Oh, but we're fine, hon," I said, drifting off again. "Jesus, I can't believe how tired I am," I said, turning away from her.

Suddenly, Norma leapt to her feet like a cat. In a second, she was back in her smock, closing it at her throat in a fist.

"Kyle, I can't stand it," she said. "I want you. But I can't find you. No matter what I do, I can't ever find you."

"But Norma," I said as I sat up and followed her with my eyes, "what's wrong, honey? What did I do?"

"Kyle, I think you should leave." She turned to face me, her eyes full of tears boring a hole in me.

"Honey, no," I said, moving toward her. "You don't know what you're saying."

"Spare me, Kyle," she said, angrily, pushing me away. "I'm not sixteen years old anymore."

"Honey … I don't know what you're talking about. You know the stress I'm under—"

"'Tired,' you said. "I asked if you remembered your promise and you tell me you're *tired*. Well, I can do you one better, mister. I'm *sick* and tired. Sick and tired … of *you*."

"Now, hold on a minute, I don't know—"

"Kyle, I asked you to leave," Norma said as she struggled to button her shirt. "If you know what's good for you, that's what you'll do before I say something that I may regret."

My eyes held hers for more than a beat and I slumped back to the floor. As I look back on that moment, I see it as less of a decision than an accident. That split second when you see disaster coming, a speeding car through an intersection, an opponent's hockey stick swung at the open space between your helmet and shoulder pads. And you freeze. There's nothing to be done.

"Kyle," she said. "Words are very important to me."

"I know. For me too."

"You think that's the case. But I don't think so. Maybe enough for other women. But not enough for me."

"Norma, I—"

"I've trusted you for everything for so long," she said wheeling in my face. "I always come to you for advice with my feelings. When I feel sad about a friend or need to talk to you about my parents. You name it. You're always there to listen—in my work, even about my stupid job. I took so many of your suggestions for the 'What's New in Snowshoes' issue that you got a co-editing credit. Do you remember that?"

"Sure, but—"

"I've trusted you with everything, big and small. Whatever. But now, after all these years, I want to help you. To really be there for you, and you won't let me. You won't even let me make love to you." She burst into tears and threw herself onto the bed.

I willed myself to go to her but I couldn't, found myself rooted to the floor. Perhaps Norma was right; I knew nothing about love, wasn't up to being with someone like her. Norma may have rescued me from myself after hockey, but now she needed something more. Like the owner of a trading post in the wild, waiting for the supply ship. But it was delayed, held up by bad weather. If the ship didn't arrive soon, she'd starve.

After a while Norma stopped crying and gave me an ultimatum. If we were going to stay together, I would have to work with Dr. Strachan, the psychiatrist. It wasn't just our relationship, she said, but my health itself that was at stake. I had to see that.

I closed my eyes and pressed the floor hard with the flat of my hand. My first instinct was to run, to push myself up and get the hell out of there. But I knew that was not an option. I knew Norma wouldn't be there when I got back. Not this time. I froze with a terror I hadn't felt in a long time.

Finally, I nodded yes. I would call the Hall tomorrow; I would make the arrangements.

"Good, Kyle. That's good ... Now can you please tell me one thing. At least try. How did that Tannenbaum dream make you feel?"

I stood up and walked to the window. The moon had risen above a block of apartments, making clearer my reflection in the glass. Not a line was visible on my forehead.

"Each footprint in the snow was a casket that I had to keep scrambling to get out of," I said. "But even as I climbed out of one, another presented itself, and I wasn't getting any closer to my goal." Tears welled up, and I turned toward Norma. "But what was my goal?" I said, clenching my fists. "What do I know except playing hockey? Tannenbaum, the funeral director, is the angel of death. He's my new goal, because now my life is over ... That was what I was going to tell you when I walked into the room. That I wish I didn't feel this way, but I feel my life is over."

"It was a dream, Kyle, honey," Norma said. "It's not the way things have to be."

"I don't know. Maybe."

"Not maybe." She came to me and massaged the bridge of my nose, where she kissed me. "See, the worry lines have gone. This is good. I believe in you."

"I don't know."

I reached for her and held her, fighting the urge to take over as she kissed and then hugged me. Sometimes, I thought, as I looked at myself in the reflection of the window, it was amazing even to me how I got off the hook. I wanted to love Norma Hanford the way she seemed capable of loving me, but she was right: I had never been up to the task.

chapter twelve

The dashboard clock was stuck at 12:01 p.m. Wayne pulled his white
Camry off the Yellowhead Highway and down a country lane.
"Turn right," I said, "then left at the tree break. It won't be long,
you'll know when you see the sign." I was able to find my way back
to the roads that led to the picnic site I'd visited with Ron and Jim
Cowpland without too much trouble.

The Hall was amenable to me taking some time off. It was slow
anyway—more than a month to go before the NHL opener. They
also agreed with Norma that I should spend some time with this
doctor Wayne. He was a shrink but a retired one with a lot of success
treating pro athletes. A bit unorthodox, but he understood hockey
players, had a lot of success treating them, they said. Talk to him a
bit and then c'mon back home. Okay, I said, but I'm not crazy. We
know that, they said. But see him for a while in any case.

It was Wayne's idea to return to the place the Cowplands had
taken me. Perhaps explore some of the feelings that might have led
to your panic attack, he said. It was a sunny day, so we'd brought
a picnic—and Doug and Norma and two hospital workers. He'd
asked me if I minded bringing these guys along, that they were
hockey fans keen to be up close to some former NHLers. Sounded
okay to me at first, so I didn't object. "You might not be up for it,
but we'll bring some hockey sticks and play a little shinny," the
shrink had said. "Just relax, no pressure."

Doug and Norma were in the back seat, hitting it off—yakking about gardening, of all things. Doug's harvesting of Yukon
Gold potatoes from a plot behind the rink at North Battleford, and

broccoli and Brussels sprouts, his favourite. Norma's oak-leave
hydrangeas. And lace caps just past peak. "The word *flamboyant*
is lost to us, Doug," she said. "But red peonies define flamboyant.
With colour that dances off the petals, hangs fuzzy in the air."
Behind us in a Buick LeSabre, the hospital workers followed with
fried chicken, coleslaw, and soft drinks. It was mid-afternoon,
but the sun was still high in the sky, wouldn't begin its descent
for hours.

"I don't know about you, Kyle, but I do my best thinking on the
open road," Wayne said. "Some people it's not that way. They sit at
a desk with a pen and a pad of legal-size paper under a lamp and
they put down things. Not me."

The thrumming sound of the road caused a low-level pain
at my temples. My jaw tightened. I breathed deeply and felt the
twinge in my chest. "Santa Cruz Banana Slugs?" Norma said with
a laugh. "You've got to be kidding."

"I know young folks like yourself are inclined to think that
retired guys don't do much thinking at all," Wayne said, squinting
into his discount-bin sunglasses. White-grey wisps of hair fluttered on his tanned head. "The truth of it is, retired guys don't
do anything else but struggle to stay in touch. That's the thing.
Otherwise we might as well curl up and die."

Wayne stretched his arm over the top of his bucket seat and his
hand gripped the backside of my headrest. "With these satellites,
even when I'm on a hunting trip, TV brings you Comedy Central,
Bravo, the BBC. Of course, the last thing I need a thousand miles
into the wilderness is a one-liner from *The Colbert Report* or a sit-
down with *49 Up*, that dreary British documentary tracking fourteen ordinary people from all walks of life, but satellite TV does
keep you up on the serial killings. Retired shrinks love that stuff ...
And impotency-treatment pills. The news about impotency pills is
very popular."

He cut me a look, but when I didn't respond he returned his
attention to the road.

"Where *do* they find these beautiful men and women who read
the news, anyway?" he continued. "A few years ago they looked
like my father in a thousand-dollar toupée. Peter Mansbridge on

Cheez Whiz. Now they're something else, eh? Clean-cut, of course, but tawny brown, with piercing blue-green eyes, shiny hair, teeth like pearls. Just the ticket for high-def TV. Can you imagine what these people will look like when they're even more enhanced by the next generation of HDTV? Maybe Viacom and News Corp. are investing in gene pools for news anchors in order to guarantee a steady supply of the right look—say with Dene hair, Javanese skin, Parisian cheekbones, Russian eyes, Danish hands, Thai fingernails. Control for sex. They could copyright exclusivity."

"There's been a lot of change," I said, looking out the window. A roadside sign, "While They Snore, We Pour," advertised a local cement company. A wheel chock that I imagined fell off a tow truck lay on the shoulder of the road.

"Change? You betcha," he said, pounding the steering wheel with the heel of his driving hand. "The truth is I don't know how it is for young people like yourselves. I was one of those who thought old President Bill wouldn't have lasted a week after it became clear he was getting his oil changed between checkups by young Miss Monica. What do you think, Kyle? I know I don't get it. People don't have kids like they used to. And when they do, families break up and youngsters are left to fend for themselves. Grown kids at ten, say, piss in their pants and weep non-stop, or are serene and suck-faced, loaded up on psychosocial drug cocktails courtesy of my esteemed profession. In America, of course, they load up Papa's automatic and blow off some steam. The nuclear family, they call it. Nice."

Wayne slipped a package of Lifesavers out of the front pocket of his blue and white striped golf shirt and offered me some. Lemon was on top so I peeled back the paper to grab a cherry along with it to get a sweeter taste. He offered them to Doug and Norma, but they were preoccupied. Doug was sitting on the edge of the seat, waving his arms. "It's the sound of the prairie sage grouse that you can't forget," he said. "Palummp bump, palummp bump. One otherworldly love call. The lord of the mating-dance pirouettes, doing quarter turns, green sacs swelling on his breastplate. But the sound. Palummp bump, palummp bump. That's what you can't get out of your head."

Wayne and I fell silent for a while and I wound down the window. In summer, the Saskatchewan prairie smells as sweet and clean as the air in the middle of a northern lake. The hot afternoon sun beat on my arm. For hours, my father drove on roads like this by himself, not saying a goddamn thing.

"I don't know where you are going with this yammering of yours, but I told you, I don't have anything to say. I keep my feelings to myself, understand?" I whispered with one eye on Norma, convinced she wasn't able to overhear me while she was talking to Doug. "There is nothing wrong with me." I closed my eyes and the underside of my lids glowed red in the bright sun. My chest pain eased and for the first time in I don't know how long, I relaxed.

Wayne brought both of his hands to the wheel. He finally stopped his blather, and Doug and Norma's chatter softened as I lay back on the headrest and fell asleep.

For a year or so after the war, Dad worked in a factory. I remember it before it was torn down. Windows so black you couldn't see in. Then Dad took a job at the Keppel airport. He ran the mower, patched the runway for quack grass that sprouted through the asphalt. Roddie Firth, the Sunday school teacher, would take a different boy up in his Cessna four-seater for their first plane ride on consecutive Sundays after class. And grommet-maker Will Scabbard flew to Kitchener for meetings five times a year. But no one of any real importance ever landed at the Keppel airport. Even politicians from Toronto chose to drive the campaign bus north, rather than fly into town. High-and-mighty lost votes in Keppel—even the fools from Toronto could see that.

Instead, it's Dad's life on the road that I've imagined. What he seemed to love, what worked to tamp down his war within. Up in that cab, Fleming Cartage. A logo of two rounded rectangles atop wheels made oblong to convey speed and purpose. The front rectangle was oblong, too, as if yielding to an external power but not quite, showing the resistance that makes it personal. Father didn't read books, but he smiled at the signs: Continental Laminators, Flowers by Don, Blind Man Driving on the back of a panel van owned by a vertical venetian maker. Trucks of the U.S. Post

Office—205009, 4777001; Nice 'N Necessary, a notions semi; a giant pink Looney Tune pig—Porky, Servicing the Food Industry. High above the road, Father was like a sahib on an elephant, minus even a nuance of enlightenment.

Because he had sports, not war, in his head. Hockey, my hockey. The touch of the hand on the wheel like the shaft of a stick, guiding the rig down the road, like the stick to the puck. Behind the wheel, Father looked for an opening, and when he anticipated it, he sped up, pointed the truck in the vacant space, assertive and clear. Like the power forward before the goalmouth. He didn't yield, because if he did he felt his balls shrink.

For road is like ice. What you have to feel to succeed. Where men live for the challenge of being pitted against other men.

We ate the picnic food in no time, and I popped my anti-anxiety pill with a swallow of Snapple. The two hospital workers collected the road hockey sticks and rigged a playing surface on the parking lot. Norma and Doug against the two orderlies, no body checking. Wayne and I were sitting on the picnic table I'd sat on only a few nights before with Ron Cowpland. A steady breeze cooled the heat of the sun.

At faceoff, Red, a big orderly in a carrot-top Afro, dropped the ball between Doug and the swarthy-looking worker, who Wayne said was named Jobey. Doug drew the ball back to Norma, who stickhandled wide of Red. She tried a pass before Doug was clear of Jobey's check and the ball caromed off Jobey's leg out of bounds. Possession, Jobey and Red.

Like a talent scout in the playoffs, Wayne propped his elbows on his knees and rested his craggy face on his folded hands. Perhaps the Hall was right. Wayne may be a regular guy, I thought.

"I'm reminded of that Philly/Pitt game in 2000," Wayne said. Red flicked the ball high in the air with his stick and Jobey got a step or two on Doug and ran under it. "The one that went five overtime periods before it was decided."

"Yeah, what about it?" I asked.

Jobey one-timed the ball as it hit the ground and fired it into the open net. "Beauty," Wayne cried, slapping his knee with his open palm.

"It was like Coach Dick Irvin of the Montreal Canadiens once said, 'When your team gets a goal, it's sudden; when the opponent gets it, it's death.' It's either over in the first ten minutes or it seems it will never end," Wayne continued. "The Game endlessly playing, a dream come true."

Norma flashed me a wave and blew a kiss. A strand of hair fell over her left eye and she tried to blow it back into place. She blew a second time, and then pushed the strand behind her ear.

I felt a stab of love for her, blinked back a tear and moved down the bench from Wayne. He was too pushy for my liking. The closest I had ever come to working with a therapist was the personal trainer I'd hired in my final two years before retirement. Jay did a good job on muscle stretching and leg strengthening. In the beginning, I'd liked his war stories about Vietnam, yarns about his buddies on the road, but after a while I'd told him I wanted quiet. It surprised me how much Wayne reminded me of Jay. Wasn't Wayne supposed to get me to talk on my own terms? It seemed odd to me the way he was acting. But unlike Jay, I couldn't tell Wayne to just shut his yap. I knew I was at the end of the line with both Norma and the Hall. I didn't know what I could do but sit still and take it.

After the goal Jobey and Doug dropped their sticks, began roughhousing on a grassy knoll. Norma and Red sat on the pavement, talking. I wanted to grab a stick and play, but Wayne said he had only four sticks. We were to take on the winners.

Suddenly, Norma leapt up and yelled for a pass. Doug snapped one that hit the heel of Norma's stick and ricocheted to Red, who spun and golfed a long shot into the open net. 2–zip for the Orderlies.

Wayne whistled and shot his fist into the air. "Yes. Good one, fellows," he said. He cut me a gloating smile.

"I'd like to play. I'd like to play now," I said.

"Soon, Kyle. Let's just talk a bit more first," Wayne said, raising both arms slowly and plaiting his fingers at the back of his head.

Damn him to hell, I thought. Who did he think he was, treating me like that? Patronizing me. Suddenly, it hit me like a blindside bodycheck. The Hall wasn't interested in seeing me back to good health, or getting me to return to my job. They couldn't continue to trust the safety of the Cup to someone like me. To such a fuckup. Didn't Wayne say in the hospital that he had talked to Myra, who must have told him about that scene I'd had with her? Wayne had his orders: monitor my instability, even provoke me to the point where I might go off on him, with remarks like that one in the car about impotency pills, for Chrissakes. And Jobey and Red? What a deluded dope I was to think that they could get worked up about seeing a couple of hockey has-beens like Doug and me. Why else would they be along if not as witnesses, or bodyguards in case I went ballistic? Later, in his report to the Hall, Wayne would make the case to let me go. Out on my fat ass again.

Norma surprised Jobey from behind, poke-checked the ball from him, and fed a lead pass to Doug on left wing. Red appeared to have the goal covered, but Doug fired a gem between Red's legs for Norma and Doug's first goal. "Lovely pass, honey," I shouted as she stopped and blew me another kiss.

"Besides, I thought we'd give them the first go—I'm getting a little old," Wayne said. He stood up and arched his back like a bear against the hard tabletop. "See, I sit on a picnic table without support and my back starts acting up. My doctor says it's arthritis. You have no idea."

He reached over to me and put his long-fingered mitt on my shoulder while toothpicking chicken with his other hand. A dark tuft of hair flagged his inner ear. "Imagine you've got a few aches and pains yourself, Kyle," he said.

"What is it with you?" I said, jerking away from him. "Why don't you just be straight with me, eh? Tell me what you're really up to." I glared at him until he looked away.

"C'mon you guys, tighten up, don't let them get another one," Wayne said, ignoring me.

Wayne watched the game for a beat before he lifted his grey eyes toward me. "Retirement is no easy stage of life, Kyle," Wayne said. "In the beginning anyway. I'm kind of an expert. I can help."

"Fuck retirement," I said, spitting on the ground. Jesus, I thought, everyone must be in on this. Even Norma. So damn determined that I get in touch with my feelings that she'd push me to the point of collapse. That way she'd have me, be in control, I thought with a shudder. Just like after San Jose. "Give me a stick and I'll show you."

Norma and Doug criss-crossed, catching Red flat-footed. A pass put Norma in the clear but on the backhand, and she lifted the ball too high, over the net. Red didn't run worth a damn, but he was good with his stick. Jobey had no hands but was fit, always seemed to have at least a step on Doug, leaving no room to make a play.

"You can piss on my shoes, Wayne, but don't tell me it's raining," I said. Ron Cowpland told me he could sense something about me. Maybe that was it, I thought. His sixth sense was warning him that I was going to be forced out of The Game.

"No, Kyle," Wayne said. I could feel his eyes on me like a soaked rag. "It's not like that at all."

"Well, I don't want out, Wayne," I said. "You can do your damnedest, build your case with Myra's lies, your mind games. The Hall is going to have to fire me, and I'll sue them for wrongful dismissal. Put that in your fucking report."

Jobey got the blade of his stick on a long clearing pass from Red, and the deflection slipped between Norma's right leg and the "post," a painted yellow line on the parking lot. 3–1. Couldn't Doug see that Red was vulnerable to an outside-in move? Deke to the outside to his strength, move the ball through his legs and around. At this rate, Red would bat down everything. The Orderlies would win going away.

"You can be more involved," Wayne said. "Play Old Timers hockey. I can talk to the Hall about helping set that up for you. There are others who feel just as you do."

"Thanks," I hissed, looking at the game. "When I'm ready for that kind of company, I'll let you know."

Yeah, right, sure I will. If death was when The Game ended, then Old Timers hockey was death's dressing room. Consider yourself done, I thought, suddenly spent. A second ago I was as angry as I'd been in my life, now I couldn't feel a thing. Maybe it was the meds, I dunno, but I felt myself drifting. Empty as a gourd with Wayne distant, an echo. No threat at all. Strange how he could hear me from so far away. So much like my life: the further away, the deeper the connection. Soon, if I played my cards right, Wayne would be gone and I would confide in him.

"I don't know, man. I feel so weird."

"How's that, Kyle? Tell me."

"I've been wondering about these men I saw at the airport with Sheldon and Bobby," I said after what seemed a long time. "Two European athletes and this odd man. A fat guy in a beard and dark glasses."

Play was bottled up as the Orderlies bore down on their checking. Boring hockey. "I saw them, Kyle. At the hospital. They seemed quite concerned about you after what happened at the airport."

"Do you know who the fat man was? I can't seem to place him."

"It's funny you should ask about him. Doug saw him at the hospital and said he was certain it was Virgil Hadfield. He could've sworn it, he said."

Virgil. Of course. How could I have been so stupid? And Doug had to have known. That explained his strange story in the Caddy about his father, the violent legacy of Eddie Shore. His solicitous behaviour at the hospital. Why hadn't he just told me that he had seen Virgil? Why couldn't he have levelled with me?

Doug barrelled into Red and they both went down. From the ground, Doug held the blade of Jobey's stick long enough to give Norma time to stickhandle around the three of them and into the clear. Easy goal. 3–2, Orderlies.

"What do you know about Hadfield, Kyle? Kyle?"

I froze like a statue, my arms flat along my thighs. Norma and Doug were in the goal crease, slapping high fives. I thought if I kept still, the pain wouldn't come. Mind over matter. I'd beat back the panic attack. The point of a blade of grass touched the leg of a picnic table next to where we were sitting. Red ants swarmed where the green paint of the table had worn away. A bird I couldn't see in a pine tree was calling like mad: CREE-CREE-CREE-CREE-CREE-CREE-CREE. Over and over again.

Why couldn't I have seen the resemblance? Because he never showed that face behind the beard and dark glasses. The beard was new. And he had put on a slew of weight since I'd last seen him.

"He represented me," I said.

CREE-CREE-CREE-CREE-CREE-CREE-CREE. Sticks clacked. Red heaved and laughed like a cartoon giant. CREE-CREE-CREE-CREE-CREE-CREE-CREE. The crow wasn't a fan, a boo-bird. He just wanted us out of there. Which was exactly what I wanted. And silence, for once, wasn't going to do it. That was the crow's message. If I were to get out of there, I had to sing, too.

"I wasn't one of his star clients, but there was a time when Virgil Hadfield represented half the pros in the National Hockey League," I told Wayne. "When I was playing pro, I did my share of school visits and for a couple of years, summer hockey camps. The jocks, of course, were stuck on the dream of playing pro, but the brainiacs had their eyes on Virgil Hadfield. He was the one—the great agent to the stars—they all wanted to be."

A give-and-go from Norma to Doug caught Jobey leaning as Doug burst past him. Then Doug head-faked Red, deked to the outside and through the legs. Tip in, 3–3. "All right," I yelled, punching the air. "Hey, Doug, about time you saw that."

Norma ran to Doug and they leaped in the air, slapping high fives. "One for Eddie Shore," Doug cried, as he bowed deeply toward me. I turned to face Wayne: "It's not the move, but when you make it."

"He represented you?" Wayne asked, his interest in the game gone.

"Yeah," I said. "Signed me to my first contract when I was seventeen ..." Wayne reached to touch my sleeve, but I shrugged him off.

"Virgil was into the gullible ones. Big-time. Billy Burlington was only the most famous. Remember the press when he came up? 'You can take Billy out of the country, but you can't take the country out of Billy.' But Billy never got his face to the trough. Or anywhere else for that matter. Billy couldn't go to the bathroom without first asking Virgil if it was okay."

"Hey," Jobey yelled at Red, who head-manned to Jobey in full flight, smack on the tape. From nowhere, though, Doug was on him, taking away the inside move. The ball skittered into the bush.

"It was all part of Virgil's carefully laid plan. He'd get players and their parents to trust him like a member of the family so that later, about a year after signing, he could screw them and they'd never know what hit them. He'd draw up a contract extension and bag payola—in travel, cash, and entertainment from the team brass—and in exchange settled for peanuts—basic cost of living increases, when salaries in other sports were going through the roof.

"But that wasn't the worst of it," I said, grinding my teeth and glaring at the game. "We trusted Virgil and he negotiated new pensions for us—and then skimmed a fortune from them. He was just too slick to ever get caught, but in the end hundreds of thousands of tax-free dollars were gone, salted away in the Caymans, they say, while retired hockey players, even guys with big names in their day, twenty-goal scorers and shot-blocking kings, are reduced to signing pucks by the basketload, slipping them out as legit on eBay for sales to hockey nerds for $5 per."

With a grunt, Red fired a long shot. It sailed but Doug got a hand on it, passed to Norma, who, rather than stop the ball, tipped it over the blade of Jobey's stick, sidestepped him and scored. 4–3 for Doug and Norma. In the waning light, Red leaned heavily on his stick and gasped for air. Jobey and he whispered something and then waved at their opponents, pointed to us at the picnic table. Surrender. Norma and Doug hugged and kissed, briefly—on the lips.

"Shit," I cried, bounding off the table. "Grinning, back-slapping liar. He'd get me this, get me that. Instead, I'm left with squat for savings, grunt work to get by. How is a lawyer like sperm? Do you know that joke, Wayne? Overhear that one at the hunting lodge? Because both have a one in ten billion' chance of becoming a whole person ... You didn't see Virgil buttering up Mom, lapping up Dad's best whisky. 'Mr. and Mrs. Callendar, this is one day in your life you're never going to forget.' He actually delivered such a turkey of a line."

"Grouse," Doug said in a hushing voice, as he and Norma arrived at my side. "In these parts, it's grouse, Kyle." Tiny beads of sweat dotted Norma's forehead.

"This doesn't concern you, Cowpland. Just back off," I snapped.

"Hey, lighten up, big guy."

"Kyle, honey," Norma said, moving toward me and resting her arm on my shoulder.

"Don't you 'Kyle, honey,' me," I said, pushing her arm away. Wayne cut a glance at Jobey and Red, shook his head no. I darted from them and rushed to the bush. CREE-CREE-CREE-CREE-CREE-CREE-CREE, the bird cried. In warning this time.

chapter thirteen

"C'mon, let's go for ice cream."

Virgil gently pressed the small of my back and all the tension left my body like a giant wave. He was helping me out of the deep leather chair in his Toronto office. On the walls were framed colour shots of Billy Burlington, mobbed after scoring the Stanley Cup–winning goal against the North Stars. Larry Cooper, the trophy winner for best defenceman, checking a Canadien I couldn't make out. Citations from the league: "To Virgil, For Meritorious Service." Portraits of Virgil himself. Others with Gordie Howe, Vladislav Tretiak, Bobby Hull. And the politicians: Trudeau, Nixon, Brezhnev.

A few minutes before, Virgil Hadfield and Mom and Dad had watched as I signed a paper to have the agent represent me in all my dealings with hockey owners. Virgil gave my parents free passes to the Hockey Hall of Fame. When Dad left, clutching the passes in his hand, I could have sworn he was crying.

Virgil's touch was unfamiliar to me. In Keppel, men had rough hands, hair sprouts at the knuckles, skin like leather. When Virgil shook my hand to seal the deal, I was struck by the soft pressure of it. A pencil pusher, my father would've said. More like a woman than a man. I felt as if I were liquid and could be sucked up inside him. My hair was cut too short, slicked back in a bygone fashion. The white felt bow tie Father insisted upon was awkward for Keppel, gaudy for the streets of Toronto, and outright hilarious for the posh Yorkville suite of the great Virgil Hadfield.

Virgil smiled with small tea-stained teeth. Not a hair out of place. The smell of fancy cologne made my head swim, my stomach turn. Like a sick fish in a tank.

"Sure, I'd like some," I said.

I'd never been to an ice cream parlour before. With the Keppel Grey Devils, we stopped at roadside Dairy Queens and the occasional drive-through. At home, Mother bought Sealtest vanilla— on special. In spring, Father brought home gallons of maple syrup on barter, and on special occasions—holidays and birthdays, the odd game day—we'd have vanilla ice cream smothered in maple syrup. Father ran a tight ship, except when it came to maple syrup. He'd pour syrup out of the gallon jug until the ice cream glistened in an amber pool at the bottom of the bowl.

Men in blue suits and briefcases hurried along the streets, crossing against traffic. Women were ravishing in dark silk stockings, trim cotton skirts, sweaters draped across their shoulders. Never had I felt so self-conscious about the way I looked. My bow tie clung like a fuzzy fungus to my brown polyester shirt, whose beak collar made my long face even longer. With each step I took, I felt the flap of my bell-bottom trousers ride further up my leg. Wisps of facial hair sullied my upper lip. But as we walked along Bloor Street, the anxiety faded. I may as well have been invisible. Because everybody was looking at Virgil.

The parlour was lit like Maple Leaf Gardens and must've had a million flavours. Virgil went for the macadamia butterscotch; he ordered me double-dark maple walnut.

I'd never had anything that tasted so good, and I couldn't help myself, devoured it like an animal. Another twin-scoop, double-dark maple walnut cone appeared. Virgil stood holding it for me, as I shook my head no. Not for me, no, I couldn't. But as a drip began melting down the side of the cone, I took it. I licked the melt and then ducked into the mound on top.

"I don't want you to lose sight of something," Virgil said, eyeing his rounded cone like a sculpture. "The poet Al Purdy calls hockey the Canadian specific. What defines us, our soul, our passion. In Canada, more than any other place in the world, it stands to reason that people fall in love with The Game ... And what's purer than love? Take a mother's love. What's purer than a mother's love, Kyle?"

"Nothing, I guess," I said, twisting the cone where the licking was better.

"That's right, Kyle. Nothing. But every year, I guarantee you, young hockey players like yourself enter The Game with the wrong idea. They love The Game in that pure way that they love their mothers ... You see as many boys as I do and you can tell the thinkers from the hockey pucks. And you're a thinker, Kyle ... Here, you want to get this spot here." He reached out with his index finger and ladled some melting ice cream from my cone and slowly drew his finger into his mouth.

Virgil took a long, slow lick of his ice cream so that it whorled in the shape of a woman's breast.

"I think what Purdy was getting at is that love is only part of the story," Virgil said. He flicked the tip of his tongue at a macadamia nut. "That there are a helluva lot of ways to show your passion. I mean look at the way you wolfed down that first taste of maple walnut. Did you love that ice cream? Of course, you did. But woe to the poor bastard determined to stand in your way of eating that cone. He'd have soon seen how quickly love becomes something else."

Virgil put down his half-eaten cone and gestured toward the soda jerk, who in several quick steps was at his side. The jerk took Virgil's cone and stashed it in the trash. I had never seen such waste.

"A nation's passion will never be as pure as a mother's love," Virgil said, his shoulders hunched. He peered at me like a badger in a hole. "I see from the times I've spent with your mother that she is a beautiful person. A person can be a beautiful thing. A nation, on the other hand, can be a messy thing, an ugly thing.

"Look at fighting in The Game," Virgil said. "Grown men thrashing each other to within an inch of their lives. Remember Ted Green and Wayne Maki in that stick-swinging fight that left Green with a steel plate in his head? Or the bloody mess of Bobby Hull in those slugfests with John Ferguson. The biggest heartthrob ever to play The Game, Bobby Hull, the Golden Jet, one of the smoothest skaters and greatest scorers to ever play. God, did he suffer. One year he played with his jaw wired shut after it was broken in a fight, sucked mineral drinks through a straw to keep his strength up. Every game day had bruises the size of grapefruit up and down his perfect body."

Virgil looked at me then in a way I'll never forget. A little cross-eyed and with that hunger that was all badger—and wolf and coyote, too. Animals that prey on inconstancies—and fear. On hesitation and weakness.

"Nothing's simple, Kyle boy," he said. When he smiled his cheekbones lifted, his eyes disappeared. "Folks always want to reduce life to simple terms. Hockey's no different." He pointed to another drip of ice cream that I was missing. I found it and lapped it up. Virgil gave a little wave of permission, and I took a big bite at the cone. Ice cream squeezed out of the cone's bottom, splatted the Arborite.

Virgil pressed his chest against the table, his arms down flat. His eyes narrowed to piss spots in the snow. His breath minty stale. "In places like Keppel you're closer to knowing what it's about than here in Hogtown, Toronto. Poor Hogtown. You saw some of our so-called sophisticates on our way here. Men and women in their eight-hundred-dollar suits. Culture barons spinning cockamamie dreams from their ivory towers. If they watch television, if they read the news, they know who I am, but when they pass by, the cowards turn up their noses and sneer. Hockey, the game of and for brutes, they sniff. The national disgrace, boxing on skates.

"But do you know what I would tell the worst of these bigots if they were man enough to challenge me?" Virgil asked, raising his voice, clenching and unclenching his fists. His black eyes bore into me, as I sat back in my seat, cutting a glance around me to see that the ice cream parlour had cleared out. Except for the soda jerk the place was empty. "I'd tell them what ordinary Canadians know. Not the culture Gestapo, the bilingual Shakespeare lovers in peacekeeping khakis. But ordinary Canadians. I'd tell them that this isn't a country of lawyers, this is a country of truck drivers. A place of real people, rough and ready people. Like my dad," he said, almost hissing, his red face inches above his hands. "And your dad.

"And The Game—what these real Canadians are left with is hockey," Virgil continued, flopping back in his seat and jabbing a finger on the counter. "And inside the rink, for eight long months in the cold, anything goes."

The soda jerk wiped the table and then placed before us two tall lemonades with ice. The straws weren't plastic but of stiff, waxy paper. The taste was new to me, too: sour from freshly squeezed lemons, and ice-cold. My hands shaking, I downed the drink in two halting swigs. Sharp pain throbbed at my temples. Before I'd placed the glass down on the tabletop an identical lemonade appeared.

Virgil sipped lemonade, closed his eyes, and breathed deeply. When he reopened them he looked again like the dignified man who had sent off Mom and Dad to the Hockey Hall of Fame. Laugh lines deepened as his mouth slimmed to a dolphin grin.

"I've seen a lot of boys come up," Virgil said. His voice was soft, with a touch of gravel, barely audible, as if the last few minutes had exhausted him. "They are the most innocent, the most guileless, the most well-bred boys you can imagine. They come to me and I do the best to steer them in the right direction, to educate them."

Virgil fell silent and slowly drained his lemonade. A fractured note accompanied each breath.

"Even the best families can fuck you up," Virgil whispered. "And unless you've got someone like me on your side, The Game can fuck you up, too."

chapter fourteen

Pucks on ice. Coach had a way of tossing them from a bucket so that they slapped the ice and glided like arrows through a vacuum. No tension. Black on white. Pucks on ice. Lying by the sideboards, at the faceoff circle, just inside the blue line, along the backboards, a shade off centre. Pristine, ineluctable. Kubrick's monolith in *2001*. What will always be.

Early winter mornings in Keppel, the birds hover above the waterfront. Big white birds, but they're grey in the half-light of dawn, forever circling. Or so I imagined them. From the road that first time with Coach aboard the team bus, the all-night trip from Pennsylvania.

"Don't move like them, Kyle, like those gulls," Coach said. Smells of diesel fuel and the sour puke of rye whiskey clung to the heavy curtain that separated our seat from the rest of the team. I was on the floor and Coach lay on the triple seat above me, on his side. The team, I felt certain, was fast asleep. The motorcoach rumble soothed me like a mother's heartbeat.

"Never be a floater, coasting on the wind," Coach whispered, stroking my hair. "Learn from the crows. Dodge and weave. Badger and batter. Hack and cling. Call out, seek help, turn back. Watch a crow fighting off a big hawk. Do you ever see them one-on-one? Do you ever see the big, circling hawk gain the upper hand on the crow?"

It was gulls that came to me when Coach touched me. Not attack birds, tearing flesh from victims, like nightmares, *The Birds* of Alfred Hitchcock. But those damned circling ones. That climb ever farther into the air. So that no white man can see.

When Coach touched me I didn't open my eyes. Not once. I screwed them shut and thought of the birds in the air. How I could be like them. Imagine the approaches, get there first. If there's time, a backside touch with the stick, moving the puck to forehand. If not, just do what you have to do to get the body between the puck and the opponent. Feel him. Will he come wide, backstab, poke check between the legs? Hold the position and wait for the first move. Always wait for the first move because he will surely expose himself. Timing and patience, the good twins of the athlete. Remember. You are the puck. And the bird in pursuit.

chapter fifteen

The ice was keen at Keppel Arena. That hadn't changed. The puck moved smooth and clean, flip passes landed true, didn't bounce end-over-end. In warm up, I feathered a pass net-side to Doug and it went on a line, perfect. I thought as Doug buried the puck past backup goalie Al Smith that this Old Timers game would be something to see, a real crowd pleaser. That if the true fans were watching they were going to have a night to remember.

We were about a month away from the Stanley Cup playoffs. I had been on leave from the Hall. Upon recommendation by Wayne, who said he was pleased with my progress, the contours of the long-gone memories that were taking shape in our talks. A game in your hometown can only help, he said, stir deeper into the past, perhaps touch the source of the pain. Where the healing can begin.

I had agreed to play a few games with the NHL Really Old Timers, a team of hockey's past greats and not-so-greats, a cross-Canada promotion strategy to build fan interest for the playoffs. If Old Timers hockey were death's dressing room, then you had plenty of good company, Wayne said. I had made my peace with Doug, too, who said he didn't mention having seen Virgil at the hospital because my health seemed so fragile. He was afraid of how I might have reacted, he said. The Hall and Wayne arranged for Doug to join me in the Keppel game, which was more than okay with me. Doug and I worked out together, were back on the ice for hours of practice. My pains had subsided, and Doug was being a friend—at a distance. The way I liked it. If all went well, sometime during the playoffs, I could go back to escorting the Cup. But until then, the Hall wanted me to continue to hang out with Wayne. Keep things low-key.

In Keppel, we were to play the town's top junior team, the Grey Devils, my alma mater, the team I played for a year before Kingston. Old Timers games were once an institution in Keppel. The highlight of the season. In those days, it was the Leafs who came: George Armstrong, Andy Bathgate, Pete Stemkowski, Billy Harris, and, of course, Eddie Shack. Clear the track, here comes Shack. The finesse of a freight train on a hairpin curve.

A part of me had forgotten what it was like. But a million practices take their toll. Or what seems like a million. I practiced from age six to age thirty-two, one a day for at least two hundred days a year. That's more than five thousand practices, half as many games. It had been an age—five years—since I'd been on the ice. In the middle of scrimmage, or practice, even games, the sharpest memories of home, my earliest days in The Game, came flooding back.

Before me the well-worn parts of my canvas bag spilled out buried treasure: the shoulder and elbow pads that had taken on the shape of me, the round Mario-style helmet, cut and blemished by slapshots, the deflection off the stick of Wayne Gretzky, the black-mark butt end by bad boy Brian Spencer. Mouth guard and teeth protector, jumbles of elastics, handfuls of half-used rolls of cloth tape, pucks. And up in the end of the bag, in opposite corners, as if they were clawing to get away, as if they had nothing to do with each other, were not equal parts of the same thing. Because together, they are the life of The Game. My game, anyway. My gloves. My hands.

In full gear, I leaped up and down on my toes, doing a little dance I first did in peewee. Not an Irish jig or Scottish fling, or ice-dance sashay. It was nothing more than a double toe-hop left, step right. Hop-hop, step. Hop-hop, step. Whack the shin pads with the flat blade of the freshly taped stick. Hop-hop, step. Finally, I felt home, not in my father's home, but truly home. At the rink.

I watched at the gate as the Zamboni flooded the ice. In the NHL, there's never any silence during Zamboni resurfacing. Always the catchy songs—Shakira, Pink Floyd, Madonna, Eminem—or upcoming games, key fob nights, Wal-Mart tie-ins, bathroom-fixture giveaways. But in Keppel, people take their cue from the roar of the Zamboni, the tractor in Everyman's field. Simple traditions that have conspired to create something wonderful and new from nothing more than the careful rendering of the exact same act, over and over again.

From the crowd above, waves of talk fell like ribbons in water. I looked for Norma's face, my mother, my father. But I could draw no distinct pictures of people during Zamboni resurfacing. I never could.

When the Zamboni finished, I stepped onto the ice. I skated along the outside of the rink, at arm's length from the boards. In the beginning, I moved slowly, carefully, feeling the whisper of sharp blades on hard ice. The leather had worn away in the palm of my glove and I could feel the hard shaft of the stick. Play it like a saxophone, light touches to heavy hits, glancing, staccato. What the other guy can't hear.

I remember an old interview of Leaf great Frank Mahovlich by television sportscaster Ward Cornell. Ward asked Frank how he got to pucks ahead of defenders, while looking like he was working half as hard as anyone else. "Well, I don't know, Ward," Frank said quietly. He doesn't say a lifetime of blades on ice, the rap of pucks on boards, end glass. The second-year point man on the power play hesitates, is susceptible to the sweep check, slow to turn on his skates. Frank sweeps away the puck, banks it like a pool shark, low to the boards. The puck glides to centre ice, where in strong, deliberate strides Frank gets to it and moves in on net. The third-year goalie drops his shoulder going right to left. Frank head-fakes, the netminder drops his shoulder, and Frank shoots in the vacated space and scores, a short-handed goal, a game breaker.

A puck hit my right inside blade, and I kicked it forward to my stick. Another glanced off the left outside blade, and that, too, I brought to my forehand. Around me, my teammates, as much grey as any colour on their helmetless heads, wheeled the perimeter of the ice, slammed pucks into the boards. I passed one puck back to Doug, and stickhandled with the other—simple moves, nothing fancy. Even along the corner boards the ice was as smooth as glass, the puck gliding just so.

"Attaboy, Kyle," Father yelled. Father was directly across the ice from the players' benches, his seat for as long as I could remember. Father had recently reconditioned his Second World War bomber jacket; the colour of his hair complemented the white ruff of the jacket. Dad was eighty-four but looked sixty, with wavy hair to his collar. He'd not put on a pound since the war years. Burning off weight in the silence of thousands of cross-country trips. Even now, when Father leaped from his seat and punched the air, the pent-up emotion jolted the place. Like a long-slumbering giant awake in the cold. I'd not done much, just fired a shot in practice and the puck squeezed through the pads of starting goalie Bernie Parent. But Father yelled, "That's my boy" at the top of his lungs.

Mom had broken tradition and was sitting next to Dad. In my playing days, Mom sat with the other hockey moms across the rink from my father. She tried in the beginning to blunt Dad's outbursts, not exactly to shush him, but to temper his behaviour, make him stop short of actually carrying out his threats to referees, opposing coaches, other fathers. But after a while Mom just let Dad be. A family dog straining on a leash, pulling with all his might, barking and snarling and snapping but not capable of getting away, of biting someone to the bone. Mom liked the games, so instead of being worn down by my father, bracing for the attack, she would sit with the hockey moms on the other side of the rink. From there she could watch my father, fix him with a beseeching look when he got particularly agitated, try to rein him in without disturbing her own pleasure, gossip with the girls, what she called "the talk," her heart's desire.

Mom smiled at me and I nodded back. She hadn't aged as well as Dad. There never had been a lot to her, but now she looked pale and haggard. Like those antique photos of pioneer wives, half again as tall as their farmer husbands and a fraction as heavy. Not as if she's been denied food; more like whatever she does eat feeds an inexorable worry, sleepless nights. Dad stirs for a moment in bed, sees that Mom is staring at the bare wood walls, but he drifts back to sleep without letting her know that he has seen her withering away.

The Really Old Timers were looking pretty good—given that some of the guys were well along the backside of fifty. Centre Phil Esposito still dished passes like dandruff. Also on the forward lines were former Canadiens Réjean Houle and Bob Gainey, and the ex-Ranger great Rod Gilbert, our player-coach, the Dick Clark of pro hockey. On defence were ex-Islander Denis Potvin; Kevin Lowe, who played on the great Oiler teams of the 1980s; and Jim Schoenfeld, the former player and coach who said, "Have another donut, you fat pig," the insult responsible for changing the way games are wired for sound. Me, I hadn't played so much on the tour. Outside of Keppel, Kyle Callendar wasn't exactly a star attraction. So, I'd come to look forward to the game. More than anything I could remember in a long time.

Gwen gave me an orbit of red shoestring licorice and held my hand as we walked toward her general store. "I talked to your father and he agreed, Kyle," she said, "that you should wait for him inside the store with me. He won't be too much longer." I peeled a single strand of licorice from the orbit and ate it slowly. Savouring each bite. I felt like a beach ball blown up and tapped into the air, as I looked at Gwen Martinson against the treetops in the dying sun. Brown hair flickered in light and shadow across her face. The hand that was not holding mine brushed the hair off her face as she smiled and then looked down, not to watch her steps, because this was a lane she knew like the back of her hand, but because she was shy about being with me.

Once in the store, she flipped the sign at the window to the "We Are Closed, Folks" side, and let go of my hand. "Here, sit at the cash, Kyle. I'll see about your father." Behind me were tins of tobacco, shoe polish, a picture of a sore-looking black cat with a paw extended. Gwen Martinson smelled of lilac and faint leather, wore Levis, the red tag a tail light on switchbacks as she walked, not glancing behind to be sure that I was all right as she went to be with my father. I sat on a stool at the cash, wrapping my arms around myself in order to hold on to the smell of her. I emptied the orbit of shoestring licorice before my father arrived alone to get me, to hurry out of the store and go home.

Herb Groat, the retired used-car salesman, beat the Keppel Lions bass drum as our line glided to centre ice after the playing of the national anthem.

"You're up, Kyle," Rod Gilbert had said at the sideboards before game time. "It's your barn. Your line will start."

Doug skated slowly to centre for the faceoff. Lionesque Larry Robinson and Jack Lynch, another Keppel favourite were on defence. Former Leaf Errol Thompson was on one wing and I took the other. Opposite from Father's side of the rink, as always.

In the split-second before the puck was dropped, I spied Norma in the stands, a couple of rows above the glass on my side of the rink. Next to her was Wayne, and above them both, two rows behind, was Virgil Hadfield himself.

I started at the drop and my opponent—a big kid with ten pounds on me—batted my stick out of my hand and onto the ice. The crowd groaned as I skated over to my stick to pick it up.

That was Virgil, all right, I thought. Of course, there was no law against him being there. But I couldn't imagine it, my homecoming game. What a slap in the face. He wasn't with Sheldon, though, which was a relief. The last thing I wanted to do was to meet up with the two of them. Next to Virgil was nobody at all, a blue-haired woman in a kerchief. Someone I vaguely knew. She ran the flower shop. No, she was the newspaper editor's wife who'd run off with the retired postmaster. Shit, I didn't know. When Keppel women reached a certain age, they all looked alike.

A Devils forward crossed the centre line with the puck and dumped it into our zone. My check burst down the wing, and I stayed with him for a piece, then peeled off, took position at the boards inside our blue line. The puck was likely to be corralled by Lynch, and I wanted to give him a target to pass to when he got to it.

That was just his arrogance. Virgil goddamn Hadfield. I had no idea what it was he had cooking with Sheldon and those European hockey players. Whatever, he couldn't be trusted.

Lynch's pass came off the dasher, end-over-end, and I couldn't control it. I put my head down to locate the puck at my skates, a kiss of death but I couldn't do anything else, like the motorist inching out from a crossroads in one-way traffic, with cars double-parked in the first lane, creeping forward, hoping against hope that there wasn't a car barrelling down in the second lane, because if there was, there was nothing he could do, he was going to get nailed. Boom! Rocket flash, then darkness. Names of war movies shelled me. *Guns of Navarone. Where Eagles Dare. Bridge on the River Kwai.* Bakerbakerbaker. Medic. Dad? Where are you, Dad?

When Dad carved the roast, I always felt a little freer to think. He'd ease into his chair at the head of the table, the roast before him like a found object from an Egyptian tomb, and plug in the carving knife. On special occasions, when I'd bring a girl I was seeing the year I played on the Grey Devils, Dad stared at Suzy Hunter, say, or Peggy Simpson, like the night watchman at the nurses' residence. But when Dad was carving he didn't look up, didn't pay us any attention. He switched the knife to full power to feel the extra vibration in his hand, said it made a smoother, more even cut. He hunched over his work, a medieval artist with an illuminated manuscript, while I talked to Mom and my girlfriend, the tension lifting with each cut of the squirrel-coloured roast. Mom didn't believe in medium, much less rare, and cooked the life out of everything she ever made. Like the mush of vegetable sides made from boiling the fragments she poured from freezebags that I also used as athletic packs, placing them on sports injuries until I could feel the kernels separate and the blood rush to the sore.

How could I begin to think that I could tell Dad about Coach Fleming? I would wonder as he carved the roast. Dad, who lived for my hockey, the pretty girls who I brought around? How could I tell this man what Coach Fleming, his boss, the man who Father looked up to as much as anyone in his life, did to me at the back of the bus? How could he ever accept that about his only son?

The knife roared like a chainsaw through soft wood, birch, swamp trees. Slabs of our meal stacked like ridges on a dinosaur's back. He moved down the roast methodically, an executioner who never questioned what had to be done until every last head had been rolled, and he was free to look up, catch the eye of the girl I'd brought, and say, "Hungry?"

"Shut the fuck up," I screamed, turning to face the crowd behind me from my place on the players' bench. Try as I might to resist, I had an erection. It didn't happen when I played pro, but in the old days in Keppel when I got riled up, I found I couldn't help myself. A boner pointing due north in my hockey pants. "Shut the fuck up, or I'll kill you."

The Grey Devils had scored after I was knocked out at the blue line, which set off the drummer Herb Groat. BOOM-BOOM-BOOM. I'd blacked out for a few seconds and the defenceman who'd hit me scored on a screened shot. 1–0, Grey Devils.

"Yer Devils' food, Kyle." A boy's cry, reedy, familiar, had set me off. "Out with the old, in with the new. Throw out that old Callendar."

I looked to the black rubber floor, wet from the melting snow of our skates. It was over for me. Truly over. Who did I think I was kidding? The brat was right. "You're an old fart, Callendar. Long past time to give up."

Fancy a kid like that getting to me. Thirteen if he were a day, hair cropped short, eyes popping from his head. Way too young to know anything about Kyle Callendar, the Keppel legend. Just an altar boy sitting next to his father, whom I didn't recognize. There was a cut to the man's coat, a half-cashmere, half-wool blend, an out-of-town look to the pattern of his scarf I noticed as he bundled up, took his son's hand, and left for the exit.

"Easy, bud," Doug said, pulling on my arm. I shook myself free and glared at him. A linesman's whistle sent shivers through me as I slumped in my seat. The erection shrank and I draped my gloved hand over the boards as Doug slapped my backside, and said, "Please, Kyle. Pull yourself together. Get into the game, man."

"Our crosses won't path," Dad said. Father wasn't one to mince words, not one to confuse them. But not long after we'd seen Joan Hawthorne he told me our crosses won't path. He was talking about the rest of the summer, about how he and Mom wouldn't be seeing that much more of me when I signed and went off to play in the pros. We'd laughed at the time, and I told him I was amazed, that I'd never heard him misspeak. He was a man of the fewest words, and except for that day with Joan Hawthorne I had never heard him tongue-tied, not able to say precisely what was on his mind when he wanted to say it. I think now that I was wrong. That he knew exactly what he meant to say that day.

Nobody did the drop-pass like Espo. I don't know how many times I paid the price for it. His eyes were cool, hips betraying nothing. Esposito would carry the puck over the blue line and he could do anything: stop, go wide, or head-fake and cut inside for a shot. That would back off the defence, leaving the responsibility to the backchecking forward. That was when Espo'd get me. He'd turn, absorb my check, and drop-pass the puck to a trailing forward for a scoring chance. When Espo drop-passed the Devils, Paul Henderson let the puck fly as Gilbert raced to the net. Henderson's slapshot was low and hard, but the goalie saw it through Espo's screen. The rebound came to Gilbert, who buried his shot—not in the net—but under the goalie, who was flat on his back. No goal.

The building shook with roars and foot-stomping. In the press box, Darren Govier, the CPOS Radio guy, led a "Devils' food" chant, while Herb Groat banged his drum for all he was worth. Across the way, Father tried to catch my eye, but I wouldn't bite. I looked to the seat above Norma and Wayne, who, wide-eyed and cheerful, appeared to be enjoying themselves as if they were at the circus. Two rows behind, the blue-hair was still there, but Virgil's seat was empty and his coat was gone. If Virgil Hadfield was in the barn, he wasn't staying put.

"Now we're in for it," Doug said, his voice small in the din. Fans had thrown game programs, peak caps, and candy bar wrappers on to the ice. The Zamboni guys were sweeping up. "The goalie's got horseshoes. He's going to be hard to beat."

"Doug, I think I saw Virgil," indicating with a jerk of my head the general direction as the arena staff cleared the ice. "Two rows up from Norma and Wayne. Section K. Do you see? There's a blue-hair up there now. I couldn't say for sure, but I could've sworn I saw him."

"I wondered what had got in to you, I—"

"I can't stand the thought of him being here. Not in my barn."

Gilbert gave us a nod and two thumbs up. Errol Thompson and Doug, and then Robinson and Lynch, rolled over the boards and skated to the faceoff circle to the right of the Devils goalie. I hesitated and then I, too, went over. The crowd hushed. Then the chants came. First, a murmur, a call, swelling in my mind as only the best memories do. KY-ELL! KY-ELL! KY-ELL! What a mother drinks when she feels her child's heartbeat, not the first time but every time. So filled up, you can't imagine. KY-ELL! KY-ELL! KY-ELL!

She was there, all right. Behind the glass at rink side. That I couldn't mistake as I glided to the faceoff circle. How could you? Gwen Martinson. Of course, even at eighty, she would be there. Gwen was slipping something out of her pocket. While the cheers waxed and the linesman crouched in the faceoff, under the flat of her hand she placed against the rink-side glass a trading card face-forward, my rookie card with the Pittsburgh Penguins.

Late spring days were all one when I played hockey. What former Flyers' coach Fred Shero said: "Life is just a place where we spend time between games." There was golf, the job at The Beer Store, girls at the beach. But one spring day during hockey playoffs, just before I left for the pros, I drove Mom's Chevy Vega to Gwen Martinson's to learn more about my father.

Even in warm weather, Gwen wore a sweater. Light, something you could see through, that touched the contours of her still-lithe body, even at fifty. Soft and round, inviting to the touch, her elbow, as I helped her down the stairs at the front of the store, which she'd left in the care of the after-school help while we went for a walk. "We'll talk, sure," she said, but first she wanted to show me something.

At home, Father offered nothing. Only the ceaseless quiet of numberless meals. The whir of the electric carving knife, the leer at the girlfriends I brought home, the ones I least cared for because Father showed attention to them, not to me. I loved my mom, but before my father she was a background player. Laughing at his jokes, anticipating his needs, jumping up to snap on the switch before he called for more light so that he could best carve the roast, handing him the salt and pepper shakers—the Gals, we called them because they were tiny milkmaids, faded blue and yellow, three holes in a white hat for salt, a hollow for pepper. "Here are the Gals, dear," Mom said, searching the table, her memory, for what he could possibly be wanting next.

So it seemed right that Dad had someone else. Not often, I don't think, because Gwen was a loner. Happy with her unhappiness. She had a story of her own, that was certain, but what it was I could guess. Lost someone in the war, when she was young, and she and Dad talked about those days. Dad drew her pictures from his memory because Gwen had earned the right, loved a man who didn't come back and had chosen a life that Dad in his righteous way could respect. Never once forsaking her love. Even in the arms of my father, in the confidences they shared, the tears for the darkest of the memories he did not spare her, because she wanted them, needed them, like the pine-scented air that even on this, the hottest of spring days, kept her one with a man who had perished in the woods.

"Here, take this path, that way. We don't have far to go now," she said as she took my hand. Her fingers were long and soft. I'd never had my palms read, didn't believe in the stories they held, but I was amazed by hers, by how clear they were, unetched. Like mirrors.

"Let's stop here. Right, that's right." We were atop a knoll in the forest. Miles from the river so there were no blackflies or mosquitoes. Just orchestras of gnats in splashes of sun. Gwen pointed to a sawed-off tree crowned with what looked like an old woman's hat. She pressed a translucent finger to her lips.

I couldn't keep my eyes off her, so I missed when the hawk first appeared overhead. I heard his flap, like a flag in a cutting wind. I looked up to the old woman's hat and saw the flash of red. Another hawk rose from the hat like a magician's assistant unfolding from a tiny space. The hawk flew off as the first one arrived and settled out of view.

"I've been watching them since they first got together. Sharing a meal on that tree over there," Gwen said, pointing to a gappy maple. "Rabbit kill and mice mostly. They've never seemed to mind my company." She smiled and shook her head. "Now, of course, they have eggs. My guess is the chicks are due any day.

"Reds are survivors, Kyle," she said, looking off in the distance where the mother bird had flown. "Redtail hawks will filch eggs from weaker birds, fly all night and into the next day hunting for food. They don't give up, not ever. When it comes to their young."

Strands of brown hair blew across her face, but she didn't lift a finger to push them back. She smiled and her teeth glistened in the sun. A moment later we were walking again. Gwen told me that she could understand my awkward feelings around my father. That he had made up his mind after the war not to burden his family with those memories.

"More than anything else he felt the need to protect you and your mom from that, Kyle," she said. "You have to respect his decision. I can see your father does not love in your style, but he will never forsake you. He will always be there, flying back to the nest. You can count on that. Perhaps one day, he will tell you what you seem so desperate to know. But I can't say for sure."

Gwen touched my elbow and warmth of a hearth fire filled my chest, coursed down my legs to my toes. She put her arm around me and we walked in silence back to the car. Before I left, she kissed me on the cheek and then she turned and went back toward her customers in the store.

Hockey was my war. There were no rules for Dad, but he demanded them for his son. Where the stakes were contained. I was protected from the war, but he couldn't yield on my hockey. Which was always more his than mine. To Dad, it was always better than a fair trade.

I thought when I went to see Gwen that it wasn't about me. That it was about my father that I needed to know. What was it about my father, the stern man that I knew, that could capture the love, the beauty, of a woman like Gwen? Why had he left me alone with these feelings? Walking back to the Vega and my life in hockey, my heart pounded wildly in my chest as I struggled with the urge to call out to Gwen, to run to her and tell her everything. To fall on my knees and weep for my life.

The puck fluttered toward my hands. Chipped up from the drop as Doug's stick and another's scissored at the faceoff. I caught and cradled it in my hand. Then I dropkicked the puck to Robinson, whose one-timer was high and hard, and it glanced off the goalie's blocker, where Errol corralled it, two Devils on his tail. Now was the time to strike. If the goalie made the ten-minute mark without a goal against, he'd really settle in. Didn't matter who was shooting, whether it was forty, fifty, or sixty shots, from close in, screened, breakaways, dekes. He was going to beat you.

Errol passed to Doug behind the net. Doug looked for me out front, but a Devils defenceman, a tall drink of water, had me covered. I bumped him with my hip, and again chest-to-chest, but despite his slender build he wouldn't budge. Instead, Doug passed the puck to Errol who redirected to Robinson, then to Lynch, who snapped it toward the goal.

Suddenly, I was falling. Chopped down, a slash at my ankles, or at least that was what the boys told me later, but I had no lasting pain so it couldn't have been that. The puck was going into the open side of the net when I lost my edge and fell, and the puck hit me in the middle of the back. My check cleared the puck, the whistle blew and with my bad back aching like hell, it took two guys to lift me up and off the ice.

"You're not going to believe it, Mom, but guess who Dad and I saw at The Beer Store today," I said, grinning from ear to ear. The meal—spaghetti and meatballs in red sauce—was on the table. Dad had downed his tumbler and Mom was refilling it with tap water at the sink. I wasn't waiting until he was out of earshot, away enough so that he couldn't pin me down with a gaze, a warning scowl. Who was I kidding? My father would never tell me anything. So, I decided to tell my story with gusto, with a sense of excitement that was rare in our lives together.

"Mr. Shanahan? Your history teacher? Did she come in from out Port Elgin way?" Mom said. Mom liked to play the Guessing Game. Mom came back to the table and placed Dad's glass before him.

"No, Mom. I'll give you a clue. Butter tarts. And that's a good one."

"I can't imagine that it would be your Aunt Toot," Mom said, as she speared a meatball. "She'd sworn off the beer."

"No Mom. It wasn't Aunt Toot. Give up?"

I could feel Dad on me like an arctic wind. Fierce and unyielding. Or a boxer daring you with his rock-hard body. C'mon, take your best shot.

Mom handed me a plastic tumbler that we'd won with Esso coupons. Red and white stripes to commemorate the new flag, which Keppel was finally getting around to accepting. The glasses had faded some, but Dad was really partial to them, insisted that we used them for everyday.

Dad picked up his fork and plunged it into the red mass, half-turned his wrist and snared spaghetti, sauce, and meat and shovelled it into his mouth. The napkin he'd tucked into his work shirt splayed over his stomach like a tarp. He leaned forward and down, inches from the table to receive the second forkful.

"Gals?" Dad said, trying to catch Mom's eye. But she was already up at the counter and had them in her hands. Dad snatched the salt from her, stared into the hat to see that it was the right one, and shook it over the food.

"You'll never guess," I said, too hepped up to prolong the game. "It was the famous artist Joan Hawthorne. In our store. Can you imagine?"

While Mom nearly dropped her fork in amazement, waggled her hand in the air like a moth, and told us about the woman in the Wittichs bread outlet who had a poster of *Butter Tart and Toast*, was the artist's biggest fan, would probably faint dead on the spot when she heard that Joan Hawthorne had paid a visit to Keppel, Dad fixed me with a wicked glare. That said how much I can't trust you, boy. Next, you'll be telling about that day out at Gwen's. You can't know when or where to keep your mouth shut, boy. That's for sure.

"Tell Rod I'm going to go for a walk, to stretch out my back," I whispered to Doug on the players' bench when the pain subsided enough so that I could stand on my own. "Or like my father says, 'Tell him I've got to see a man about a horse.'"

"Eh, whazzat?"

"Tell him I got to make an equipment adjustment."

"You'll be long?" Doug said, looking concerned.

"No, partner," I said, giving him a fake punch to the head. "Not at all. I'll be back before the snow's melted from my blades."

"You just be sure you do."

I looked up in the stands toward Wayne and caught his eye. I pointed to the exit, behind our players' bench, and Wayne stood up and began to make his way down the crowded rows. I didn't dare look toward my father.

I slipped away from the bench and hobbled down the main corridor. A few steps along, I paused before a framed headline notice in the *Keppel Advance*, the story about my signing with the Penguins: "Callendar to Sign With NHL's Pens." There were two pictures: a backlit ice-chip shower of me and one with my dad, "Lowell Callendar, Dieppe veteran and Fleming Cartage operator." The photographer had us embrace, and looking at the photo now after more than thirty years I could hardly believe it. At the time, our wooden postures seemed so obvious that I thought everyone could tell. Now I wasn't so sure. For the first time I was seeing it the way everyone else had, the way they still were seeing it a generation later. From the picture alone no one could tell that that was the first time my father had ever hugged me. Outside of myself and my father, no one could have known.

"Hey, champ. Reliving the big one, are you?" Wayne said.

Wayne wasn't alone. Norma had come with him. She touched the back of my hair and reached toward my face. Startled, I stepped back. Jesus, I thought, couldn't she tell she wasn't wanted? Not now. That this wasn't about her? That she reminded me of what I wasn't? Of what I could never be again?

"This has got to be quick," I said, glaring at Wayne. "I've got to get back. Virgil is here. I saw him in a seat above you two, Wayne—"

I grabbed Wayne by the arm and moved down the corridor with him.

"I don't want her here," I whispered. "I don't want Norma to see me like this."

"Like what, Kyle?" Wayne said. In my skates, I was a foot taller than him and his round head looked ridiculous as it tilted to look up at me. "Virgil is certainly a bad guy, but to tell you the truth, I just don't get it. Is there something more that you're not telling me, more than the fact that Virgil robbed the pension funds? I wish you could tell me why he gets you so upset. That could really help."

I shifted my leg, and the back pain shot up my side like a bullet. I crumpled along the concrete wall and doubled over to try to catch my breath as Norma rushed to me.

I gestured with my head for Wayne to leave Norma and me alone, and he stepped away. We were between framed pictures of me with my hat-trick puck from my game at Maple Leaf Gardens and one of the championship midget squad I played on in '72. Norma didn't give the pictures a second look.

The pain eased some, and I raised myself slowly up from the wall, looking down the corridor to see if anyone had seen us. Thank God, the corridor was empty.

"Kyle," Norma said. Her scent was maddening, heart-holing. "You have to tell me. You have to tell me what's going on." I felt her touch on my face like surrender.

My stomach plunged as I groped for breath. "I have to get back, Norma," I whispered, finally.

Norma stared at me as tears filled her eyes. "Yes," she said. "Of course you do."

"C'mon Norma," I said. I took my glove off and touched her shoulder. "You don't know what it's been like for me," I gasped. "But I think Wayne was right. The hockey is a good idea. I'm a little out of shape, but for the most part I'm feeling good, looking good, too, wouldn't you say? That last play was clumsy, but—"

"Kyle, honey." Norma put a finger to my lips. "Don't waste it. Not now. You're right. I don't know what it's like for you. I never have. I feel it when I touch you."

"Norma, don't—"

Norma leaped off the rubber path to the concrete of an adjoining corridor and ran. She knew I wouldn't follow her for fear of dulling my game skates, of running the risk of further ruining my edge. She knew me well, perhaps in the end too well, I thought, as I looked down and saw puddles of water from the snow that had melted from my blades before I hustled toward the roar of The Game.

chapter sixteen

"Look at that, son. It's a funny world, eh?"

It was the weekend of Mom and Dad's golden wedding anniversary. Dad and I were at Sauble Beach on Lake Huron, watching two young girls walking in the surf. Tank tops and short shorts, dense dark curls trailing down their backs. The slender hand of the taller one lay on a forearm of her companion. They must have heard Dad's loud comment but they never let on.

"I can't begin to know, Dad." Maybe, I thought, to keep wolves at a distance. Or perhaps they were close family, or less likely, lovers, what Dad thought so funny.

Later, Dad and I drove to his golden anniversary dance at the Keppel Lawn Bowling Club. In attendance were Mom's elderly brother and sister, a chirpy aunt who kept family like a Swiss cabinet, well-groomed and austere; cousins; Mom's gambling pals; lawn bowlers; a former neighbour in khaki fatigues with a new digital camera. Buy broadband, he said. The menu was triangles, squares, and circles: sandwiches of meat goo cut in wedges, homemade desserts carved from aluminum pans, a punch of ginger ale, sweetened juices, jaundice in Styrofoam cups. Dad showed me the supply shed he'd built and before a lonely Pink Flamingo, pointed out the anthills on the bowling green. "How many do you think there are?" he asked. "Go ahead, take a guess."

"Fifty," I said.

"More than two hundred, if you can imagine." On weekends, Dad worked as the volunteer greenskeeper. Five drops of poison will kill them all, according to Dad, not burn the grass, disturb the lies.

Norma insisted that I give a little speech, and before the cake
with an edible photo from my parents' wedding day, my father in
his Second Canadian Infantry Division dress, my mother a blur of
white, blood-red lips, I said how much my parents meant to me,
how I couldn't have realized my goals without them, that they held
the secret to a long life of love and devotion in the warm attentions
and admiration that I saw in the eyes of the people before me. I
said, "Let's all raise a glass and toast these two, Mom and Dad, to
their first fifty years." Mom threw herself into my arms and hugged
me close and I shook hands with Dad. He said, "Thank you, son,"
and put his arm around my shoulder, actually touched me without
a photographer telling him to do so, and before he could react the
man with the digital camera took our picture to mark the occasion.

"Movement," Rod said, his finger of authority in the air, during
a pep talk between periods in the dressing room. "Their goalie's
quick but let's have movement, sharp passes. Shoot before the boy
sets up. Fire on the bottom of the pass, not the top—"

"And keep the puck away from that Rod Gilbert," Doug said.
"He can't put the puck in the ocean."

With that we balled up hand towels and fired them at Rod,
who took a couple in the face before covering up. Then big Larry
Robinson tapped Rod on the shoulder, and dumped a tumbler of
ice water on his coif.

"Hey, that's enough, non?" Rod cried, the room erupting in
laughter. He looked like Moe of the Three Stooges, pushing back
his hair with both hands, desperate to recover his puff.

"And bury the rebounds, Rod," Doug said. "Bury the rebounds."

"Okay, okay, you've had your fun," Rod said, as he ducked into
his equipment bag and unsheathed a large comb. He walked to the
mirror attached to the back of the door and began to rebuild his
hairdo.

Suddenly the door swung open, and to avoid getting bonked,
Rod leaped toward the wall where the door barely missed him.
"Hey, Rod, best move of the night," someone blurted to more gales
of laughter.

"Where's my childhood hero, Rod Gilbert?" Mayor Armstrong said, scanning the room as he entered with his entourage. The mayor's face was heavily pancaked. He'd probably been to Wilda Nelson's for the makeover, and she'd insisted on the exaggerated look. A smile as toothy and frozen as a cartoon shark's.

"Back here" came a muffled sound. "But shut off the TV camera, would you?" Rod gingerly stepped out from behind the door where Mayor Armstrong looked like he'd swallowed a bug.

"I love the Rangers," Armstrong said above the noise of laughter and stick-slapping on the floor. The mayor was a campaigner; he would tough it out. After all, he was into it for at least fifty bucks at Wilda's. "They are my favourite team. And you, Rod, my favourite player."

While the fat fan in pancake makeup and a cheap suit stared dumbly at Rod Gilbert, looking as vulnerable as a country boy at his first prom, even members of Armstrong's entourage broke into smiles. Finally, Rod, grinning ear to ear, sat on the floor, and with both hands deliberately mussed his hair.

"The camera's not on, right?" Rod asked.

"No, Rod," Mayor Armstrong said. "It's not. But we would like to get some footage. That was the deal, remember?"

"Just a moment." Rod pulled himself up and went to the mirror, where he again unsheathed his comb.

"First, I'd like to compliment their goalie," Rod told the television interviewer after he had his 'do to his liking. "He's really holding the Devils in there. Reminds me of little Roger Crozier of the Wings. The first goalie to win the most valuable player in the Stanley Cup playoffs in a losing cause. But like the great Montreal Canadiens did to Crozier, we'll get to your boy. Consider our collective professional hockey-playing experience. Seventeen guys, about fifteen years per career. What's that? Well, you do the math—"

"Consider the booze and steak dinners, the cholesterol, the heart disease." Wayne had slipped into the dressing room and was whispering in my ear. For purposes of the team, Wayne Strachan was my Uncle Lloyd, a know-it-all hockey fan. My mother's side. As far as I knew, only Rod and Doug were in on Wayne's true role.

"Hockey players, always one step away from the really big time ..."
Wayne said.

"Uncle Lloyd, give me a break, would you?" I said, playing
along.

"Sure, The Game is changed, the clutch and grab gone, the
centre line erased," Wayne said, raising his voice. "But with NHL
the fix is always in. When new arenas are built do they go for bigger international-size ice sheets, reward the swiftest skaters, the
pinpoint passers? Nope. In an NHL rink only the skyboxes and
ticket prices are big—that is if you don't count the giants on the
puny ice surface with sticks the reach of Yonge Street that get you
zero flow, a slew of extra penalties, and every game decided in the
penalty box. Jesus, Kyle boy, if the NHL can screw it up, it'll screw
it up." Gainey and Potvin gave Wayne a disgusted look and went
to another part of the room. Deep in the rant of the hockey nut,
Wayne had cleared out our corner so we could talk.

"There's no sign of Virgil, Kyle," he said, draping his big hand
on my shoulder. "He didn't return to that seat, and I just don't
see him anywhere. But he can't get to you here. This is your barn,
remember?"

I raised my head and his earnest glare pressed me down like a
fly under glass. Sure as hell, I thought with a shudder, he was taking me out of The Game. His report would finish me. "I might be
losing it," I said, digging my hands in my hair. "Maybe you're right,
maybe the Hall is right. I am crazy ..."

"No, on the contrary," he said, shifting his hand to my back.
"I'm proud of you. Keep letting go like you've been doing. That's
the boy. That's the way we're going to beat this thing. Nobody said
it was going to be easy." Wayne asked me if I felt I could go on, if
I wanted to leave with him. I said I thought that I would be okay,
that it was important for me to finish. "After the game, we'll talk
then," he said. His grey eyes softened behind long white lashes.

"Yeah," I said, looking to the floor, "you know where to
find me."

I felt a tap on my back and I turned to see my father. Knowing
Dad, there was no telling how long he had been in the room. The
shock of the possibility of him overhearing my conversation with

Wayne, of him finding out that I was seeing a shrink, ran through me like an electric current.

I leaped to my feet and shook hands with him. You can never approximate shaking hands with yourself, but whenever I shook hands with my dad I came as close as I ever would. The pressure, the way our fingers grasped, the timing of our clench were exactly the same. It always made me feel equal parts happy and sad. Like so much of me I'd never quite know.

"You're looking good, Dad," I said. Soft silver curls touched the top of the white ruff of his bomber jacket.

"You, too, boy. You've still got the hands, don't you?"

"Got 'em from you, Dad. You know that."

Dad looked down to the floor, then his hip bumped mine. An involuntary move, a twitch? A real attempt at physical contact? I didn't know, but the thought amazed me. In the next instant, though, Dad backed off a step, looking toward Wayne who had snatched up one of Kevin Lowe's gloves and was demonstrating to the cameraman in the mayor's entourage how best to fling it off, to get the drop on an opponent.

"Brutal toughness, yes, but trash-talking is definitely out," Wayne hollered. "Hockey is for gentlemen brutes, I'd say, who say darned not damned, shoot not shit, who live half their lives in ladies' garters holding up their stockings."

"Strange company you're keeping, son," Dad said, shaking his head.

"It's the business, Dad. You know, hangers on, autograph hounds. Never know who is going to crop up next."

"Yeah, guess so," Dad said, as he pulled at the elbow of his bomber jacket. A nervous habit. From years behind the wheel of the truck, making sure there wasn't any drag from his sleeve to mar his driving. "You're going to want to get ready to go back out there," he said. "Give those young bucks something to remember. I—"

It wasn't like Father to pause. He was either silent, or delivering lines. Telling a long, pointless story. With Dad, if he had something to say on the telephone, he'd wait for 11 p.m., when the rates went down, tell me what it was—usually a relative was ailing or dead—and then he would hang up.

"What is it, Dad?"

"Nothing, son," he said, finally. "Just wanted to tell you that I noticed a hitch in your stride. What you did in midget, remember? On transitions, mostly. But it's there. Push off with the left first, then go hard with your right. Remember?

"And use your finesse, boy. These kids aren't that good on their skates, you can see that, can't you? Show 'em some different looks."

Father's voice was stern, unyielding, and I was right back. Eleven years old. My father, Solomonic, all-knowing. Compared to him I was just a snot-faced little kid. Always something off, something missing.

"Yes, Dad," I said. And I glanced away and noticed Wayne watching us before the shrink left the room.

Norma was gone. Out of there. I was gliding on the ice moments before puck-drop in the second period and could see clearly into her and Wayne's seats. Her overcoat wasn't there, so that was that. There was no Wayne, either, but his coat was on the seat.

I whacked my stick on the gate of the players' bench. Who did she think she was? Imagine, splitting like that. My homecoming game. So much for loyalty. I sat down with no pain. I'd stretched after the visit with Wayne and Dad and my back was feeling a lot better. With the palm of my glove, I tipped my helmet up my forehead and then draped my gloves over the boards. Mayor Armstrong was at centre ice with Butch Goring and the Devils' top centre, giving each of them a plastic key fob. Something Armstrong had dreamed up from a customer, no doubt, somebody with too much time on their hands, with a videotape library of international hockey tilts. Never mind that such gift exchanges were supposed to take place before the game, and to have some significance, like stuffed Inuit Ookpiks from Canadian players and softwood doll sets from the Russians. Of course, Armstrong, the self-made man, would do it his way.

"I noticed that Norma is not in her seat, Kyle," Doug said. He was sitting next to me on the players' bench. "Is everything all right?" We ducked as an errant clearing shot slammed into the wall behind the bench.

"That's my business, friend," I said, face to face with him near the floor. The trainer scrambled over to the puck and flipped it back to the referee.

"Careful, Kyle," Doug said, flashing an Eddie Shore as we sat back down.

"Maybe I should call you Dougie," I said, standing and rising above him. "Being friends is your way with girls, isn't it? I've seen how you've been with Norma."

"Save it for the ice, Callendar," Gilbert called from down the bench. My voice had risen to a shout. Everyone along the bench and the first row of seats behind us was staring at me as I sat down beside Doug. Even Darren Govier, the broadcaster, looked my way, muttered something in the mike. Hell, even Govier had turned against me. Norma, and now him. But media goofs like Govier always covered for us in Keppel. And the mayors, too— Armstrong, Maury Williams before him, and Chauncey Johnson, the first black mayor in Ontario history, who acted more white than the white guys because that's the way it is. In Keppel and everywhere else. The mayors, the cops, the Crown attorneys. They all looked the other way for hockey players. Didn't matter who we screwed, where, or what drugs we took. Hits of acid in the old days, lines of coke. Cursed out blue-rinse mothers, rink rats, mall managers. Nobody told us what to do. But there was Darren Govier staring at me, Kyle Callendar, as if all bets were off and I was suddenly to blame.

I sat down, squeezed the knob of my stick, and slapped the top of my helmet. Glared at my father, who was scowling at me, his hate-by. I had to admit that Wayne might know a thing or two about getting a life off the ice, but Gilbert was right. The rink was the place to take out your anger. Before Gilbert gave us the nod for our next shift, I stole a glance at Doug. Frozen in his Eddie Shore leer. As I hopped the boards with my linemates, though, I realized that I was probably mistaken. That Darren Govier wasn't going on about me. It had to be Doug. The man whose father was a folk hero for holding hostages at gunpoint in order to see his boy's game. Ron, the father, whose manic moral purity blazed through Doug's eyes.

Not far from Govier I could see Suzy Hunter. She was looking good and I winked toward her. Face lit up like a goal siren. It would be Suzy, for sure. Her stooge husband sitting next to her looked away. Peggy Simpson or Victoria Blackwood wouldn't do. With Norma leaving me like that, I needed a girlfriend-type, at least.

"Your guess is as good as mine, Kyle," Mom said. "I can't begin to think of what happened to the two Negroes."

The year I got my job as Cup escort, I went to visit my folks in Keppel. Dad was away, gone most weekends on trucking gigs, but he'd built a deck out front at the place on the lake for Mom. With wide-plank ledges for her lawn gnome collection. The frog couple in polka dot swimwear was in the basement. They were weathered, Mom told me, and Dad said he would touch them up when he returned from the road. On display were Mom's seven red and yellow lawn gnomes, the deer, the Brer Rabbit, the Woolworth Building, the family of moles, and the Arc de Triomphe.

"It was the Negroes that went, though," Mom said. "You hadn't seen them, I don't think, had you? No? Well, one was dressed as a butler, very prim, and the other was more of a working man, you know, in overalls. He was pushing a wheelbarrow that fit a houseplant as nice as you please. Glads. Glads worked best.

"Can you imagine the gall of someone coming right up on our porch and taking my two Negroes?" Mom said, as she leaned to get up and out of her lawn chair. Dad had installed an outdoor speaker so that you could hear the phone when it rang, and she was rising to answer it.

"Of course, I was thinking it was just kids, but you can never be too sure."

When Paul Henderson got position on his check the Devil had to cut him down. Paul had their goalie on his back and the puck on the sweet spot of his stick. Wristed in, tie game. So what choice did the Devil have? He chopped down Paul, and the ref sent him to the penalty box. Power play, Old Timers, with only a few minutes left in the game.

I hadn't done much. The first shift in the second period my check got free in front of our net. Lucky for me, Robinson poke-checked the puck off the shooter's stick. Later, I passed the puck through centre trying to hit Errol at their blue line, and it was intercepted, forcing Bernie's best save of the night. What with my colossal miss in the first period, the puck slamming me in the back when Lynch had a sure goal, I couldn't blame Gilbert for benching me.

"We're ready," I cried at Gilbert. "One shift," I said, holding up an index finger. Gilbert was about to send Goring, but Butch and his mates were hurting for air. The Espo line was baked, too. That's par for the Old Timers. If the grey-hairs don't score enough early, they lose late. No wind.

"I want it, Rod," I said.

In his day, Gilbert played on some terrible Ranger teams, but he was no quitter. Up until that moment, he was convinced that our line wasn't up to the task, that there was something off about us. Finally, though, Rod nodded, and as one the five of us—Doug, Errol, Larry, Jack, and me—leaped over the boards for the power play.

"Ready?" Doug asked me. He was at the button in the faceoff circle in the Devils' end; I was in front of the net. Their goalie was giving me a skate more than he should have on the short side. Late in the game, he wasn't trusting his reflexes long side quite like he was early on, so he'd moved off the post, gave up a sliver more of the net. I nodded and Doug watched as the linesman's thumb held the puck at the red and yellow flame of the Devils logo. The ref snapped his wrist, the puck dropped, and Doug and the Devil scissored the puck as it hit the ice, sliced flat toward me, and into my wheelhouse. The goalie didn't move as the puck whizzed past him and bulged the twine. But the crowd did. Every single person was on their feet, cheering and hooting, "KY-ELL! KY-ELL! KY-ELL!" as I grabbed the puck from the net, kissed it, and threw it to the rafters.

At the end of The Game, there's this perfect moment. Men in various degrees of undress, the smell of sweat and beer and hair oil and farts. Melted snow on the black floor, wrappers with gum, phlegm, twists of foil. All visible in the caged light. Before light bulbs jailed in metal.

My mind filled not with Suzy and the sex we would have, or my father, whom I dreaded to see, even after such a game. Even when I was the hero he made me feel somehow lacking, never quite good enough. I didn't think of Wayne Strachan or Virgil Hadfield, Myra the ticket taker, Gwen, or the Cowplands, the Shrivers, Sheldon, or Bobby. Or Norma. None of them.

I saw Doug, smiling broadly, his hand behind his back. A half-bottle of champagne lathered my head before I leaped, feigning rage. Champagne corks popped and ricocheted around the room. Bottles lay submerged in the icy water of a galvanized tub, stickered "Courtesy of Mayor Armstrong. Upstate New York's finest."

My eyes stung from the champagne as I chug-a-lugged from a bottle. "YEE-HAW!" "WOOOO!" "KY-ELL!" the boys yelled. Reggie Houle uncorked a bottle and swung it into my hands. I tipped it back, and Doug grabbed it away, passed it down the line, to Lynchy and Lowey and Schonny.

"Hey, man," I said. "Would you quit being such a boy scout?"

Doug took me firmly by the arm, hissed in my ear. "Jesus, Kyle, I'm on your side," he said. "What I did for you with that set up. What I asked about Norma. Careful, man. I'm worried about you."

An old feeling swept over me. It happened with my father that first time at the Hall. And when I left home for good, went away to camp tryouts with the Penguins. Dad had spent a bundle on steak and red wine at Louie's Chop House, and the old man was tipsy, not soused, and he looked at me with so much pride in his eyes that I felt incredibly light-headed.

"Yeah, so what do you propose?"

"Let's say our goodbyes here and go for a walk. There's stuff we should talk about."

"What stuff?" I said, suddenly remembering Suzy. She could stall that lame husband of hers for only so long. If I were going to hook up with her, I'd have to get a move on. "Can't it wait? ... You forget, Doug, this is my town. Don't you want to get laid? Let's get laid first, and then I'll talk to your heart's content."

"Sure, man," Doug said, shaking his head and patting me on the back as we made our way out of the room. "Whatever you say."

On the other side of the door stood a clutch of boys, acting polite. Rather than rush the door, they had backed off a few steps. Like Mom's lawn jockeys, holding game programs in outstretched arms.

A few rows down the corridor from a towhead boy—not even six years old I'd say but there was something familiar about him—I caught a glance of Suzy. Time hadn't treated her well after all. Dark circles under her eyes, mottled skin that slipped the disguise of her makeup. She'd shaken her old man, or so it seemed, and had taken up with Peggy and Victoria, but her friends didn't look much better either. Hungry, even starved. Like I'd imagined the dames Father was with in France. Desperate, sad-looking women putting in their time, waiting for the war to end.

I had just scrawled my name on a program, a little ragged even for me and my lousy penmanship, but the towhead seemed happy with it as he scampered away with his father. I was a bit out of drinking condition, so I wasn't seeing too straight as I scanned the crowd for babes, Doug holding my elbow a little too hard. Suzy and her crew wouldn't do. We didn't have to settle for dried-up wenches with nubile puck bunnies to be had. Then I saw him. It was a distance, but he was directly under a jailed light bulb, where years ago you couldn't see two feet in front of your face for the swirling cigarette smoke, but now you weren't allowed to smoke so the air was clear, and I could see it was him. Coach Fleming. He was standing with my father. Coach reached out and touched my father, ever so lightly on the shoulder, pawed the leather of Father's bomber jacket. Then he pulled my father toward him and embraced him.

That's all I remember. If Doug hadn't been with me, held me up, then rushed me out the exit, as all Keppel it seemed stepped back, gave way, I would've fainted. Or screamed bloody murder. Screams that would never end.

chapter seventeen

Doug and I ended up at the Boy after the game. Wayne may have wanted to go with us, but I imagined Doug had shooed him off, said it was better if it were just the two of us. Maybe I had fainted again, or blacked out at least. When I came to, I was resting my head on the tabletop, peering up into a glass lamp, a narrow dust-caked shade. I marvelled at how black the bottom of a light bulb could get. How if you don't clean, nothing can get through.

"Here, drink this, bud," Doug said. He shoved a cup of java under my nose and I jerked awake. Beside me was a pot on a plugged-in warmer and a half-bottle of Canadian Club with two mugs. We had a booth in the back. The Boyson House was the first hotel in Keppel to go wet after the temperance vote. The vote was thirty years ago, but the place looked like it was yesterday. A week before the vote, The Boy served tap beer, jug wine, and spirits, not only to thirsty adults but to minors like I was. Arresting officers, blinking from the harsh light outside, stood in the foyer while we kids and adults hightailed out the rear door or up the back stairs, dumping drinks as we went.

That night, though, The Boy was mobbed with hockey fans. No women, of course. Only men in team jackets and wide-checked lumberjack shirts, hunting vests and shepherd coats. Every single one of them knew that two ex-NHLers were sitting in the back booth but nobody let on. But then Elvis Presley could've been in The Boy with John Lennon and nobody would've raised an eyebrow. If Elvis bought rounds for the house, say, there'd be nods of acknowledgement, then folks would've gone back about their business. But Elvis wasn't Keppel. I was Keppel, so while there were the occasional furtive glances toward me, nobody interrupts a local man in a private talk.

I drank the warm coffee, which was laced with more than a few drops of Canadian Club—what we called Windsor—and Doug splashed in some more Windsor and poured the brew to the brim. You could stare into the top of the mug and see to the bottom. Even in that light.

I gulped the drink and Doug touched my hand. "Easy, bud. Easy."

"Yeah, whatever," I said, pulling away my hand.

"I don't know what's got into you. Man, it's like I don't recognize you."

"What? And you're a piece of work too, aren't you? What do you expect after what you've done to me," I said, leaning forward in my seat. "You see Virgil Hadfield, keep that from me; charm my girlfriend and turn her against me. Then, pardon me, but wasn't that you who twisted your sweater in a knot when I was lining up some action on the side," I said as I drained the rest of my drink. "Sure as hell looked a lot like you."

"Stop, Kyle. I didn't turn Norma against you. Not at all. You know I think you guys are great together."

Doug poured two more Windsors and I slurped mine. The picture framed on the wall was a faded landscape with water spots. Ireland or Scotland. Likely snipped from an old *Toronto Star* magazine. I scanned the room again for girls and came up empty.

"So then wassup, Mr. Cowpland?" I said, lounging on the wooden bench of the bar booth. "You've got me here. The Boy for Chrissakes. Not even the scent of a woman. Lay on the homo shit."

"Kyle," Doug said firmly, a tear in his eye. "We've got to talk. You can't go on like this."

It was like Doug took a shot at my face. Hard knuckles on cartilage, soft flesh. In fights on ice, with arms flailing and heads wheeling, you don't usually get or deliver anything but glancing blows. This was between the eyes. I'd run from Norma and Wayne, left them both behind. Was shaken at the airport in Saskatoon when

I thought that I'd seen Doug, welcomed his visit at the hospital after my panic attack but then didn't give a moment's thought to his veiled warning over a Tim Hortons breakfast a few days later. Hadn't he been there for me? Wasn't he someone I could trust? I patted the inside pocket of my jacket, felt the bottle of anti-anxiety pills. Jesus, what the fuck was I doing?

"Yeah, I guess," I said, with what little wind I had.

"Well, let me be a friend, would you? Maybe, just maybe, I can help." Doug gestured to the barkeep, who sent over a waiter with a pot of fresh coffee. He took away the Windsor, the half-empty mugs, and the pot of mud, installed the other one on the warmer. Then Doug poured a black scalding stream into a clean mug. He gave it to me and I held in my hands and watched the heat curls at the lip until I couldn't see them anymore. I blew on the drink, took a sip, and burned my tongue but didn't let on.

"What's in it for you, Doug," I said. "Why stick your neck out for a fuckup like me?"

"I got my reasons ... Why do you think?"

"I don't know ... Listen, Doug, I—I got to go. I'll be right back."

He grunted sure, and I took the first few steps toward the men's room. As soon as I was out of Doug's view, I lunged forward, scattering people as I went. In the men's room, I fell on my knees and coughed up my guts into the toilet. The Big White Telephone. How many nights had I spent calling into her, weeping into her? Give me long-distance information, get in touch with my Marie. Or Francine. Or Bernadette. Or Willow. Sure, I could get them, I had them, but in the end this was always my last call. Doug may be right, I thought, as I fought my way back to my feet. I'm getting too old for this. Either something had to break, or I was going to.

"Feeling better?" Doug asked, when I made my way back to the booth. No judgment. Not even a smirk. Only that Louie's Chop House gaze of concern.

"Yeah," I said, sipping some coffee.

"Kyle, can I ask you something?"

"Sure ..."

"What happened back there? By the dressing room."

"I don't know," I said, running a hand through my hair. "Maybe the excitement, the champagne. A long time between goals. It's not like the roof has been blowing off at home every night with people shouting my name."

"Uh-huh."

"I got light-headed and, um ..." I took a big gulp of coffee. "Lost my equilibrium, maybe; I'm back, you know, playing before my hometown fans thirty years after the place made me out to be its one true hope. I pull myself together and score the winning goal, and the place is so loud with cheering, with cheering for me, I can't hear myself think. I'm feeling feelings that don't even have names. Anything can happen."

"Please," Doug whispered, leaning in closer to me. "I'm not some reporter. I'm a friend, Kyle. Anything didn't happen. Something very specific happened. You were fine, signing an autograph, and then you saw your father in an embrace with a man. All the life drained out of your face. Man, I thought you had a heart attack."

I tried to blurt something back. Something mean, ugly, something to put him off. A gorge rose in my throat. But it stayed put. And, surprisingly, so did I.

"What was it you wanted to tell me?" I muttered as I signalled to the barkeep for some water. Bar patrons passed a pitcher of water to me and I filled my empty mug to the brim and took a drink.

"The first thing I want you to know, Kyle, is I'm behind you. One hundred and fifty percent. You're a helluva hard guy to get close to, but if anybody has half a chance, it's me. You're not the only victim in the world."

"You've been watching too much *Oprah*, Doug."

"Would you stuff that shit, Kyle," Doug said through clenched teeth. "My old man went down in a hail of bullets because of me. He was full of life and humour with a woman who loved him and friends who cared for him; now he's a ghost driving a beat-up truck up and down back roads all over Saskatchewan. All because of me and my hockey."

"I know, Doug. It's sad, and I'm truly sorry for you—and your folks. But you can't blame The Game for that."

"Oh, I can't, can't I? Kyle, I love you. You're too rich, too chocked full of what they want you to be chocked full of. That pure sense of loyalty to The Team. The Team above all else. Do you know, Kyle, that for ten long years after my father was shot up and sent away to prison, I had nothing but The Team? I lived for The Team. And you know what The Team did? Did The Team protect me, replace the family The Game had taken away?"

"It has done. It can do."

"Bullshit, Kyle," he said, slamming his fist on the tabletop. "We put up with it, the hell of it. Would you forgive Norma if for every other Friday night since you've known her in high school, instead of her Night Out with the Girls, she'd put on trousers, a fake moustache, two-tone Oxfords, and went to pick up a woman? Not on your life. You wouldn't put up with the lies, the betrayal. But for The Team we'll forgive anything. Year after sorry year. Because The Team is all we've got, man. Our one pathetic shot at glory."

I felt Doug's eyes like sun through glass. Then he looked to his hands, which lay flat on the tabletop. If I were going to get up and out of there, that was the time. Before Doug had a chance to regroup. I tried to move, and my shoes stuck to the floor on spilt beer, or lemon gin fizz, or lime cordial, Clubman's, a cheap-booze favourite of the teen set, with a green grandfather sofa on the label.

It wasn't a long time before either of us spoke. Not as I think back on it now. Long enough to recall Doug, the first time we met. During a scrimmage at training camp in Kingston. I'd feathered a pass up ice, snatched a glimpse to follow its path when Doug nailed me with a shoulder, sent me hard to the ice. I blacked out and when I came to I saw Doug's face, an eyebrow raised. Doug pulled me back onto my skates and we raced back into the game.

Now Doug was sweet and forlorn, a native in prayer. I looked up and down The Boy to see if we had drawn anyone's attention. Not a soul.

"Kyle, you can choose to be invisible," Doug said. "But I can't bear to see you blind." His eyes narrowed and he leaned forward so that we were nose to nose.

Kingston's Initiation Night. What I'd always tamped down. The room began spinning and I closed my eyes to stay still. Doug put his hands back on top of mine and I kept them there. The empty warehouse. Doug's voice, like a storyteller in kindergarten. Big pillows and primary colours. Safe territory. Boys, naked on wooden chairs, hands bound, nooses taut around their necks. Senior players, Coach, the team owners, a town councillor surrounded Doug, me, and several other rookies. Fat men wearing nothing but fedoras with PRESS cards in their hatbands and wide forties-style neckties snapped photos. Marshmallows stuffed in asses, a scorekeeper with clipboard and stopwatch noted the fastest at shitting them out. First star. Second star. Third star. Strings tied hard to our knobs, a pail attached. Pucks dropped into the pail until the string broke. Clunk, clunk, clunk …

"I'm going to be sick," I said. Doug's lips a crease in stone. He looked away to the floor. I finished off the water to ease the gorge, then Doug filled the mugs with coffee. We both sipped some.

"I wasn't much older than eleven or twelve," I whispered, breaking a silence. "Beginning to discover girls." Ribs on Doug's fingerless gloves, as if I could snuggle into them.

"The class toughs were harassing the two best-looking girls in the grade. One was Trudy Phillips. A new girl, pretty thing just arrived from Toronto in pedal-pushers and bobby socks, with Maureen Stockton, the dentist's daughter.

"I came up on them with my pals. Together, we formed a big circle and pushed Trudy and Maureen in the middle. One boy pulled Trudy's blond pigtails so hard the braids came undone, her hair fell wildly around her face. Trudy rushed toward me, but I shoved her in her breasts so hard that she fell, dress hiked up her thighs. First, she cried, then through madwoman's hair she glared at me with such hate it took my breath away."

I gazed at a wet spot on a panel in the booth, a flaw in the wood.

"That night in Kingston, Doug, through it all, I couldn't get Trudy out of my mind. I wished to God I could tell her I was sorry." I stared blankly, willing tears.

"It's okay, Kyle." Echo on tundra.

A swirl of smoke froze in air. I shivered with the cold. Who left a door open? Why couldn't I feel my hands, my feet? I snatched the bottle of anti-anxiety pills from my pocket, swallowed two with a swig of water. I should've stayed away from Ron, from Norma, from Doug. Why couldn't they leave me alone? Why couldn't everybody just leave me alone?

"That man," I said, gulping air like water. "The one with my father. He was my coach in Keppel. Coach Fleming."

Doug's hands swarmed mine. I had never felt so small.

"I didn't know the first thing about Trudy, Doug. That maybe she was into horseback riding, or could play a mean game of tiddlywinks, or had the ripest farts when she ate pork 'n' beans."

Doug leaned his head toward me; a waft of stale coffee and smoke.

"I'm not going to tell you what happened between Coach and me," I said. "I'm not sure I can ever tell anyone what happened."

"What he did to you, Kyle. We were just kids. What he did to you."

"Yeah. I'm not sure I can tell anybody about that."

"One day. Given the right circumstances."

Doug never once let go of my hands. It felt good, right. I became aware of my breaths. Not shallow, broken. But breaths like before. Like the beginning of the calm before I stepped onto the ice.

"You can't imagine what it's been like for me," I said. "I really don't know what to do. Who to trust with this. Maybe Wayne? He's somebody you'd trust, no?"

"Uh-huh. Of course he is, Kyle."

"But all these years, man, who was I going to go to? Dad? Who if not for Coach Fleming would still be doing yardwork at the Keppel airport? Instead I told Virgil. My first years in hockey he was a god to me. I believed him, that hockey was my family, that it was all about being strong, about trusting him. He promised me he would get to the bottom of it, that Fleming would be exposed. But in the end he did nothing, and later with the pension theft he was a traitor to everything I cared for. I got so I couldn't think of him and not feel my blood boil, my stomach tie up in knots."

"I get it, Kyle," Doug said. "Of course, it makes perfect sense ... But Norma, Kyle? What do you think? Wouldn't she understand?"

For a long time we just sat, lost in our separate thoughts. Strange calm of booze and the anxiety pills shrouded me like cashmere. I was surprised with the sudden comfort I felt.

"The reason I always thought I was thinking of Trudy that night in Kingston and when I was with Coach was that I felt like I knew what she was going through. I remember that crazy look in her eyes. Like an animal in a trap. Like she was saying to me, 'How in the world can you be so cruel?' Then, a worse thought struck her. If a decent boy like me was capable of such cruelty, then what hope was there? That was the horror for her. That was what I saw in her eyes."

"And what was in your eyes. When you were with Coach Fleming."

I nodded, and then I stopped and looked at Doug as if for the first time. At the puck scar above the eye he'd gotten one night in Owen Sound that had broadened and softened like a kiss. Nostrils flared to his philtrum, the hollow between the tip of his nose and his upper lip, where it seemed to me he had long pressed shut with a finger the shouts that he, too, wanted to make but never had.

PART THREE

chapter eighteen

Once Dad took me on the road. To Niagara Falls. I was small, so I don't remember much about it. Mom didn't come; it was just the two of us.

We went up in the Skylon Tower, with its views to America, wore rain slickers, and walked to a place under the Falls where the water poured around us, a million baths a second. Stand in that spot, boy, and I'll tell Mom you'll never have to wash again in your life. In a picture that someone took of us, we stood chests thrown forward, arms back, the cords of the slicker hoods pulled tightly across our throats. Chinstrap penguins in a monsoon.

I remember the thrumming on my heart. What meeting a giant must be like. He picks you up in his hand and carries you off, and it's not so much the far horizons you see from his palm, the thumb the size of an ocean liner, but the thunder on your heart. *Onguiaahra*, the Indians call it. "Thundering Water."

And I remember Howard Mann. He was a Dieppe veteran like my father. One of the good guys, Father said. Every night Howard Mann put on his shoulders a child—beyond their bedtime, that was a must—and showed them the Falls at night. After the war the town fathers gave Howard Mann the best job in town, Niagara's lamplighter, and every night he could he let a child do his job for him. From Howard's perch, I learned about the pilgrimage to power, how people came from all over the world to stand at the railing before the Falls, for hour after hour, mesmerized, unable to take a step. What people do at Peace Park in Hiroshima, or at Trinity Site, New Mexico, where the atomic power of the first Ground Zero is remembered.

Then Howard Mann let me light Niagara. I turned a knob and bridal white poured on the Horseshoe Falls. I did red and blue and purple and orange, always turning the knob first and running back to leap up on Howard Mann's shoulders to see what I had done, to hear the oohs and aahs of the pilgrims below, to feel my father's eyes on me, the official Lamplighter of Niagara.

In forty years of volunteering and working in amateur hockey in Keppel, Bob Fleming had never been accused of as much as a parking violation. He was a family man, a father of two boys, Rick and Ron. His wife, Marge, wove baskets for Keppel United Church, her father was a direct descendant of United Empire Loyalists. Fleming himself fought in the re-enactment of the Battle of Ogdensburg at Fort Wellington in Prescott, Ontario, every summer. He flipped pancakes for the Kiwanis, arranged for pro-hockey speakers to come to the Lions, did Career Days at the high schools. His company, Fleming Cartage, donated trucks for the annual Christmas parade; Bob himself drove the cab escorting Santa. The *Keppel Advance* stock photo is of Bob and Marge as guests of honour at a benefit for a hospice for children with incurable diseases.

An untouchable, I thought, with a sly grin. A hockey man.

I expected the gun to feel a lot heavier in my hand. It felt smooth and tapered. Like a fist-sized trophy.

A hockey player relies on strong hands. Bobby Orr had such strength in his hands that he'd cock his stick no more than six, seven inches and hit the puck so hard it flew like a rocket. As if there were no friction. If not in the net, the puck hit a place the goalie was least expecting. So that he had to make the save of his life.

Dad never touched a gun after he came back from the war. I asked and he said the last guns he had anything to do with were the tin soldiers on the wallpaper he'd put up the first month he was home. Then he wallpapered the rest of the house and went out on the road, trucking. He also would do a little home repair. Dad built a workroom in the basement where he fixed things, and when he wasn't on the road he walked around the house with a tool. The gun

I was using, the .38 Special, an old police issue, felt no more alien in my hand than Dad's wood drill. And just as easy to use. Release the safety, aim, and make the hole. The noise is something different. But something you don't notice. Like the drill. Once you've concentrated on the job, the noise isn't something you notice at all. The noises that make the difference are inside, anyway. And until you do the job, there's no way you're going to quiet them.

I was holding the gun at an indoor shooting gallery north of Toronto. It was Wayne's idea and we went there together after I'd told him about The Boy, my conversation with Doug. The gallery was affiliated with one he belonged to in Saskatoon.

"Just go along with it," he said. "Consider it part of your treatment. Tell me how you feel, what memories come."

Hockey storage rooms don't smell like dressing rooms at all, I explained to him at one of our more frequent sessions. Of piss and sweat and must and rat farts. Storage rooms are where the Cup is kept before it's presented to the champions. For five seconds of every year, I wheel the Cup out onto the red carpet to centre ice and then retreat to the shadows, I told him. Back to the smell. Of piss and rat farts, the universal stink of hockey storage rooms.

It was 1998, the year the Detroit Red Wings won their second championship in a row. Before the Cup presentation, the camera at the near boards got a close-up of my profile. I was in my white linen gloves, blow-dried hair with feather-like texture. Then I bowed my head as I stepped onto the ice and my bald spot showed. On national television. You're flying over what you thought was a snowy mountain, majestic and beautiful, and you look down and you see it's not a mountain at all. It's a volcano. Raw, ugly, dangerous.

"Just keep talking," Wayne said. "Your father and the story of Niagara was simply beautiful, really meaningful. Your feelings for him are complex, not so cut and dried. The more you can recall, the deeper the memories, the better progress we can make. And we are making progress. Did you know that a certain species of orchid, with the most delicate and complex blooms, grows only in the fertile mouth of a volcano? Orchids grow wild everywhere but Antarctica, and before the Ice Age, there, too. We've been amazed by these gorgeous primitives for thousands of years. Recently, an entirely new species of orchid was found in Belize, one that had never before been seen."

"That's matterless," I said.

"You mean meaningless," he said.

"No, matterless."

I like the way the gun feels before I squeeze the trigger. Not like anything else I've ever felt. Before the squeeze I feel a remarkable quiet. A relaxation I've never known. Like a baby's breath before its first cry.

Before I used the gun, a hockey stick was the closest I'd come to holding a weapon in my hand. In peewee, I jumped my own teammate. The opposing goalie had ankle-chopped the boy with the heel of his stick blade, and he fell heavily, only to leap to his feet and swing his stick like an axe across the only exposed part of the goalie's body—the back of his neck. The boy netminder went down in a heap and would've certainly been maimed by the next blow if I hadn't swung my stick at the back of my teammate's leg, sent him crumpled to the ice.

The gun felt like the weighted darts my father used. Dad liked darts. As a young man his father served in the British Army in South Africa, and he brought to Canada his passion for darts. Father kept a board in the basement and occasionally fellow truckers and dispatchers would come over to play. When I was a boy, Dad's weighted darts felt like iron ingots in my hands. It was only as I grew older that I learned to use them well. I even came close to beating Father with them. But I knew better than to beat my father. Not at his own game.

I felt impelled to let Father win at darts. There was something inside me that told me winning wasn't a good idea. I'd have lined up the game clincher, the double-ten, my easiest shot—and I'd miss. Choke. Then he would seize the advantage and win. Before the dartboard, with my dad standing beside me with his weighted darts clutched in his hand, I never felt safe.

I could feel Wayne's eyes on me. He was next to me, shooting. Wayne approved of the gallery, said whatever it takes, you must get your anger out. In that, Gilbert was wrong, he said. Better that it happens here, and not in the hockey rink. Where threats you recall from your father's rage are real, like the taste of blood from a blow to the head. Because the violence doesn't stop with career-ending backstabbings from the likes of Todd Bertuzzi and Eddie Shore. Beware the traces of murder in the corridors, the stands above. What police seldom tell, like spectacular suicides from the atrium of a downtown hotel. In hockey, too, the horror is hidden. We've only rare glimpses. A Massachusetts truck driver beating to death a carpenter on a summer day. On the ice, the truck driver's hockey-playing son cries in frustration, wheels away, is taunted, pushed, elbowed, and kicked by the carpenter's boys.

"It's supposed to be fun," the truck driver says, as one of the carpenter's sons is ordered to the penalty box for his crime.

"No," the carpenter says with a smile, "that's hockey."

If you are angry, Wayne said, then it's best to show it in a safe place. He told me he'd advised grown women who'd been abused by their father to build a mannequin in the father's likeness and then viciously beat it up, slash it to ribbons with a knife, blow a hole in it with a revolver. For men with irrational fear of intimacy, he prescribed a weekend in a sweat lodge with cross-dressers. Face your fear, confront the source of your anger. Two wrongs may not make a right, but they can help.

If only I could see Coach Fleming. Or Virgil Hadfield. See the whites of their eyes. It's true about that. When you really have a target that you want to kill. The whites of the eyes. When you see them. You squeeze the trigger. So sweet. I imagine it like nothing I've ever had in bed.

Everything converges to the central spot. Like traffic around the town green. So much movement on the outside, but on the inside, quiet and permanent. An island of peace, of calm. In Keppel, the courthouse square. In Mexico City, the zocalo. In Italy, the piazza. A lightness of being that I've never known. I wore headphones that muffled the sound from outside shooting lanes, and I eased ever so slowly, peacefully, into a place deep inside myself. The divine centre of revenge.

I couldn't look down the end of my lane and see the shadow outline of my shooting target and not imagine Coach Fleming. Yet with each bullet I squeezed out of my .38 Special, it wasn't hate that rose in me. Not anger, either, I'd have to admit to the shrink. Doctors' prescriptions, I've found, never get to the crux. They can close a gash on your face, set a broken bone in your foot, come up with the right care for a severe groin pull. But when the disease or the hurt is deeper, doctors are like everybody else. They don't have a clue.

I was out of bullets and the target began to move. It was on its way forward from the end of the lane on an overhead track. I shot again and again, but the gun's chamber was empty and the silhouette kept coming. But before the arrival of the target, the wide fleshy forehead of Coach, his beady pig eyes, that small, thin-lipped mouth, as I heard the swooshing sound—the speed of the paper in air—I imagined the voice of broadcaster Foster Hewitt, that unmistakable play-by-play, "Good evening, hockey fans in Canada, the United States, and Newfoundland. Welcome to *Hockey Night in Canada* ... The Leafs are behind the eight ball tonight ... Pulford eludes a check, headmans to Bathgate, to Duff. He shoots! He scores!"

I looked at the target and smiled. Six bullets in the head. They made a hole the size of a puck where the mouth should be.

chapter nineteen

New York is nothing like Saskatoon. Gretzky and Messier and Shanahan played out their hockey lives there. Lindros said it's his favourite American city. I don't know about that. To me, New York is a big, dirty town, with loudmouth cops and even loudermouth women. When the Cup finals roll around in June, the place is literally crawling with German tourists, Japanese shutterbugs. New York is the only place I know that is surrounded by rivers but isn't defined by them. At the Battery, where the waters connect, you could live a lifetime and not see a heron in flight, a trout on a line. Instead, you've got Hong Kongers in photo flashes. Wealthy ones in tuxes and mammoth bridal gowns, posed before the towers of the World Financial Center, bringing home mementos, replica buildings on chains, the emptiest place on earth.

If there was a place where I truly needed Norma it was in New York. My sessions with Wayne had gone well, I could consider myself on the mend, he said. On the question of Norma, he said, of course, it was up to me. A million times since the Really Old Timers game I'd thought to call her. Once, I dialled the number at the place she'd moved into a week after the Keppel game. It rang once, twice, and she picked up. But I froze, couldn't get a word out. "Hello? hello?" she said. Then I hung up. The next day I tried her number again. With a little script this time, some words of apology, "I miss you, Norma. I'm a lot better, but I'm in New York and it's hard for me. You know how I am in New York. We have to talk. Maybe, if you let me try, I can make it up to you. I can't not have you in my life." But I never got through. The phone said only, "This number is not in service." And when I called long-distance information, they said Norma Hanford had taken an unlisted one.

"She'll come around. You'll see," Doug said. He and I were sharing a room in a chain hotel across from Madison Square Garden. The Stanley Cup and its carrying case were on the floor by the bureau. Wayne had convinced the Hall that I was up to the escort duties, as long as Doug worked with me. That given my years of service, they owed me at least one more chance. Doug was combing his freshly shorn hair before the mirror while I drew a lint brush over his NHL blazer. It was the day before the third game of the Stanley Cup finals.

"I don't know, Doug."

"She loves you, man. She won't desert you. Anybody can see that." His comb carved a wide line down the middle of his florid scalp.

"On the side, buddy," I said, smiling. "Part it on the side. It'll look better.

"Think so?" he asked, flinging me a glance over his shoulder.

"Sure, sure, let's see." The left side took a narrower part and the comb-over made him look ten years younger, until he showed his jack-o'-lantern teeth.

"So, what do you think?"

"Beauty ... You know, Doug," I said, looking at the Cup on the floor. "I can't thank you enough for all you've done. If there is anything I can do for you. Anything. All you have to do is ask."

Doug looked at me with slightly crossed eyes, his brow knitted as if I'd somehow lapsed into a foreign tongue, a Russian rookie in training camp. "I like the sound of that, man," Doug said, as he pulled two Diet Cokes from the mini-bar and tossed me one. "Maybe I'll take you up on that someday. Now, though, you just look after yourself, okay? You've had a lot happening, after all. Take it slow. That's my advice." We pulled the tabs and took a swig. I was dying for a beer or a whiskey, but Doug and Wayne had been keeping me on a short leash.

After a while, Doug got up and snapped the television on and we sat down to watch.

I'd gotten no closer to understanding Doug. You'd think after that night in The Boy, the hours we'd spent together since, in hotel rooms with the Cup, we'd have got beyond the surface. But for all of

Doug's smarts about other people, he was guarded about himself. This was particularly hard for me because I felt like I was digging deeper, was desperate for a real friend. Bullets into a paper heart had tapped an anger long withheld, but it was a demon not easily exorcised. I hated Coach Fleming, but I wondered how I would have responded if I had seen him alone that night in Keppel. Instead, it was his embrace with my father that had me floored. When I thought of them together, I realized that it was my father, too, who unglued me. That everything—from his encounters with Gwen to my first visit to the Hockey Hall of Fame to Howard Mann, the Lamplighter of Niagara—was about him, about his feelings, his needs, not mine.

Without Doug's help I would've still been in the dark. Now I found I wanted the same from him. I wanted to be able to touch him in the way that he had me. But with Doug, it seemed, everybody was a project. Me, the hot dog vendor, the chambermaid, even the homeless man fishing for quarters down an elevator shaft with dental fixer, yo-yo string, and a cheese grater. All were subjects to be studied: a girl with a fresh haircut in a rainstorm. A donut's glazed sugar on waxed paper. A puck slapping ice.

Doug never talked about his own family, about women, in a serious way. He'd speak brusquely about himself, his father, Ron, and poor Dead-Eye Jim, then clench his jaw and go silent. If he didn't have something or someone to take care of, he didn't have much else to say. Once, we watched Alfred Hitchcock's *The Man Who Knew Too Much* on television and Doug danced around the room singing "Que Sera, Sera," dipping and sashaying like Doris Day in that Moroccan hotel room, except Doris was dancing with her son who would soon be kidnapped. Doug had no partner.

The front desk called an hour before game time. On television was a report of a murder in Queens. In soft-focus promotions, an announcer said a reporter had an exclusive on the killer. Broadcasting live from the scene, the reporter said police had found only a bloodied ashtray next to the body.

Bobby Shriver had left a message for me. He was in town, staying at the Brooklyn Marriott. I scribbled down his number while watching a news report on Willies Buttons. Willies Buttons changed its name from Willies Bottoms, with two dabs of white paint on its sign, in order to conform to a new anti-porn law that banned signs with sexual references. Dark-haired women, censor bars on their privates, slunk in and out of shadow on the screen.

Bobby picked up the phone on the first ring. He and Sheldon were in town for the finals. He'd heard that I was escorting again, and he'd wanted to look me up. That he really couldn't believe that ten months had gone by since we'd last seen each other. Over the years, he said, he and his dad had often come to New York, to visit museums, the Statue of Liberty, the new Forty-second Street. Earlier that day, Bobby said, they had played tennis at Grand Central Station, got a bird's-eye view from the most fantastic toilet in the world at the pinnacle of the Chrysler Building.

"Dad is busy tonight and I'm going to be coming from Brooklyn," Bobby said. "Why don't we meet at the main support of the Brooklyn Bridge, on the Brooklyn side, this evening? You can see so much from there: Lady Liberty, the Staten Island Ferry, City Hall Park ... No, nowhere near The Hole. Don't worry."

Brooklyn? It was no place for a Keppel boy. I didn't want to have anything to do with Brooklyn. If Manhattan was a swamp of humanity, Brooklyn was its sewer. Where the filth travels. From Brooklyn they come in droves to Manhattan, up and out of the subway, with their foul airs and twisted accents, jouncing up and down the street, blocking crosswalks. Menacing types. Black, white, all sorts of blended colours. Who to hell knew what horror actually waited for you in Brooklyn?

"What do you mean, Brooklyn?" I asked.

"Just on the bridge," Bobby said, "high up above the river. You can see for miles from there."

Like maybe back into my old life, I thought. Before Saskatoon, when my problems began. With big, sad-sack Bobby, about as self-aware as a garment bag. I don't know what I was thinking, standing holding the phone, listening to the empty air, before Bobby most surely would've said, "Kyle, are you still there? Are you still on the line? Whaddya say? Wouldya like to meet me?" I said—surprising the hell out of myself because it was the last place in the world I wanted to go—"Yeah, sure. I'll be there at eight o'clock."

chapter twenty

In Keppel, you couldn't go across town without stepping on a bridge. The Crowder Street Bridge, the Jubilee Bridge, the Keppel Harbour train bridge. Pedestrians Beware: Not a Thruway, the sign said on the train bridge. By the time I was a boy, the train spur into town had been long abandoned, so the warning didn't seem reasonable. Only slick railway ties and the places where some of the ties had fallen through. Places in which you had to watch your step because if you slipped and fell there was just enough room between the ties for a boy's body to squeeze through and plunge into the icy river fifty feet below.

Before I went away for good to Kingston, my friend Cody Rhéaume would come over to the house. Funny how that time, my friendship with Cody—all of it would have stayed lost to me if not for my work with Wayne. Everything I'd tamped down, everything I didn't give attention to because it was outside The Game: the sweet taste of Father's approval, what I felt that day as the "Lamplighter of Niagara," or when we went off, hand in hand, in search of the Stanley Cup, or at Louie's Chop House a generation ago. So many memories locked under ice, slowly breaking up, taking shape.

After midnight, Cody would shine a beam from his flashlight onto my bedroom window. I'd be dressed except for the boots I kept at the back door and I'd tiptoe through the house careful not to rouse my mother, which was really not necessary because Mom was a chronic insomniac who woke at the lengthening of a shadow on the wall. It was our unspoken arrangement that if I was quiet

Mom wouldn't rise and stop me when Cody came to get me at night. Instead, she'd say prayers to herself for me and watch to see that my father didn't stir.

Once outside, I raced with Cody in the night air. When we ran it was step for step, not as if we were petty thieves, pressed equal parts by fear and excitement, or sprinters, born to the task of winning. We ran as shy friends do, down back streets, snorting and cackling as we went. Unintelligible phrases, yet repetitive, in serial. "Aiiiii-Oooooo-Ahhhhhhhh ... Aiiiii-Oooooo-Ahhhhhhhh." Lights blinked on in the apartments above McDonough's Drugs, Ted's Sporting Goods, Alma's Gifts. Once a man threw open the shutters to yell, "Pipe down out there," and I ran backwards a few strides, threw him an exaggerated shrug.

We flew through the train alley of steel ribbons and pavement fragments. One night Cody stopped in front of a brand-new tractor-trailer tire. "I'm taking this," he said. "No, don't ..." I cried, as he heaved the tire down a slight incline, and bounded after it. I chased after him, losing ground, slipping on the rails, nearly going down. "Forget it, man," I said. "Put it back."

Cody had stolen the tire from Fleming Cartage. Fleming's office was two doors away in the train alley. In its window was a mud flap. Beautiful pressed rubber. The depth of the crown, the tapered stripes, the serrated border. Canary yellow, royal blue, with fire-engine red piping. You could tell a Fleming transport two blocks away from the gleam of its mud flaps. Once, I'd tried to pry loose the flap on my dad's truck but was stunned by its weight, the bulk of a full-grown man.

That night the truck tire soared over the cracked pavement of the train alley as if it were rolling along Millionaire's Drive, the road in Keppel where doctors and plant managers and Coach Fleming lived. At the train bridge, Cody paused, made as if to throw the tire into the water below, jump in, and paddle away. *Papillon* was playing at the Roxy that week, and we had sat through it twice. Imagined ourselves as Steve McQueen, making a great escape.

"It's not high tide," Cody said, as I arrived beside him. He'd leaned the tire against the bridge railing. The dark water beneath us was deep, maybe twenty, thirty feet, but still as bathwater. "We'll have to wait for a current to take us away from this Devil's Island," he said, as he looped his arm around my shoulder.

Cody hopped onto the bridge and scaled its iron wall, stood on the narrow ledge, the height of a man on stilts above the railway ties, and spread his arms high above his head. "C'mon Kyle," he said. "Follow me."

But I couldn't move, couldn't take a step on the bridge over the dark water. I watched Cody as I ran my fingers over the surface of the truck tire, let them slip into the deep grooves of the tread.

Cody walked along the ledge, halfway across the harbour bridge, which wasn't long, only a short distance from the intersection of Crowder and Valley Road; even in a boy's memory, it was nothing, seventy feet at best, only half of which was over water. "C'mon Kyle," Cody cried, angry, insistent. "What's wrong with you? Let's go."

Instead, I turned and pushed the tire back the way we'd come, retreating as fast as I could, while Cody yelled at me, cursed me for the betrayal from the parapet of the Keppel Harbour train bridge.

I can handle myself. That was what I thought as I stepped onto the Brooklyn Bridge, a wooden walkway, the pedestrian path above the noisy car traffic on the drive portion of the bridge.

Of course, I needn't have been afraid. Water was for girls, I'd always told myself. I don't like water in my drinks and I don't like great heights over it, either. If you didn't look down it would be okay. I'd been aboard boats and that was what you did, look toward the horizon, where the sky meets the water, the thin blue line that looks as solid as any ice surface. Except in Madison Square Garden in May. Much more solid than that.

But I was afraid. Finally, I could admit that to myself. I ran from Cody Rhéaume that night on the Keppel Harbour train bridge because if I had climbed to the ledge I would have certainly fallen in. Or jumped. At least that is what I believed that night. Since I was little, my place was over ice, not water, particularly not dark water. There was no telling what would drag you down from dark water. The thought of it put me in a cold sweat.

Which was what I was feeling on the Brooklyn Bridge, looking toward the edge. Of course, I was hemmed in by a web of steel, could no more jump to my death than fly to the moon. But the knot in my stomach was real. That I could squeeze through these openings, jump to the road bed below and if a speeding car didn't get me, race across the road to the edge, climb the steelwork there and jump to certain death, hit the water with a terrible smack. From beginning to end, no more than five seconds and it would be over.

But there were witnesses everywhere. Like Broadway over the East River. Cyclists, joggers, rollerbladers, mothers pushing sport strollers. Even fiercer-looking faces than the street, if that were possible. For the first one hundred metres or so there'd been no water, just the bridge rising above the city streets, no horizon to look at, only high rises, Pace University, and a massive brown wall, the colour of most of the faces fleeting by. Now there was nothing but witnesses. Bike riders with wide asses, roaring down the wooden track, cutting in and out of the walkers, racing up behind Hispanic families, Jews in long beards and tall black hats. Cars roared below, and the bike riders, everyone with headphones on, soaked in sound, not the din of the traffic, but hip hop, soulless pounding of another world.

Without headphones what you heard were the cars below. Many lanes of cars, bumper to bumper at sixty miles an hour, the road bed sounding much more hollow than it should, a super-loud thrumming that went right through you, lightened not only the head but the bowels so that as you walked in that melee of runners and cyclists you were like the deaf walking the plank. With only the vibrations to alert you to danger.

Why did Bobby choose such a place to meet? I wondered. Jesus, why did I let him get me into this? I swallowed an anxiety pill from the bottle I kept in my blazer pocket. Couldn't they just leave me alone? Why did everybody want a piece of me?

Slowly, I started to make my way to where Bobby and I had agreed to meet on the bridge. I snatched glances behind me every split-second, ready to twist and turn away from an attacker. Thousands of people, it seemed, were gaining on me. By giving an opponent only a bit of shoulder to hit, a half a hip, I would not only survive but retaliate, I thought. A darting elbow to the gut, a punch to the back of the head. Next time, he'd think twice about taking a run at Kyle Callendar.

A group of Midwesterners with sculpted white hair and Sears clothing seemed just like home so I'd stopped in my tracks to look at them, setting up to take a picture, two grandmas in foreground, with the Statue of Liberty in the setting sun. I was beginning to relax when I felt the vibration in the balls of my feet, whirled around to see a blur of blue metal and muscled body, black spandex head to toe, except for a bare white midriff. It was jetting toward me, would've run me down like a dog had I not been game-ready and barely got out of the way. "Hey," I cried, punching a fist in the air. "Hey, stop bitch," I shouted, but the black rider never heard a thing. She was gone, roaring up the bridge, parting the sea of people, unstoppable, like Sidney Crosby on a breakaway.

The Midwesterners with the camera turned their backs on me, the grandmas tut-tutted. A sour-faced man with a briefcase shook his head no, as if my fist were holding flyers for a new restaurant. A theme place celebrating vigilantes, Bernhard Goetz, Stephen Bunce, Michael Douglas in *Falling Down*. Others—women, children, men, it didn't matter—no one looked my way. I could've been in a chicken suit, standing on the edge of the bridge, threatening to end it all. So what? Get out of the way.

It was close to eight o'clock and I still had a fair piece to walk to get to our meeting place, the bridge support on the Brooklyn side. But after the close shave with the woman bike rider, I moved even slower along the edge of the walkway. As long as I didn't look down, I was okay. In the distance I could see what must be Brooklyn on the other side. Warehouses along the waterfront, not-so-bad-looking houses, church spires. Lots and lots of church spires. More like home than I would ever have imagined possible.

Except that black demon on the bike lived there. In Brooklyn. I only saw it for a moment, but that woman's face was as menacing as anything I'd ever seen on the ice. It wasn't that she was looking to kill me, I thought. I'm sure she'd see it as my fault. She was on a record pace from Manhattan to Brooklyn; her previous best: three minutes, sixteen seconds. Hey, maybe even tonight she did beat it, the world record, something she'd post on the Internet, collect the reward. She did the bridge run three hundred days a year, knew it like the back of her hand, so who was I to intrude? She'd timed my walking pace and was keyed to speed through the spot I had vacated when I had stopped unexpectedly. It was my luck and her sheer skill that there had been no collision. An accident would've set her training back weeks, maybe months.

I stopped halfway across the bridge and stood pressed tight against the railing, away from heavy traffic. The wind flapped my trousers like flags as I watched the sun set. The last time I'd seen a face like that black demon's, Cody and my schoolmates were there with me. That day when we'd penned Trudy Phillips, the new girl in sixth grade. She was scared, sure, who wouldn't be, with boys pushing and pawing at her as if she were a dumb animal. And then she approached me, Kyle Callendar, who if there was a God, she was thinking, would've given way, let her escape. But instead, I pushed her hard in the breasts, sent her crashing down on the ground to the roar of my friends. I felt as alive as I ever had in my life, and then Trudy Phillips gave me the blackest, meanest look I'd ever seen until that bike racer almost ran me down at forty miles an hour.

"Excuse me," said a girl's voice. A toddler had pushed her stroller and grazed my feet as she passed. Blond curly locks spun down the back of a sky-blue sundress. She was in bobby socks and Nike trainers. "Thank you," she said with a smile. Walking next to her, in matching green jogging gear, was a handsome couple, talking a mile a minute, "Merck and Lilly," "sixty points," "BAM," "bouillabaisse"—snatches of words, all rammed together, as if on a string, like the interwoven steel girders that lined this bridge to Brooklyn, where even this good-looking family seemed happy as could be to be heading. "Bye, bye," said the little girl with the bed-time of a grownup as I stood and stared, dazed, fighting back tears as she walked away and disappeared into the crowd.

Not far away, I saw Bobby standing before a plaque. It was attached to one of the castle-like bridge supports, which wasn't so much in the shape of an Absolut bottle but I could see where they got the idea. Bobby was just as I remembered him. Struggling, even as a tourist, lips mumbling the words on the plaque. And for some reason, New Yorkers were showing him a touch of kindness. Pedestrians, joggers, and cyclists weaved about him like spring runoff around a rock.

"Bobby boy," I said, clapping him on the back, "I would've thought you'd got your fill of reading engravings last summer."

"Kyle," he said, as if he were surprised to see me. "Kyle Callendar." If it were possible, Bobby looked even dopier than the last time I'd seen him. Paler but with bigger muscles. Like he'd spent the year working out under a forty-watt bulb.

"What are you reading here, Bobby?" I said, not trying to hide my annoyance.

"I was waiting for a while, Kyle. I tried waiting in different places and I was beginning to think that I'd missed you. So, I thought if I stood here in the middle of the bridge, in front of this plaque, that'd you'd see me." He smiled blankly as if he were back home on a bridge over the South Saskatchewan.

I didn't know what I was thinking. More lame hope, it seemed, that I could somehow get close to a man. Of course, a stooge like Bobby Shriver was incapable of being anything like a friend. I had half a mind to turn around and leave. God, what I would've done for a drink.

"So how is your old man, Bobby?" I asked, tugging on my sleeve. I looked around me and patted a front pocket of my jeans, felt my wallet at my thigh.

"He's fine, Kyle. Busy as always," Bobby said. A gust of wind blew his hair back from his forehead, and I imagined Bobby at fifty, a round head in the reflection of a glass jar of scrub nails. With many projects on the go but nothing that he cares about.

A Chinese man bumped me and didn't say sorry. I said, "Hey," but didn't push back. Meanwhile, Bobby kept reading the plaque like early translation software. With so many words that didn't make sense that all meaning was distorted.

Emily Warren Roebling, I read on the plaque. The wife of Colonel Washington Roebling, the bridge builder, and daughter-in-law of John Roebling, who designed it. More than any other person, a woman was responsible for the bridge.

"So what do you make of that, Bobby?"

"Pardon me, Kyle. What'd you say?"

"This woman, Bobby," I said, pointing to the plaque. "Emily Roebling—what do you make of her?"

"Quite a woman, Kyle ... that was what I was just thinking when you arrived."

Bobby folded his hands on his stomach and returned his gaze to the plaque.

"Was it easy to get here?" he asked.

Damn him, I thought. Goddamn them all. Why did I come? And why in the world here, in the wind, forty stories above the river? I could see people walking along the Brooklyn waterfront like ants, and my stomach sank.

"Piece of cake," I said, shrugging my shoulders. "Except for a woman bike racer that nearly ran me down. Thank God for Emily Roebling. She's made it possible for criminals from Brooklyn to walk to Manhattan in twenty minutes, or ride a stolen bike in three-sixteen flat."

"Gosh, I'm sorry you had that scare," Bobby said, looking down to the boardwalk. In the waning light, his hair looked good, even thick. "New York can be a bit much."

I sighed, nodded my head, and shot glances around us to see if we were alone. Nobody. Just joggers and tourist families, bikers and a businessman with his sports coat on his shoulder, holding a briefcase.

Again, Bobby returned to study the plaque. For a moment, his eyes looked focused, even thoughtful. "You know, there's something to this," Bobby said. "I had no idea how amazing this bridge would be. I mean look at the people who come up here to see it." He jerked his head toward an overlook where Japanese tourists were rooted to their spots like pegs in a cribbage board. "Can you imagine what it must have been like when it was being built? It must have been one hell of a big deal. Like the greatest thing in the world. And you know what? It was all because of a woman," he said with an ache of wonder.

"Yeah," I said. I reached out and touched him on the shoulder. "That's right, Bobby."

"I was standing here thinking that I don't know the first thing about women, Kyle. Not really. Groupies and party girls, sure, but what do I know about real women? About somebody like Emily Roebling? What do I know about somebody like her?"

"I don't know, Bobby. I don't know what to tell you."

He closed his eyes, just like he did that first moment with the Cup, and rocked back on his feet. Like he was in a trance, reciting a meditation he'd long rehearsed that anyone with good sense would know not to interrupt.

My heart was racing. I felt the paper target rushing toward me. If only I had a gun, I thought. I'd blow a hole in Bobby and not blink an eye. Men would always do that. Promise closeness then shut down. Cody and the Great Escape. Doug and his vague need to help. His father, Ron, and brother, Jim. Wayne, the therapist. Virgil, the backstabber. My own father. The promise of a million connections buried in silence. Lost under countless yards of wallpaper stuck to last.

"Dad wanted me to ask you, Kyle, if you'd consider being a governor in a new league, the World Hockey League," Bobby said finally. "News of it hasn't broken in the press yet. It was what he wanted to talk to you about that day at the airport. Later, Virgil came to that Really Old Timers game in Keppel to discuss it with you. He said he looked for you after the game but couldn't find you. Remember? With your contacts with minor hockey associations, kids' groups, and Lions Clubs, we could really build support."

Do you know about the "show" as it relates to women, Bobby? I thought, my lips trembling. I was away, lost, imagining my own script for the plaque. Bobby, his eyebrows raised, was frozen before me, waiting for an answer. Moon-faced, less because of the empty whiteness of his look than because, except for one fleeting moment, neither the moon nor Bobby had ever encountered human life.

The show was sex with a girl, the rest of the team watching, Bobby. Related to the "rodeo" when a girl is penned in and rode, and the "pulling train" when one guy after another has sex with a girl.

Bobby grabbed my arm or I would have collapsed on the boardwalk. "Kyle, can you hear me? Are you all right?"

I shook my head as I struggled to regain my balance. I had never been so tired. Of living with silences, I thought. Was there a man I could trust? Or a woman? And Emily Roebling and Gwen Martinson were angels, not women. Like the angel I'd heard about who rescued a teenaged girl who was starving herself to death, took her to France, and fed her crackers, cocoa, and wine, saved her life. Gwen had moved to town in Keppel, an apartment on the bay. Where birds hovered in a finger-paint sun at the Grain Elevator, squawking gulls, dervishes on the wind, riding the updraft, the curlicue of Arabic, each one slightly different, spelling a psalm. I imagine Gwen, a woman I hardly knew but who had my father in ways no one else had, can't read the psalms but somehow understands.

Of course, Bobby and all of them didn't want me. Not really. They wanted only one thing. For me to clam up. Like a good little girl. Like my own mother, cowering before my tyrant father. Lying in bed at night, hoping against hope that the old man didn't wake up and hear me leaving the house before a game day. He'd have whaled the tar out of me if he'd known. I'd have been thrashed with the strap while Mother clammed up to beat the band.

Bobby held me tight by the elbow until I could stand on my own. I thanked him and we watched as a tugboat pulled a barge out to sea. Why didn't I follow Cody up and along the Keppel Harbour train bridge? Now more than anything, I wished I could be on that barge. Away from Bobby, Norma, everybody.

I pulled my arm from Bobby's grasp, jammed my hands in the front pockets of my trousers. In my life, I'd always done what was asked of me. Never said what I've truly wanted.

"Dad just wants you to think about it, Kyle," Bobby said. "No need to get back to him right away. He had taken such a liking to you. Doesn't happen every day, I can tell you."

Darkness fell like a castle gate. Bobby, a great shadowy lump, and I walked closer to Emily Roebling's plaque, now indecipherable on the immense stone wall.

Bobby jerked his head around to look at a clock tower. "I don't have much time," he said. "Can I tell Dad that you'll think about it?"

"Go," I said, avoiding his outstretched hand. Bobby and I talked a bit longer about nothing in particular, and eventually he left and walked to Brooklyn as I stared at the horizon and the empty barges heading off to sea.

chapter twenty-one

It was always at night. That's what comes back to me about Saskatoon, the golden prairie sun slipping away. That evening on the picnic table with the Cowplands. The Brooklyn Bridge. When everything begins to unravel.

We didn't get on the bus until 11 p.m., going back to Keppel from Tiverton, Keady, Desboro, Walters Falls, Wingham, Goderich, Peaver, Rondeville, Galt, Shelburne. Forty times a season. Always late. After the game, we'd all be bushed because Coach travelled with only three forward lines, four defence pairings, and two goalies—the lightest bench in junior hockey. Coach Fleming stressed cohesion and consistency. That's what mattered, he said. That built champions. Maximize ice time for maximum effort—and maximum fatigue on the road home.

You never get used to the smell at the back of the bus. You'd think you would but you don't. Coach strung a blue velveteen curtain across the two seats adjacent to the toilet. It was heavy, like a wall, trapping in the stink of shit and piss, laced with the blue noxious chemical that makes me sick as a dog even now. All the air travel I did with the Stanley Cup, and never once did I visit the onboard washroom because of the slimy swirl of that blue poison.

"C'mon," Coach said that first time, touching me on the top of my head. He stank of musk and whisky. I had been sleeping in an aisle seat next to pint-size wing Nelson McConachie. In the middle of the night, a highway motorcoach is white-trash romance: the thrum of the motor, faint lights at the luggage rack, deep-pile headrest.

"C'mon, Kyle, I want to talk to you."

I was exhausted. (Where were we? A sign for Dundalk, Mandrake, then black, a void.) But it was Coach, so I snapped up and out of my seat, followed him down the aisle. Except for the driver, not another soul was stirring.

"This way, walk this way."

I look back and hate myself. Those wide-pipe corduroys were dead giveaways. Keppel was a town of cotton work pants, polyester dress slacks, overalls. No one else wore trousers like that. And it'd been weeks since they'd been washed—let alone folded. His shirt-tail was out, trailing down his leg. I told myself Coach Fleming was allowed. He was the best in the business, eccentric in his way, a man who'd throw hockey sticks on the ice to protest what he saw as a bad call, who never failed to protect the rights of a player defending his patch of ice, give hell to teammates who didn't do the same. A team guy whose players made Junior A year after year. A hockey man. All the way.

Coach pulled back the velveteen curtain and asked me to go inside. That was all he said. No promises of being made captain of the team, of more ice time, even sitting in the front of the bus. Coach peeled back the curtain and invited me to join him. He had deep smile lines and dimples and ear lobes that were two and a half times normal size, but otherwise he was an attractive man. He smiled at me, touched my butt, held the curtain open and I didn't even hesitate. Despite the stench of shit and piss and that terrible blue poison. In silence, because that was the way it was done, was always done.

My guilty pleasure.

chapter twenty-two

Madison Square Garden has the worst ice in the business, but everybody wants to play there. It's Broadway for plays, Carnegie Hall for bands, the Garden for hockey. You want to win in New York because of the little phrase, "If you can make it here, you can make it anywhere." And in pro hockey, not only can you make it but you don't even have to sweat it. All you have to do is show up to beat the Rangers.

That wasn't so in 1994, the one year in the last seven decades that the Rangers won the Cup. But this time around, the final against the Dallas Stars was shaping up to be a real stinker. In the first two games in Dallas, the Stars won by 7–1 and 6–0, and writers with a sense of history were recalling mismatches like the New York Islanders–Vancouver Canucks series of 1982, back-to-back lopsided losses by the St. Louis Blues to the Montreal Canadiens in 1969 and the Boston Bruins in 1970. The puck began bouncing the Rangers' way in the third game, and they held on to win 4–3. But the game we were working in New York returned to form: fans roared when a third-liner potted a rebound after only two minutes of play, but before the first period was over the game was 3–1 Dallas, and out of reach for the Rangers. At the end of the first period, half the audience had split uptown to buy T-shirts at the Disney Store, while others hailed beer men in the stands.

Doug and I were in a Garden storage room, guarding the Stanley Cup and watching a TV monitor mounted from the ceiling. The game may've sucked but New York was good for leather-padded recliners and beer and soda in an ice bucket. Diehard Doug was watching TV with the intensity of a cat, occasionally swallowing long draughts of beer. Earlier I'd told Doug about my visit with Bobby, his offer to me about the World Hockey League. He'd nodded said it sounded like a good deal to him, what did I have to lose. Then he fell silent and turned to watch the game. What to me was friendship, the distance of not telling.

"I saw this boy in Central Park today," Doug said, staring at the boxes that lined the place. Kootenay Spring drinking water, Mr. Clean, sweep compound, wax polish, bum wipe, paper towels, air fresheners. The TV was showing a baby chick between two eggshells. An insurance sponsor.

Doug twisted the top off a beer and gulped half of it down. "I like to go up to this place, Bethesda Fountain. You've seen it. Remember that Mel Gibson movie we rented the other night? Where the kid was snatched? That's the place. To get to Bethesda Fountain, you have to go down a slew of stone steps that have attracted skaters like you've never seen. Inline freestylers go up and down those steps at breakneck speeds, doing mid-air spins, jumps, flips. Unbelievable."

Mike Modano fired the puck into the Rangers' zone, veered to centre, glomming to Rangers as they crept up ice. Neutral-zone trap. Wet blanket on the fire wagon.

"Did you ever see these new Rollerblades, Kyle?" Doug said, as he pulled from a bag a pair of silver and blue inline skates and handed them to me. "The best boots are feather-light now, with wheels that'll spin in a strong breeze."

The skates were beautiful. Leather and Lycra blend, light but sturdy, with a form-fitted boot. The wheels were big and did spin freely with barely a touch.

"Put them on," I said, giving them back to Doug. "Show me." I popped a Coke from the bucket and sipped it. The second period was ten minutes old, and neither team had had what you could call a scoring chance. A long shot by Blair Betts rebounded off the Dallas goalie's blocker. The camera hadn't shown the Dallas end enough to identify Marty Turco between the pipes.

Doug slipped on the skates and did a series of back-crossovers, circling the recliners. Faster and faster he went, then in wider loops, as if he were on ice, not concrete, until he was skating backwards along the periphery of the polished floor, skirting the supply boxes, leaping a mop handle. He stopped and picked up one of two hockey sticks tucked in a corner, and threw a street-hockey puck from a trouser pocket onto the floor. With one hand he knocked down the second stick and with his skate kicked it to me. I pushed the recliners aside, yanked a Kootenay Spring box out from against the wall as one goalpost, and arranged the Cup in its case as the other one. I'd just picked up the stick and struck the goalie's stance between the two "posts," when I saw a flash of orange out of the corner of my eye and kicked out my right foot to catch a piece of the puck that Doug had fired low to the stick side. It hit the Cup's case with a wallop and lay outside the goal.

I whirled into a shooting position and let fly a slapshot. It slammed knee-high near Doug, breaking the surface of a toilet-roll box, where it burrowed somewhere inside.

Doug punched the hole bigger, dug into the box, and flipped out onto the floor a roll of toilet paper still in its wrapping. "Time to slow it down a little," Doug said, as he skated in a figure eight, stickhandling with the paper roll. Doug stopped at the top of the slot, and with the blade of his stick jammed into the fold of the wrapping, he raised his stick to his shoulder so that the toilet-paper roll was attached to his stick like a ball to a lacrosse stick. He whipped the roll and stick in the air, twice, I think, but it was a blur, I couldn't really say how many times he whipped his "puck," and a cloud engulfed me, a swirl of white that I couldn't size up, and I lunged forward, grabbing as much white as I could, but it wasn't enough and it wasn't the main part with the cardboard roll, just shreds of toilet paper that I clung to in my arms as the bulk of the paper was in the net, resting a good foot or so beyond the left goal post, the Stanley Cup.

Doug fell to the floor beside me and we laughed until we cried, dabbing tears with the paper.

Wayne Strachan opened the door a crack and peered inside. "You guys all right in there?"

"Peachy, Wayne. Just peachy," Doug said.

Wayne walked into the room. He was in parade form—for

retired shrinks from Saskatchewan. A double-breasted suit layered with a topcoat, narrow lapels. His fedora was sharp and small. Except for his Dumbo ears I wouldn't even have recognized him.

"You look great, Wayne. Just great," I said, getting up from the floor.

"You, I'm not so sure about," Wayne said as he peeled a toilet-paper shred off me and held it in mock disgust.

"Just letting off some steam," I said as I stretched an arm to him and he pulled me to my feet. Doug watched us from a prone position on the floor, a bent arm propping himself up.

"Hey," Doug said, "c'mon Wayne, let's see what you can do."

"Nah, I don't think—"

"C'mon, you've seen me cut the ice in Keppel, even doing a little road shinny. I'd like to see what you can do," Doug said as he skated to the far corner of the room and picked up a third stick. He dug into the toilet-paper box, snatched another wrapped roll, rung it with two twists of electrical tape that he found on a shelf. Doug skated back to Wayne and me. "For you, m'lord," he said, dropping to one knee and presenting the stick and toilet roll to Wayne as he bowed his head.

"Okay, you win," Wayne said, laughing as he slipped off his topcoat and jacket and hung them on a hook on the wall.

"That would appear to be so," Doug said. "Ah, yes, how could I forget? There's one more thing." He pulled an ice-cold Molson from the ice bucket and twisted off the cap. "Down the hatch," he directed as Wayne accepted the beer and drank about half of the bottle.

Wayne polished off his beer in the next swallow and Doug batted a pass to him. "I got it in me, boys," the shrink said, stick-handling the "puck." "You know, Wayne, the Great One?"

"The Grey One, you mean," I said from my goalie crouch.

"No, my boy," Wayne said, getting into it, lord of the lame line. "The Great One," he said, with a sneaky smile. "My namesake. The man known the world over by a single name. Think Pelé, Jordan, Gretzky. The boy who at twelve years old skated in alone between periods against the old pro Les Binkley, gave him a head shift, a

backhand deke—and was stopped. Only this twelve-year-old
didn't hang his head, look away, or shrug. He slammed his stick on
the ice in disgust … The Great Ones, my friend, don't ever think
they are going to lose."

I did the splits to my left, but the puck scooted by me ankle-
high, just inside the post. While yakking, Wayne had slid the puck
over to Doug who'd one-timed a shot into the net.

Upset with myself, I fished the puck out and passed it back to
Wayne. "C'mon let's try that again, Grey One."

"Sure," he said, smiling, "if you like."

Wayne and Doug huddled for a moment at the back of the
room. Wayne stayed with the puck and Doug skated in hard toward me as Wayne fired a shot. At the last second, Doug tilted the
blade of his stick, redirecting the puck between my legs. Another
goal.

"Now you get in net," I said, pointing at Wayne.

"I'd like to, Kyle," he said, with a half-smile. "But as you can see
I'm a natural as a forward, I don't think—"

"No, I insist, Wayne," I said, as I stepped out toward him. He
pressed his hands down his knit trousers, grey with blue flecks,
tailored to cuffs. Italian loafers. Try as I might but with Wayne
sometimes I couldn't help myself. With Doug, it was easy, just
guys together. Wayne, though, for all his hockey knowledge, his
tired one-upmanship, obscure stories of Gretzky for God's sake,
knew nothing of The Game, the call for your head from shooters
between periods, mullet heads, beery and wide-stepping, ditzes
in pyjamas, the puck every time missing the gap in the net, the
prize, a commuter flight to Boston, a dinner for four at Two
Guys. Maybe I was right that day back in Saskatchewan, when
I had my doubts about him. Wayne'd help me, sure—right to
the unemployment line. Jesus, why didn't I see it, what he was
really about? He made me sick—that smile, that smirk of the
Saskatoon shrink, not aiming to help, to bring me, along, to
insist to the Hall that I deserved one last chance, but to double
deal for the man, to put Kyle of Keppel out of there, out on his
big faggot ass. Again.

"You get in net," I said, biting off each word.

Doug skated in between us. "C'mon guys, let's break for a bit. Have a drink. Watch the game, the Rangers are starting to get some shots," he said. I looked up at the set. Four minutes remained in the second period. Still 3–1, Dallas. The Rangers did have the Stars by a two-to-one advantage in shots, the TV guys said; it was only a matter of time before the Rangers broke through. Sucker lines meant to keep the viewers from surfing, the advertisers happy. The Rangers' shots were all from outside, bad angles. No movement through centre ice. A ratings bust.

"I'd like to take a shot at you all right," I said to Wayne.

"Kyle, please. This isn't any way to act," Wayne said, putting his hockey stick on the floor. "Let's sit down and talk this out."

"I've had enough," I cried, flinging my stick. It thumped against the wall and clattered on the floor. "Talk, talk, talk. I don't see where it's got me."

"We've been helping you, Kyle," Wayne said. "It's been working." He stopped and looked at my stick on the floor. "It was you boys who wanted to play," he said with a shrug. "It wasn't my idea."

"Good that you should be doing something that's not your idea," I yelled at him. "Now get in that net!"

Doug turned to face me. "I think we've had enough, Kyle," he said, putting a hand on my shoulder.

I jerked away from Doug and glared at him. "Don't you patronize me, Doug Cowpland. Don't you think I know what's going on? You guys want me to believe that you're my friends, but you don't give a damn about me," I said, poking my finger hard into Doug's chest.

"And you," Doug said, grabbing me hard by the shoulder. I swung to take a punch at him. But he grabbed me by the wrist and twisted my arm behind my back. I struggled, but Doug pressed on the arm and it hurt like hell so I stopped. "What about you?"

"What's that? What do you mean?"

"When are you going to start giving a damn about yourself?" he hissed into my ear.

chapter twenty-three

Cody Rhéaume's family had the biggest front lawn on our street in Keppel. Our place was one of several row houses across the street and our neighbours were mostly a sad bunch, retired couples with too much time on their hands, who played canasta on plastic table covers and in mid-afternoon, puttered in a backyard big enough for a button rose garden but not much else.

So the kids on the block played at Cody's. His house was a dump, with windows boarded up, half-filled buckets and pots in the kitchen and dining room to catch the roof leaks in case of rain. But we never played inside. Instead, we grabbed a sponge rubber ball and wooden bat in summer, a hockey stick and skinned tennis ball in spring and fall, and played on the lawn.

At first, Roland Miles liked it that we played there. Roland's father, Stan, was Cody's next-door neighbour. Roland lived away most of the year, but late in the spring he'd come to his father's house and stay until Labour Day. Once, I was inside the place. Mom was holding a package for the Mileses, and one day she had me deliver it to them when I came home from school. Roland's house was a freestanding bungalow with white aluminum siding and faux stone. But a few steps beyond the door it was another world. The walls were lined with books from floor to ceiling, shelves upon shelves of them, packed in like bricks in mortar.

Roland was nice enough as I walked into the vestibule and handed the package to him, which had to be more books, more printed words. In my father's house we had no books, only manuals for gardening, home repair, *Reader's Digest.* "Please do stay a while. I've baked some biscuits," Roland said in what sounded like an English accent. Roland Miles was a university professor in Toronto. Mom said he had more learning than everyone on the block put together. Rather than take him up on his offer, wander through that place of room after room of books, I found I couldn't breathe, as if I were in *Dr. No* with walls of books closing in on me, smothered by words that I'd never know, places I'd never visit. "Thanks," I muttered, "but I got to go," and I turned and dashed to the safety of the street.

That summer Roland and Stan, who ran a hardware store on Main Street until he retired, would come out of the house with webbed lawn chairs, unfold them at the edge of their property, and sit down to watch us play ball. Cody's house was built on the back of the lot because a stream ran underground through the middle of their property. We played ball on his front lawn, which was sandwiched on either side by houses that were built in the middle of their lots. To hit the north wall of Stan's place was a pretty good smash, a ground-rule home run, and it would happen from time to time. But it seemed okay with Roland and Stan. In fact, when the ball hit the wall, they would rise from their seats and give us warnings, finger-wagging sessions that first worried us, but then made us smile because we could see them grinning to themselves afterward.

Roland, a fat man in sweatpants and a grandfather's shirt, would sit in his lawn chair with a book open on his lap, smoking a pipe and watching us play ball for hours, even after Stan had grown tired, folded up his lawn chair, and gone inside the house. That summer we played morning, noon, and night, only breaking for meals that were wolfed down in a flash, and Roland would eat then, too, and return to sit, smoke his pipe and glance at his open book, and watch us boys at play until there was no light in the sky and quietly he would go inside.

Then one morning, Roland didn't come out. And neither did Stan. Mom said Stan was having spells, that he was lucky to have a devoted son like Roland to take care of him but that it was only a matter of time for Stan.

I hit my streak then. We played a game in which you retained the right to continue hitting with each consecutive home run, and I found I couldn't miss. As a boy athlete, Gretzky once told CBC Radio that it was okay with him if he had a life in either hockey or baseball. The same was true for me. I slugged dipsy-doodle curves, caught up to fast balls, golfed pitches inches from the ground—all of them, it seemed, landing with thuds against the wall of Roland's father's house. I clobbered home run after home run, an amazing streak, my pals were saying, a record that would stand on the street for ever, until as Cody was preparing to throw another pitch, one that if I slugged would set that mark, a man who at first I didn't recognize came running onto the playing field. The body in the baggy off-white trousers was Roland's. But the face was beet red and wrinkled. Smushed berry on barn board.

"Stop it! Stop it!" he cried as he ran through our short centre field. Roland lunged forward as players scattered. "He's dying. You're killing my father."

I looked at Roland from home plate as if I'd seen him for the first time. Everyone else had fled from the game, left the field in fear. But I hadn't moved. Roland had never done anything to me. Never more than a howdy-do after that invitation to stay for cookies. Nothing beyond "Hi, Kyle. Beautiful day, isn't it? Tell your mother and father I said hello."

Roland stopped at the pitcher's mound, and I didn't take a step out of the batter's box, didn't drop the bat. He raised his soft white hands. "Please, please stop. My father is on the other side of that wall. You can't believe what it sounds like in there. The last one you hit, I think it brought on a heart attack. An ambulance is coming."

"We're just playing," I said.

"You're killing him," he shouted. "Don't you get it? If you keep it up, I'm going to call the police." Then Roland ran back to the house like my mother in an emergency—elbows and knees flopping like fish.

Roland slammed the door to the house. I ran my fingers up the shaft and nodded to Cody, who had run back onto the pitcher's mound. His last throw was a slider, breaking low and away, but I managed to get the barrelhead of the bat on the pitch, and drove it with power, my best of the day. The record homer hit our neighbour's wall of books like a cannonball.

I had no more to drink than anyone else after the game. Outside of my Gardens hat trick it was the best I'd ever played. There were no drugs, no uppers or downers, no Benes, not a sniff of coke. Rounds of draft at the "I," the Islington House in Toronto, on the house, sure. What would you expect? I was in the second year with the Kingston Canadians and we'd doubled up on the Baby Leafs, 4–2. I scored the winning goal, set up Doug for the empty netter. "More beer for the Canadians, the Kingston Canadians," the bartender said after I was carried in on the boys' shoulders like a native chief on a travois. "Good on you, Kyle," he said, clapping me on the back. Sawdust and worn oak flooring, the back of a sleeve across our kissers. Sixty-cent beers for free, one after the other because we were going to stay over, spend the night, a matinee the day after tomorrow in Oshawa, so Coach had given us the evening off, and draft beer after victory will go down like gulps of air on a mountain trail.

"Hey, Callendar," Doug said, "wait up." That's what he told me he said anyway, because at that point my memory got patchy. He and the guys were stuck on the idea that I was going to be somebody. On that night they could smell it. "Watch and learn," Doug said his dad told him. "That Kyle Callendar is the one." Nothing ordinary about you, Doug told me afterward, even the way I left the "I," slipping out through the crowd so soundlessly that had Doug not felt a twinge in his back where he took a late hit, and twisted to ease the pain, he would've missed me. "Kyle, wait for me," Doug said.

Snow slithered off my team jacket. Soft flakes that didn't grip, not even on the seams. In the gathering storm Doug could see me, a red beacon in the fog, moving steadily, relentlessly, away.

"Stop, wait up." What else could he say? Not that he gave it much thought. Not that any of them did. They only wanted to be close, to have me by their side. So that some of me might rub off.

In a Toronto snowstorm the light smears but never so much that you can't see where to take a step. Slowly, Doug follows in my footsteps through the drifts. The story becomes his because at this point I black out, remember nothing. I am far from Doug now, a ruby smudge in smoke, but the footprints are mine. Big and sure, no slippage on the edge, Doug says. For hours, it seems, we walk in this way.

The footprints lead to a covered parking lot. On the lot are Chevys, Fords, Toyotas, four-by-fours, Volkswagens, Lincolns. More blue cars than other colours; station wagons, compacts, an Oldsmobile, forest green Delta 88. One truck, a Mack, taking up two spaces, where the footprints end, and Doug makes his way to it in the middle of the lot. He bends down under the cab of the Mack and sees me. I'm on my back on the pavement, my head propped up in my hands, staring at him with old man's eyes, not knowing him. Finally, Doug reaches in and says "C'mon, Kyle, let's go home," and after a long time I take his hand and pull myself up and out of that place.

I really didn't stand a chance. Drink will do that, I suppose. The speed of the music, ZZ Top, "La Grange." All of us in Keppel in such a hurry to grow up, like comets on a country road, never stopping for a red light. Stoked to the gills with hormones and booze and resentment for any difference you can see, a gap between what is possible and what is. Nothing that you can foresee, but when I'd come home from Kingston before I turned pro, I could see it in the set of their bones. No threat stirred hatred in the Keppel young so much as a boy who had done good. The property of the headline writers, salesmen, girls. Better to stay in the abstract. Not go to a party where I'd gone a dozen times, Victoria Blackwood's house, and leaving by myself at dawn, a little too drunk, taking the back road to avoid the cops, stopping for a boulder in the middle of the road. A crab that has lost a pincer doesn't shrink from battle, fights with even greater determination, the humiliation like an injection, a jolt of fearlessness because what he has lost can never be recovered. He is forever lost, a cripple, angered by fate. Like the drunk who burst out of the darkness that night. Who before I could react, to slam down the car door lock, had thrown open my door and begun to kick and punch me in the face with such speed and ferocity I thought that I was someone else. Floating above it. Only now as I touch a spot near the bridge of the nose, pinch it so that I feel a hint of the pain, do I think how lucky I was that night, that people can be killed in such gales of hatred by men, cripples without headlines.

Until now, my life had always been open and shut. Respect where you come from. Do what comes natural. In many ways, I'm not much different from that twelve-year-old boy whose love for The Game killed a father in his bed. I'll read game sheets, box scores, but probably never crack open a book, get to some deeper place where respect goes beyond where you come from. I wanted understanding, sure, but at what cost? What really did I know about my own father? What but these collected memories of a man who, for reasons that I'd never really given much thought to, had always shown a conflicted but genuine love for me? Didn't he take me to be the Lamplighter of Niagara, build the rink in the barn, take pictures of me with the Super 8, grab my hand at the Hall? What value did I place on that? Wasn't he doing the best he could? He was no Coach Fleming for God's sakes. I'd never found the courage to tell him about what Coach Fleming did to me, or the hazing I'd suffered in Kingston. Instead, I was driven to see the worst in Dad because of what I'd been through. Forever bracing for the blow to the head that had never come.

When I close my eyes, two memories come. I'm on a lakeshore at summer sunset with a beautiful girl, desperately wanting her, but playing catch with myself instead, throwing the ball again and again with all my might into the air against the rose-coloured sky. The other I'm in skates on ice, an endlessly shifting variation with legs moving like wings in flight.

The summer beauty rolled her eyes and let me be. Saved herself. To love an athlete is to be in the shadow of The Game, the blank spaces of feelings withheld, a half-life. What Fred Shero said, "Life is just a place where we spend time between games." I wanted Norma, sure. But until now these had always been the only terms.

I'd imagine Dad's country was of first things, too. If another truck hit a crossroads at the same time as him, Dad jutted his finger at the rival, an attack inches from the wheel. Proceed at your own risk. I see him, too, as a farmer in haying season. Standing on a hill against a sky by the sea. From his spot on the hill, Father can see for miles, arms akimbo, watching to see that his boy on the tractor is doing the job just right. We were in so many ways the same man. Yet we lived as if were we gays in the military: don't ask, don't tell. Countries devoted to containment, living lives of undeclared war.

But that was then. I was determined to know more. If I were going to heal I needed to better understand my father. I was the boy who killed a father in his bed, who showed no mercy in menacing a girl, who in a moment of personal glory walked in a snowstorm to lie under the cab of a truck, the kind my father would drive. Kill the silence, I finally realized. What I had to do.

The night after the row with Wayne I had a dream. Doug and I are skating onto a rink, for more than a moment blinded by a light, able to see only shapes of people in the stands, as we glide to centre to find, on either side of the faceoff dot, two brilliant red sweaters. With no fancy designs. Only the letters C-A-N-A-D-A stitched large in white, and on the back our last names and the numbers we used in the NHL.

We give up a goal and Sheldon Shriver fires his straw boater from the grandstand, and others a see-through visor, a Dow 10000 cap, a prim fedora, a flapper hat that looks like a converted bra cup, triple C.

At the faceoff, Doug draws the puck cleanly to me, I get a step on what looks like Rostov, the Russian I'd met in Saskatoon, and put my body between him and the puck, pass to Doug, who works wide on Bjorn Skajjit, the Norwegian, dumps a saucer over Rostov's outstretched stick, to me in the slot and I don't miss. The goal siren whines, 1–1.

In the stands, Bobby Shriver lifts Myra into space, backs arched like Russian pairs. Wilma Rangford heaves her bonnet onto the rink.

Sweat pours from me like a bath. A single item hangs on the bare walls of our dressing room: a vintage Stanley Cup calendar of the Toronto Maple Leafs, 1967. The last time Toronto, the great Canadian hope, had won the Cup. The months are torn through May, with the winning date circled.

Stanley Cup Callendar.

You never know what's going to come to you between periods. Coach can't foresee the steam shovel digging up the bottom of a swamp. A garden rake over your intestines. Coach can only keep the door closed, try to stop what's outside from coming in, put his trust in what's inside.

So much is known without being said. Before you take in the fluids you're like a waif in the desert. A hair-trigger from fainting but incredibly aware. A plant sending tendrils deep in the earth, taking root. Doug says nothing to me, and I convince myself he, too, will never go back. Not to Old Woman's River Community Arena, where Doug's the rink rat, the mongrel of revulsion and awe. He knows our secret is safe.

Me, I didn't know what would become of me after The Game. What about Norma? My father?

Then I see the Cup, the one in which in an earlier dream I couldn't for the life of me make out the single name engraved on its surface. We go out to the rink for the final period, and for the first time I allow myself to think that it could be my name. My name on the Stanley Cup.

On the ice we see openings, the places where possibilities begin. A boy shudders on a bridge. A man struggles with the terror that is his past. For that single moment, skating around the rink, holding aloft the gleaming Stanley Cup for all to see. A light that will never go out, not now, not ever.

The Game is ours, the score just a statistic, like the temperature. Which is hot. As hot as I'd ever been.

It's teenagers, mostly, who come to Bethesda Fountain in Central Park. Some are older, in their twenties, early thirties, with shaved heads in yards of cotton clothing, with no elastic bands, material fluttering in the breeze. Just after dawn the skaters approach singly and in pairs like great black birds. Their features are feral too, sharp and bony, suggesting a hunger that isn't about food. Not easily filled up.

It was a short walk to Bethesda Fountain from the hotel. I awoke with a start from my hockey dream and rose to see the skaters that Doug had talked about.

The skaters sweep over the stone steps without breaking stride. One after the other, with no headgear or padding, they soar, touching down in ways that seem to increase their speed and control, as if they haven't rushed headlong into certain accident but have shot on a course through space. At the flat surface by the fountain they stop, and each pulls from a sheaf that is tied close to their chest, a metal hockey stick, the expandable, lightweight kind. Someone throws a puck on the ground, and the boys start to play.

They skate backwards around the fountain, passing the puck without looking. One boy sends the puck with his stick through the air to another, who draws it down from mid-air as if the stick and puck were made of Velcro.

Along the ledge of the fountain a motley collection of homeless men and women is gathered. More shadows than people, blots on concrete, amid dark plastic bags, terminally soiled cloth sacks.

A boy driving down the wing with the puck cuts back to an inside lane to avoid a check, drags the puck through his legs and switches the stick from his right hand to his left, and fires a snapshot. The puck slams into the "net," a family-size yogurt container. A homeless man rises to his feet and claps. "Attagirl," he says, as he moves among the other vague human shapes along the fountain ledge.

Suddenly, a player blows a whistle and pockets it. Two cops on mountain bikes appear on a pathway from the direction of the Central Park boathouse, and are pedalling like hell toward the skaters, who I now see are not boys at all but girls. Down the waterside path and up the Bethesda steps the girl skaters flee, vanishing like cockroaches from a light. The cops take the playing field, unsheathe their walking sticks, and poke the homeless bodies awake. Get up, get a move on. The park is open now. The tourists are coming.

When I was young I could no more allow a girl in my confidence than fly to the moon. Who did they think they were? No, life was defined by boys. In grade school, I remember Cody Rhéaume—and Smiley Picard and Tommy Marlboro.

Smiley knocked over the forty-seven parking meters in Keppel. Buried the loot in grandfather socks in Smiley's garage. And Tommy Marlboro once stole a shoebox full of Charlie Brown paperbacks from Ireland's Stationers. Tommy had bigger hands than the rest of us, and he palmed them and slipped them under his waistband so that Mr. Ireland couldn't see: *You're the Greatest, Charlie Brown*; *There's No One Like You, Snoopy*; *Here's to You, Charlie Brown*. On the playground, Tommy gave them like diamonds to his closest friends, and *There's No One Like You, Snoopy* still burns on a shelf of mine.

Smiley died in a Malaysian jungle, people say, carved up in chunks and shipped home, a different box once every five weeks for a year. Keppel lost track of Tommy Marlboro and Cody married a Toronto girl, works in computers in Scarborough, sends e-mail jokes to me that aren't meant for reply but never let up.

Sure, then, it is the girls that I've neglected, I thought on the way back to the hotel from Central Park. What Bobby was getting at when we were talking about Emily Roebling. Women not as victims and whores, but as winners, as champions. What I saw in those skaters, who weren't boys like Doug had thought but women, fighters like the demon bike racer on the Brooklyn Bridge and little Trudy Phillips, which of course now that I thought of it was who I had seen in Norma. What was always unfair of me. To see Norma as the girl who looked to me as saviour, as someone capable of being real. But I had denied Trudy, and in my relationship with Norma I'd laid on my own punishment, had always denied her what she wanted, the simple truth of my feelings. To ask her to take me back was the wrong question. Rather, more than anything else, I just wanted to talk to her. To share these thoughts with her. Norma would be, I told myself, happy to hear that.

I was a few blocks from the hotel when a newsstand headline stopped me in my tracks. "NEW ICE AGE," it said. For twenty-five cents I picked up a copy. "Lords of the Rink Start World Hockey League." The morning after the NHL game between New York and Dallas scored the lowest TV ratings of any sport in history, Sheldon and Virgil made their move. "The game is good, it will survive the idiots of the NHL," Sheldon said. Players in the new league would represent their home countries: Russia, the Czech Republic, Canada, Sweden, Finland, and the 3M States—Massachusetts, Minnesota, and Michigan. "Canada won't dominate," Sheldon said, "but at least we'll have a better than average shot. The NHL—how do you say it?—forget about it. During the first eighty years of Stanley Cup play only eighteen times did the winner NOT represent a Canadian team; in the past decade and counting that number is a fat zero. No Canadian teams have won. A Canadian is a northerner; we owe it to our history to bring the game back. Call it the True North Original Six."

"Congratulations," I said to Sheldon on the phone when I got back to the hotel. "And thank you for your offer to be a governor. I'd like to think about it, if I may."

"Sure," he said. "Kyle, you just take your time."

"Thanks," I said and hung up.

I didn't like to admit it but maybe Virgil was right, I thought as I lay in bed that night trying to sleep. The Game could fuck you up, and so far in my life it had. I could hear his voice, "Don't intrude on destiny, Kyle. Boys will be boys." What if Virgil had decided to inform on Coach Fleming, force him out of the game? Who was to say that the abuse wouldn't have been made public? My hockey career would've been over before it started. I never would've been the escort, had the chance to be governor of his new league, be a part of hockey history. Maybe now by joining with Sheldon Shriver in this plan, Virgil was in his own way making it up to me.

I'd begun to think I'd learned a thing or two. Like the little heckler said in Keppel, it was time for a new Callendar. But I would think hard and long before deciding. The next step had to be one I could live with.

chapter twenty-four

The raised blue of the maple leaf that I traced with my thumb helped stop my heart from racing. I'd been taking a super-aspirin for my chest pain, but the doctors said it was as important to try and contain excess stress, so on the way to Norma's art opening in Toronto I caressed the hat-trick puck in the open pocket of my overcoat. I eased into the recessed seat on the subway and felt the serrated edges of the maple leaf on the puck until I could sense the leaf on my heart itself, a soft cushion of leaves, one upon the other in a pile, fresh from the fall, no hard edges.

Norma and I had not seen each other in an age. I'd drifted that summer as far as Mexico after I'd received the offer from Sheldon, who'd given me until January to make up my mind. The Hall, too, would have me back. When I got a clean bill of health from Wayne, who I was going to see for what I hoped would be my final sessions in the fall. Just take care of yourself, they said. We'll call you.

That summer I showed up in the middle of the night on guys I used to play with in San Jose, LA, Pittsburgh. Slept on their couches, talked up old times, but they were married mostly and couldn't have me for more than a night or two, so I never got around to asking their advice on what I should do. Most, anyway, would've given their eye teeth to be back in The Game. I didn't want to lord it over them.

Later, on my way to Mexico, I stopped in a bookstore in a little town outside of Tucson. A local author had piled copies of his book, *The Christmas Tree Murders*, on a table, with a cover picture of a knife in the shape of a tree, a single glistening drop of blood at its tip. The book read like third grade, but on the flap was a description of a "Christmas tree," a knife with prongs along the side so that when twisted it pulled and tore more flesh, making a more life-threatening wound. I put the book back, and instead bought a black notebook and a couple of pens.

For a month I was in Mexico. Where Clint Eastwood and Chief Dan George were heading to in my favourite movie, *The Outlaw Josey Wales*. Where Josey wouldn't be a marked man. I stayed in a cheap hotel in Mexico City that a brochure said was once home to the writer D.H. Lawrence and wrote in the notebook. What Wayne had been saying for a long time would be good for me, keeping a dream journal, snatches of memory, but I'd never got around to it until Mexico. Mostly I sat in the hotel and wrote to the whir of the overhead fan, the tick-ticking of a little clock and the steady flow of falling water—from somewhere outside. No cantina music or nerve-rattling bus to be heard. I liked the enchiladas in mole sauce, beef tacos, messy burritos. One day in a place not far from my hotel I watched as a circle of Mexican boys—dressed in sloppy-fitting blue cotton pants and sucking on corn sweets—clustered around a water pipe on the street. One inserted some kind of stick and miraculously water, clear glorious liquid, spilled out onto the filthy pavement. The boys sucked on the spout for a long time and then collected their stick and raced away.

I wrote about the past year, from the day I met Frank Cattel in Saskatoon to the midnight interview with Ron Cowpland to the session with Doug at The Boy. But it was Norma I was stuck on. And my father. Both had shown their love for me—in different ways. Norma without reserve, for so long asking nothing from me in return. Father, too. Without him, there would have been no ice, no stage for my life. He may not have shown me love as other fathers did, but there was truth in him. I wouldn't have been able to get to the point where I was now, travelling in an underground train to see Norma again, if not for the example of my father's strength. I may never know what shaped my father's life, what it was, if anything, in the war, perhaps. Or as a boy. But he chose not to tell me anything, would rather show not tell. When architect Louis Kahn fell and died on the floor of a public washroom, he'd scrubbed the address from the only identification he carried in his wallet. Personal lives of some men would never be known; sons were left to pick up the pieces as best they could. Bury yourself in your work, son.

A month after returning from Mexico, I saw that Norma had a show coming up at a Toronto gallery and I tracked her number down on the Internet. She seemed happy to hear from me, but she said she was busy, asked if I could call back later, say after dinner, when she'd be freer to talk.

She answered on the first ring at 9 p.m. We chit-chatted about this and that, had some laughs. Got on about the weather of all things, an old joke, that people who had nothing to say to each other would obsess about the weather, an early warning sign of a relationship in trouble. Finally, she said that what she couldn't get out of her mind since I'd called earlier in the day was the avocado incident.

"What's that?" I said. "I don't know what you're talking about."

"You don't remember?" she said.

"No," I said with a laugh. "But don't hold it against me. Just tell me, okay?"

"I went down to visit you in Pittsburgh, your rookie year," Norma said. "You'd been living in a hotel, certain that you were going to be sent to the minors."

"Sure, I remember," I said. "Coach told me I should get an apartment, and I did. I was over the moon. It was one thing to get the call up, but when I got that first place—"

"Right," Norma said, "and when you did, you sent me a plane ticket to come to Pittsburgh and celebrate with you. Well then—"

"Of course. You insisted on curtains. It was a walk-up on a crappy street. Me, I was good to go without. It wasn't as if I had any neighbours who could even see inside if they wanted to."

"Do you want to hear the story of the avocado incident or not, Kyle?" Norma said.

"Yep. Sorry."

"You better be," she said, warming to the tale. "You're right, it was a pretty crappy neighbourhood, but there was this nice Italian deli on the corner and that first night we went there to get some groceries for dinner, chicken breasts, tomatoes, green and red and

purple peppers, garlic, onions and olives, lemon. At a wine store
next door we picked up the only Italian red in the place. We were
loaded for bear and as happy as could be.

"Then we spied on the counter by the cash register a basket
full of green fruit. They were hard as rocks, and the clerk said they
were avocados, but neither of us had ever seen one before, so he
could have said they were hand grenades. You sure you don't remember this?"

"No," I said, chuckling. "Go on. This is great."

"Well, you told the clerk that you were out to celebrate, that
you liked the feel of them, and we added two to our order. We left
with three bags of groceries and soon had everything spread out
before us in the kitchen. First, though, we were going to solve the
avocado. And God knows, we tried. With a vegetable peeler, a butter knife, every blade on your Swiss Army knife. You didn't have
any cooking knives then, or maybe we could've got into the thing.
But nope. We finally gave up. The avocado had beaten us. Avocado
2, the great Kyle Callendar 0, we said, toasting with the Italian red.
We cooked a helluva meal, though, and instead of lighting candles
we perched the avocados on egg cups."

"That is so funny," I said, laughing so hard that I cried. "I don't
know how in the world I could've forgotten that."

"Well, Kyle. It happened just like that. I couldn't stop smiling
all afternoon."

An old man sitting next to me on the subway was reading a
newspaper. "LEAGUE OF OUR OWN," the headline blared. I
leaned over his shoulder. God, I thought, it was only a week before
the start of the hockey season. I had totally lost track. There was
a photo spread of Sheldon Shriver and Virgil Hadfield. The first
players signed: Bobby Shriver, Vladimir Rostov, and Bjorn Skajjit. I
asked to see the paper after he was done. "OUR GAME IS HOME,"
it said on the editorial page. The new league would petition parlia-
ment for the rights to use the Stanley Cup as its trophy. It was only
right, the editorial said, to reward a league that put true hockey
supremacy first.

I slipped a hip flask of Johnnie Walker from my inside breast
pocket and took a swig. I'd been good for the most part, but this

visit to Norma had me on edge. Who could deny me a little liquid courage for something like this? I put the paper down at my side. A photograph of a man in a white coat loomed in the subway ad panel across from me, his face fleshy and dull, lifeless eyes a contrast to the bright orange and blue and red of the ad for laser surgery: "Take Off Pounds of Unwanted Fat, Recover Your Youth, the Definition of Your Calves."

The train jerked and I winced with the pain that shot down my back and leg. Instinctively, I reached out for Belle, but of course Belle wasn't there. Instead, I grazed the whorled surface of a woman's old-fashioned coat. The dark-haired woman flashed me an angry look, muttered something under her breath, got up and moved further down the train.

An apology caught in my throat. I swallowed hard, felt a contraction in my chest. I plunged my hand in my coat pocket, took out the game puck, and sat staring straight ahead, rubbing the puck in my hands like a talisman. Maybe it was a mistake to see Norma. She had turned the corner with her work, was by all accounts not looking back. Me, I was getting things together, I told myself. I, too, would do as Norma had done. That was what I had decided by coming to her art opening. I would tell her that I was going to be okay, that she should know that I was a different person than the one she had known. That she didn't have to worry about me.

I took the streetcar to the Beaches, not far from where Norma and I once lived what seemed a hundred years ago. The gallery was a Keppel-style cottage with white clapboard siding and sash-and-frame windows, doubled-paned to protect against the wind, which had picked up for late September. Weird, balmy weather with gusts that swept open the skirt of my coat.

Once inside, I slipped the game puck into the pocket of my trousers and checked my coat. The air was Lemon Pledge, tao of cigarette smoke. People in black like crows in spring, returning to a favourite tree, cawing and yakking and stabbing the air. A clutch of them had perched in the centre of the room, where a splash of laughter ran through me like a charge. I could see her between the cracks of the arms and bodies, and I pushed my way forward, saw the telltale windblown straw hair, in a wheelchair, gnarled hands not gripping the armrests but aloft, Egyptian. Joan Hawthorne, holding court.

I looked around and saw that Norma was in another room, a thousand pardons away, it seemed. In metallic blue, layers of white and sheer, hair short and spiky, before *Kingfisher in Context*, next to a man with a close-cropped beard, arms akimbo, leaning by her side, whispering something in her ear to spark a look I'd last seen on a large screen at a carousel in Midland, where a hidden camera snapped pictures of customers and displayed them for sale on the video screen, to be put on T-shirts if you said the word, which I'd wanted to have but Norma said no. The man touched Norma at the small of her back. She kissed him before he moved away.

A man with a neck scarf mounded like ten-year-old home insulation stepped slowly behind me, leaving a lane for me to see *Prairie Sage Grouse in Context*, Norma's latest. Colour and texture like I'd never seen before. A bird on the prairie, with copper and red and grey and blue, the limitlessness of the land, the mystic gaze of the bird's stare, a link with ages past, the ancient ocean floor and the life that was lived then.

"Kyle, thank you for coming," Norma said, as I stood before the painting. She had the start of the dark patches under her eyes that no makeup could touch. Tired. Caught up in the excitement and couldn't sleep, I thought.

"Norma, this is beautiful," I said, nodding toward the painting. "Mesmerizing."

"Thank you, Kyle."

"No, I mean it," I said, biting my lip. "At least something good came out of your trip to Saskatoon."

Norma started to say something but stopped and looked down, toed the floor. Then she glanced up and tried to catch the eye of the man in the beard. He had his back to her in line at the drinks table.

"Listen," I said as I fumbled in my pocket and pulled out the game puck. "I wanted to give you something. Something to mark the occasion." I turned the Toronto Maple Leaf hat-trick puck over in my hand and offered it to her.

Norma started and slowly shook her head. "Kyle," she said, her lips trembling. "I couldn't. It's too much."

"But you have to," I said. "I want you to have it. Besides," I continued, raising my eyebrows as her gaze lifted and met mine, "you know me. I've got a copy of that photo of me with the puck. Had it framed last week."

Norma looked at me then for a beat and then smiled her carousel smile. She was right: we didn't need it on a T-shirt; I would never forget it.

"Kyle, thank you," she said, as she held the puck in both hands and kissed me lightly on the lips. "Next week's your birthday. Let's try and do something, okay? We can go out. I know a place that does the best guacamole."

"Right," I said, laughing. "It's best to let go of some things, I guess."

"When it comes to avocados, yeah," she said with a wink as she gave me a kiss on the cheek.

"Of course, that would be great," I told her. "I've so much I'd like to tell you. I've missed seeing you."

"Me, too, Kyle. Me too," she said as she let an older man, with a slight nod to me, pull her away into the crowd.

Later, at the door, I picked up a show catalogue with *Prairie Sage Grouse in Context* on the cover, bought postcards of *Kingfisher* and *Crow*. Reflected in the glass at the entrance, the bearded man was talking to the guest in the oversized scarf. The man was still, like a *tableau vivant*, holding two long-stemmed glasses of cold Chardonnay.

chapter twenty-five

Father was a month away from retiring for good when I called. He had been doing the odd run. But now, finally, he was calling it quits. Until I made up my mind, I'd decided not to tell him about the governor's job offer. He still knew nothing about my seeing Wayne, seemed content with the simple fact that I was taking a leave from the Hall. It wasn't just anyone who could arrange a leave from a job, Dad reckoned. Kyle Callendar was just too important a man to the operation of the Hall. Former clients asked about me, men who came by with a load of lumber for a shed he was rebuilding never failed to put in a word. They don't give every man a leave, I can tell you that, they said. Kyle, that boy, he is something else, no?

It was December and I told Dad I had some time to kill, would he like a little company on the road? Sure, he said. That would be fine.

Our first pickup was at Nortar Oil and Paints on the Keppel outskirts: primer, flat paint, and semigloss. A northern run to a nickel mine. Father and I were at back of the trailer, guiding the forklift drivers as they moved pallets of paint. Father had his own way of doing things and he glared at me a few times as he shouted directions, but we soon did the job and I didn't think twice when I slammed the trailer door hard and fastened the lock. We both climbed into the cab and Father turned the key while I put on my seatbelt.

"Still into that, eh?" Dad said with a scowl.

"Nothing personal, Dad," I said.

Before putting the truck in gear, Dad, too, put on his belt. "They been setting up roadside checks. Getting really crazy about it. If it were up to me, though—"

"I know, Dad," I said.

North of Keppel the road is as flat as prairie. And just about as populated. In recent years, artists and weavers and candle makers have moved into town, but the farms are mostly abandoned. Windows boarded up, farm pens with holes the size of hockey nets; a horse's neigh, a cow's moo, distant memories. For Sale signs are weathered, forgotten.

Dad drove through the landscape without a word. An old man, hardened to a world that had left him behind. A survivor, not lifted by purple and red sunsets but picking through a wasteland. Slowly and methodically, as if he were on a trail of stepping stones through quicksand. We passed the spot where police had been doing the roadside checks, and Dad immediately took off his belt. He darted me a glare, but I avoided it, turned to look out the window, rested one hand on my belt. A sign before a ratty house said, "Strictly Business," with two crossed hockey sticks for a logo.

I tipped my cap down my face and rested. I could see through the slits of my eyes but I didn't let on, and my father never once looked toward me. His hands held the big wheel of his truck like the curved head of a spoon resting on rainwater in a barrel. A hint of a smile played on his face and I thought to ask him what he was thinking, but instead closed my eyes and tried to sleep. We had miles to go. And more time than I had ever allowed myself to think possible. Perhaps I would ask him what was on his mind. Or perhaps we would drive this way all day and not say a goddamn word. I took a deep breath and listened to the sound of the road.

"Roland Miles has been asking about you," Dad said, finally.

"Roland?" I said, for a moment forgetting.

"Yeah, Roland. He's retired from his teaching, but still spends a bunch of time in Toronto."

The wind had picked up. Even the Mack cab shuddered, a shred of paper waggled on the floorboards. On the horizon, the long, white, slowly turning blades of a wind farm appeared like toys, then nameless spectres, bone soldiers on a march, a stealth campaign of their own making. Across the road, as we drove in silence again, were closely arrayed slats of weathered limestone, a family's burial plot.

"Said something about you and this World Hockey League. That you might be taking up with them. Izzatso?" he said, glancing toward me.

"Maybe," I replied. "There's a chance."

"A good deal?"

"Yeah," I said, folding my arms across my chest and sitting up straight. The Keppel town posture.

"When will you know?"

"January. They've given me until January to make up my mind."

Father curled his lip and slowly nodded his head. "Sure you'll do the right thing. You always have."

"Really, you think so?"

"Yep."

Dad grinded down a gear or two as we entered Tiverton. I insisted that we stop at a coffee shop and we wheeled into the parking lot. A billboard said "Lick My Ribs." Then one for a chain of golf courses: "Do You Have the Balls to Play Us?"

"Dad, I've been meaning to ask you," I said, as we pulled out on the road with our takeaway coffees. I tried a sip but the drink nearly burned my lips, so instead just held the cup on my lap. "What did you mean when you told me our crosses won't path?"

"Eh?" Dad said. "Come again?"

"When I was leaving that summer at The Beer Store. I remember you told me our crosses won't path. What did you mean by that?"

His eyes narrowed as he gripped the wheel a little tighter. "You were a different boy, a lot different than me, I could see that real early on. You were always on your way out of here," he said, looking over the yellow and green of the farmland, lame in the warmth of another snowless winter. "It wasn't easy but at one point your mother and I decided we weren't going to stand in the way of where your life was taking you.

"All I've known," he said, "is this truck. And the war, of course. Where I suppose I could tell you now always filled me with bad feelings. The waiting was the worst of it. And, of course, what came back to me on 9/11. Thousands dying in the wink of an eye. Just like Die-down, which is what we called it 'cause Die-up didn't suit what the beaches looked like after we'd landed. The generals, of course, had their own name for it: Jubilee, like it was one big fucking party. After I got back, I couldn't see myself doing anything else but staying busy. Not waiting on anything. If I were to stop," he said, turning to face me, "I may as well be dead.

"That was something I didn't want you to have anything to do with. Why I suppose I was such a hard ass with you and your hockey. Maybe I was wrong. Could be. But I can't do nothing about it now."

I reached to my side and fingered the strap of my backpack. Inside was my notebook, pens, the postcards from Norma's show, a sweater, and a toothbrush.

We drove for a while in silence and then Dad took a sip of coffee and his face screwed up. "Bah! Tastes like your foot's asleep. I shoulda known not to stop there. Mother shoulda packed a thermos."

"Hey, Dad," I said, ignoring the shot. "I want you to see something." I took out the postcards from Norma's show and handed them to him. Suddenly, an SUV with an Oakville sales decal pulled in sharply ahead of us. We slowed down without braking hard, but Dad whaled him with his horn, three loud blasts.

"Jesus, what a jerk," Dad said, as he shook the cards in the air between his thumb and forefinger.

"Hey, be careful with those," I said, annoyed.

"What's that?" he said in a pissy tone.

"Those cards," I said firmly. "They're important to me. They're what I wanted to show you, remember?"

Dad stared at me for a beat, then back at the road. Nothing but scrub trees now, no open fields for wind farms. A sign said, "Hitchhikers Could Be Escaping Inmates." Inside, I'm sure, what those guys wouldn't give for a "Christmas Tree" shiv. Dad released his grip on the postcards, but still hadn't looked at them.

"Just give them back to me, would you?" I said.

Dad shook his head, frowned like a bullfrog. Dad always had a natural frown, but now it was a tunnel—like something blasted for the Trans-Canada.

"I'll look at them later," he said, putting them on the dashboard.

"Suit yourself," I said, resuming the Keppel posture.

"I will."

We drove what seemed for a long time, but looking back I guess it wasn't much more than twenty miles or so. Dusk was beginning to show, an hour before we were due to pull in to a rest stop for the night. Dad was wrong about one thing, I thought. That we were different. Hardly. Dad had his war and—until I was old enough to leave home—he had my hockey too. But he was wrong to think that his war wouldn't be my war as well. In the end, though, we Callendars weren't ones for being owned, which was why I had to leave for good and why Dad pushed me away—like that visit a while back when he wouldn't go out with me to look at the sunset, his hesitation in the Keppel dressing room at the Really Old Timers game. I wasn't the only one who was free to chart his own course, a freedom that I didn't ask for and maybe didn't want. I guess it was true that some memories would just be. There would be no getting to them. What Gwen Martinson meant to my father, Coach Fleming and the Kingston initiation night, the avocado incident. What was the use of words for memories like these? Whatever I'd done in the notebook would have to do. There was a place for silence, those blank spots on the page.

"Want the sandwiches?" I said.

Dad grunted yes and I pulled out his red metal lunch box that Mom had been packing him since I can remember. She'd taken the thermos out so that she could fit enough food for the two of us. White bread and canned meat goo with relish for me, baloney with mustard on white for Dad. We each finished the sandwiches in four bites, took a sip of the dishwater coffee. In a plastic container were dill slices in brine, bread and butter pickles, and a slew of gherkins—what I'd eat by the fistful when I lived at home.

"Dad, I wonder, been thinking about the Lamplighter of Niagara. About the time you took me to the Falls."

Dad paused, nodded his head—the frown at first deepening then veering to neutral.

"Yeah, that was a nice day," he said.

"Could you tell me what you remember?"

"Howard Mann, he just passed away last year," Dad said. "A pal of mine at Die-down. Loved what he did, you know. Insisting that all the kids of the guys he knew in the war be the official Lamplighter of Niagara. It's what he did to give back. Said something about getting rid of the shadows, that every kid of the guys he knew should feel the power of that light."

"I've been thinking about that a lot," I said. "About how those lights made me feel."

Dad slowly nodded his head.

"You see Norma, then?" he said, barely above a whisper.

"Yeah," I said, reaching for the postcards on the dashboard. I put them in his hand and he sneaked a glance at them as he drove.

"She's a big-time artist now. We're friends. I think I'm going to be okay with that."

Dad handed the postcards back to me without saying a word. The highway was open, not a single car in view.

"There's this woman," Dad said, in his way of starting one of his stories. "She's on her way to someplace important and her car breaks down on a strange road.

"She's worried, but then a man comes by, a motorist who knocks on the window of her car. She's startled and at first doesn't move. But the man is smiling so she winds it down.

" 'I can see you have a flat tire,' he says. 'I'd be happy to fix it.'

"Then he takes his own jack, lifts the car, and replaces the tire. He also inspects what looks like an oil leak. But not so. He gets up, brushes off, and goes back to his car.

"The woman pulls away and goes down the road a piece to a motel and restaurant where she's going to spend the night. After parking the car, she goes in for a bite.

"The waitress is strapped, her husband has recently lost his job and there's no money to pay the rent. The landlord is at the end of his patience because now they are two months overdue, is threatening eviction. Of course, she doesn't tell the woman this.

"The woman eats the meal and, feeling as good as she has in a long time, gets up to go after having left some cash on the table.

"She's stopped by the waitress, who has been very attentive despite her troubles, and asks if she would like any change.

" 'No,' she says, 'please keep it. Everything was wonderful.'

"It is the last table of the night and the waitress goes up to it and is surprised to find under the coffee saucer a hundred dollar bill. She looks around but the woman has gone. She takes up the bill and finds another one hundred bill beneath it. And another beneath that. And another. In all, she has five hundred dollars, enough for the rent, enough to get them by. Because the man is due to start a new job, could surely get an advance to cover the next month."

I don't know if that was the story he'd wanted to tell me that day at The Beer Store. Or at the end of the Really Old Timers Game. Certainly not. But suddenly, I thought, whatever it was wasn't pointless, at least when it came to feelings. Which I was free now to think that my father was having in trying to lift my spirits with that story. I realized that what I was so desperate to know was simply how to be myself with my father. That maybe we weren't beyond being able to craft some incidents of our own.

It was dark now. Dad pulled into the rest stop and before I knew it, he was fast asleep. A knack he'd never lost; four hours deep sleep and he was ready to go, on the road again. Me, I wandered into the parking lot under the night sky. It wasn't so bright as to read a game sheet, but it was quiet. So quiet that when I did slip into the seat beside my dad to rest I thought if I were lucky I'd even remember my dreams.

acknowledgements

I would like to express my thanks to my wife, Mary Morris, who, while standing before the Stanley Cup at the Hockey Hall of Fame, had an idea about a book. Above all, though, her love, support, and careful reading helped to guide me through the hard work of countless drafts. I also am indebted to Althea Prince and my agent Diana Finch, as well as Jack Wayne and Rebecca Conolly at CSPI. I also am grateful to Laura Robinson, whose book *Crossing the Line* served as an inspiration to me. And a final thanks to my daughter Kate O'Connor Morris, my friends Patrick Knickerbocker, Sue Robertson, and Greg Dunham, and readers John Blanton, Michael Kimmel, Steve O'Connor, and Naresh Fernandes whose inspiration and advice were invaluable to me.